Sweet Spot

The Sweet Spot

KIMBERLY KAYE TERRY

APHRODISIA

KENSINGTON BOOKS
http://www.kensingtonbooks.com

APHRODISIA BOOKS are published by

Kensington Publishing Corp.
119 West 40th Street
New York, NY 10018

All Kensington Titles, Imprints, and Distributed Lines are available at special quantity discounts for bulk purchases for sales promotions, premiums, fund-raising, and educational or institutional use.

Special book excerpts or customized printings can also be created to fit specific needs. For details, write or phone the office of the Kensington special sales manager: Kensington Publishing Corp., 119 West 40th Street, New York, NY 10018, attn: Special Sales Department, Phone: 1-800-221-2647.

Aphrodisia and the A logo Reg. U.S. Pat & TM Off.

ISBN-13: 978-0-7582-2876-5
ISBN-10: 0-7582-2876-7

First Kensington Trade Paperback Printing: September 2009

10 9 8 7 6 5 4 3 2 1

Printed in the United States of America

To my sister and best friend, Synetta. Thank you for always being there for me, even when I know you want to cuss me out for calling you so late at night sometimes. Or real super-early on a Saturday morning, when I had a plot idea I wanted your thoughts on and you just wanted to sleep. Sorry, but that's not gonna ever stop. *Ever*. You may as well get used to it. You rock, chica. I love you!

To my best friend, Tawny. Thank you for being Tawny when I need a shoulder to cry on, and Vivi Anna when I need someone to kick me dead in the butt and make me stop with all the over-the-top tears and many, many *many* theatrics. Although that last time, did you really have to kick that hard? You also rock and I love you.

—KKT

1

When he strolled into the Sweet Spot exuding confidence like other men sweat, looking all kind of ways good to her, Gabrielle Marlowe knew she was in trouble. Particularly in the emotional state currently holding her hostage.

His long, muscular frame was the picture of raw masculine perfection, wearing the *hell* out of a dark blue, finely striped, expensively cut suit that Gaby could tell, even from her distance away, was tailor made for his perfect form.

Despite the expensive cut, he wore the suit with a casual disregard.

As he sauntered closer to the bar, where she sat perched on one of the high-backed bar stools, she allowed her eyelids to drop low, knowing her lashes were long enough to hide the fact that she was checking every fine inch of him out.

Tall, dark, and handsome.

As soon as she thought it, she cringed. Yeah, she knew it was beyond clichéd, but that's *just* what he was.

He didn't have a typically handsome model's face. No. His was much harsher, more sensual than anything that could be termed as tame as handsome.

There was a certain . . . wildness, a barely caged sensuality about him.

Gaby shivered.

He had to top six feet by several inches, and even though he was wearing a suit, Gaby could tell he had one hell of a body. She ran a discreet glance over him, again, top to bottom, as she sipped her drink.

His sable-colored hair had a slight wave and was cut low, tapering down in the back to nearly skin in a tight, almost military-type fade, with the top long enough that several thick, wavy strands fell over his brow.

If not for the lock of hair that fell over one eye, he could have been a living, breathing, poster boy for a Marine Corps recruiting ad.

Semper Fi.

The Marines slogan popped into her mind.

Always Ready.

Damn.

Gaby blew out a breath she didn't know she'd been holding.

His jet-black, winged brows slashed over vivid greenish gold eyes, framed by sooty dark lashes so thick they seemed unreal.

The darkness of his eyebrows and lashes was at odds with his hair color, and Gaby thought perhaps he dyed his hair.

Although he didn't strike her as the type to do that. He seemed too *manly* to do something so feminine.

She casually glanced over his broad shoulders and thickly muscled body.

No, he *definitely* didn't seem the type of man who'd dye his hair.

A fine-boned, yet prominent hawkish nose, hard chiseled lips, the lower rim slightly fuller than the top, and a well-defined chin with a deep dimple completed the picture of a man who, with one look, could probably make any woman he wanted stop, drop, and strip.

Yeah, Gaby thought with an inward sigh of appreciation . . . he had it like that.

When he turned his head and glanced over at her, Gaby took another sip of her apple martini from the thin straw and hoped he couldn't see how fast her heart was thumping beneath the thin silk blouse she wore.

Or that he noticed how her nipples pearled against her useless bra.

Or maybe she did want him to notice . . .

When she dared to peek up, it was to see he'd turned away and was giving his attention to the female bartender who had scurried his way as soon as he walked to the bar.

"Hey, Sweet. Haven't seen much of you lately. Got me wondering if you forgot all about me," the woman quipped, the wattage on her smile so bright, she could illuminate the entire club.

So this was Sweet.

She should have known.

Sweet was the owner of the Sweet Spot, as well as two other popular nightclubs. Besides the one in San Antonio, the other two were located in Austin and Dallas.

Since she and Adam had been coming to the club over the last three months, Gaby had learned they called the owner Sweet because rumor had it the man could sweet-talk a woman straight out of her panties with a few well-chosen words.

She turned her body slightly around in her chair and subtly hitched her skirt farther up her thighs. *Just* so he could get a nice visual of her naked pussy.

She usually wore panties when she went out. Usually.

But not tonight.

Not after what happened between her and her lover, Adam.

When Gaby came home early from a pharmaceutical convention to which the university where she taught had sent her, she'd found him in bed, where he and another woman were going at it like two rabid dogs in heat.

His secretary.

So clichéd. So damn clichéd.

In bed with his secretary . . . the least he could have done was be original.

Gaby clenched her teeth, her face tightening as she bit back feelings of anger and betrayal over what the bastard had done.

In *her* bed, no less.

She took another sip of her martini, eyeing tall, dark, and fine discreetly from beneath lowered lashes, thinking about what she was going to do next with the mess that was her life.

She'd come to rely on Adam for so much, particularly over the last months of their relationship.

She didn't really know how she'd gotten into the situation she was now in. Didn't know why she hadn't seen it coming. Or how she was going to get out of it. She knew what she was doing, what she and Adam were doing, was wrong.

Damn. And now this.

Guess a nice set of big fake tits, overprocessed bleached hair, and a tight hoochie-mama dress made Adam forget all about his avowals of love for her.

So yeah. Gaby was definitely in a *what the hell* kind of mood.

She forced her thoughts away from Adam and his cheating behind and continued to sip her apple martini while listening to Sweet talk to the bartender.

"You sticking around long, this time around?" the woman asked him.

He accepted the glass and leaned against the bar, taking a drink. His strong throat worked as he swallowed, before he set the glass on the smoky gray glass bar counter.

"Haven't been gone, just busy with other stuff. No plans to go anywhere, anytime soon. Except bed," he said wearily, his voice a deep sexy rumble. "In fact, I think I'll head up to the loft and get some shut-eye. I'm tired as hell."

Gaby covertly ran her eyes over his face and saw the fine lines of fatigue that bracketed his wide, sensual mouth.

Just then he glanced her way and casually looked her over. She swiftly looked away, pretending nonchalance, subtly shifting her legs farther apart, in case he happened to glance down.

"Well, if you need anything—a drink, food, a pillow to rest your poor weary head on—you know where to find me," the bartender told him and winked one big blue eye and smiled.

Gaby felt the overwhelming desire to throw her half-full glass of martini in the woman's face, if for no other reason than she was the spitting image of the woman she'd caught screwing her man, hands bound behind her back, having the kind of sex that she never would have imagined Adam was into.

The type of sex that Gaby had secretly been intrigued by, but never had the nerve to engage in.

The woman's cries of passion still rang in the echoes of her mind.

The bartender leaned down and lifted Sweet's empty glass. As she did so, her ample breasts pressed against the starched white uniform shirt she was wearing. She had the top three buttons unfastened far enough so that the lacy edge of her demi-bra showed.

Gaby knew the woman wanted Sweet to see just what kind of pillow she was offering for him to lay his "poor weary head on."

"I'm good. But I'll keep the offer in mind, Sherri." He winked back at her.

With one last lingering look at Sweet, the bartender sauntered down to the other end of the bar to serve a customer. Gaby watched Sweet as his eyes stayed glued to Sherri's swinging hips as she left.

When he turned toward Gaby, she met his eyes.

He smiled and ran his gaze over her body and she knew the minute he saw her bared vulva.

His eyes flew to hers, his sensual lips stretching up into a lazy grin, and she knew she'd gotten his attention.

Pushing down the churning in her gut, Gaby wet her lips and smiled, her lips twitching in nervousness as she tried to maintain what she hoped passed as cool sophistication.

He pushed away from the counter and sauntered close to her.

Gaby kept her smile determinedly in place and maintained eye contact.

When he brushed past her, her heart sank and she felt like a damn fool.

She sighed glumly, turned around, clamped her legs together with a snap, and took another drink of her martini.

"Meet me upstairs, in my loft. Use the elevator near the kitchen entry, past the double doors," a deep voice whispered against her ear.

Gaby spun around and caught herself before she flipped out of the chair.

"Wha-what?" she stuttered out the response.

"That is, if you're serious about what you're promising."

His heated glance slid over her body like warm rain, his gaze settling between her legs, sending goose bumps to pepper her exposed arms and an ache of need to bubble in her stomach.

Her body reacted as though he'd actually touched her; her breath hitched in her throat and her heartbeat slammed against her chest.

"You'll need this key to reach my loft. It's my personal elevator. Past the swinging doors, down the hallway to the left."

He placed a small brass key into her open hand, folding her fingers over it, pressing it into her palm. Without another word he turned around and walked away.

Just like that, he left, without waiting to see if she'd actually follow him. Assuming that all he needed to do was make the suggestion and she'd eagerly jump up and trail after him.

Gaby's bemused gaze followed his slow ambling walk until he was out of sight before she turned back around.

When her eyes collided with the bartender—Sherri's—she caught the woman staring at her with a bemused expression, giving Gaby the universal look women gave one another when a fine man chose one over the other.

A "What in the *hell* does he see in you?" type of look.

Gaby had been two seconds away from jumping up from her stool and hightailing it out of the bar, getting as far away as possible from the promise of what Sweet wanted to do to her, a promise that had been shining brightly in his golden eyes.

Instead, she gave the woman a triumphant grin and eased out of her chair.

Sedately, despite the butterflies churning in her gut, she slowly walked through the crowded club, following Sweet.

2

"She's on her way up to my loft."

There was a pause before the other man spoke. "You don't waste any time. Do I want to know how you accomplished that so quickly?"

Demetri held his cell phone in one hand and used the other to pull off his jacket and shirt, carefully laying them over the small leather chair in the corner of the room. He then unbuttoned his slacks and shoved them, along with his boxers, down the length of his legs.

"Probably not."

"Shit."

He sat down on the chair with the phone cradled between his shoulder and ear and pulled off his shoes and socks before taking off his slacks.

"Yeah, well, you wanted the job done. Do you give a shit how I accomplish it?" he asked.

"No, I guess not. As long as the job gets done." Another pause before the other man continued, "You've decided to take the case, then?"

"Did I have a choice?" Demetri grunted, walking through the open loft.

"There's always choices, Agent My—"

"Don't call me that," Demetri broke in, cutting the man off, mid-sentence.

"Once an agent, always an agent. You can't escape your past. Can't hide from it, either."

"I was a pencil pusher. Before I left, I'd quit fieldwork. If you're gonna pull the patriotic card, get it right," Demetri walked, naked, across the room toward the bathroom. "I don't have a lot of time for small talk, no disrespect, sir. Can we cut this short?"

"Do you have a plan?" The man asked after a pregnant pause.

Demetri loosened his watch and placed it on the bathroom counter, then removed a ring suspended on a gold chain from around his neck.

It was the only other piece of jewelry he wore, one that reminded him of the reasons he no longer felt any desire to reenter a world of deception and manipulation.

Did he have a plan?

Good question, Demetri thought with a grimace.

Just when he was getting his life back together, Nick Panin, his former commander, called and convinced him to fly out to D.C., dangling a carrot he knew Demetri wouldn't be able to resist in front of his nose.

Completely disrupting the tranquility he'd worked so tenaciously to achieve over the last two years with an offer the son of a bitch knew he couldn't refuse.

If Demetri agreed to help him on a case involving two con artists—Gabrielle Marlowe and Adam Quick—who were involved in a Medicaid and pharmaceutical fraud, his former commander would use all of his considerable power to find Demetri's former partner.

He thought back to Siobhan and his time in the Bureau.

They'd been paired up as new recruits fresh out of the academy, assigned their first mission together. Over the course of five years as partners, they'd successfully helped bring down hundreds of con artists whose game had been so tight they'd escaped the long arm of justice for years.

Their cases usually involved criminals who preyed on the helpless, often scamming them out of their life savings. With each success, they'd gotten more and more accolades. It wasn't long before they were recruited by a special division within the FBI, headed by Nicolai Panin, dealing with criminals higher up, or down, depending on one's view, the food chain.

Their first case in the newly formed special ops team had been their last.

They'd taken months to set up a sting to infiltrate an underground BDSM cult to investigate the murder of one of their members, one they'd linked to other similar murders.

They'd first gone into "training" to learn the lifestyle. Unfortunately for Siobhan, Demetri hadn't seen the psychological effects the training and months spent living that lifestyle had on her. When the time for the bust came, unknown to Demetri, Siobhan was no longer the same woman.

She'd turned on the agency. On Demetri.

She'd informed the cult's leader, the man they believed to be the one responsible for the murders, and he'd gotten away, taking Von with him. And from all accounts, it appeared she'd gone willingly.

Demetri's gaze settled on the ring on the bathroom counter.

Siobhan had left it in the "dungeon" area of the secret club they'd infiltrated, in a small five-by-five-foot steel-barred cage.

Along with the black leather, ruby-encrusted studded collar—the one he'd given her—and a note telling him not to look for her.

He fingered the ring.

It was the ring all the cadets received after graduating from the FBI Academy.

That was the last communication he'd had from her.

"Well?" Panin prompted him, jarring him out of his musings.

"I'm working on it. I'll let you know when I have more to report," was his gruff reply.

"Demetri . . . listen—"

"I'll be in contact."

Demetri pressed the end button on his cell and flung it, as well as the ring, on the counter. The ring spun and rolled, landing with a *ting* on the marble bathroom counter.

He'd been told Gabrielle and Adam frequented the Sweet Spot, which was one of the reasons his commander had come to him for help. Demetri thought there were more reasons he'd been brought into the investigation, but if there were, his former commander wasn't telling. The most he would say was that if Demetri could bring them in, find out who else was involved, who was at the top, he'd put a special team out to find Siobhan.

For Demetri, that been reason enough for him to agree.

Upon his return home, he hadn't had to wait long before he identified Adam Quick and Gabrielle Marlowe. Quick looked exactly as he did in the many photos Demetri's former commander had given him. He was tall, with the type of muscular build that came from working out in a gym regularly.

He had what Demetri thought of as a "pretty boy" look. Women fell for that type hard.

Adam wore his dark blond, artificially highlighted hair swept back from a wide forehead, and in the photo he was smiling a lopsided, practiced grin.

With his light blue eyes, classic features, and no scars, nothing to mar his pretty-boy perfection, teamed with what most cons had in abundance, manipulativeness, women fell like a ton of bricks.

He'd dismissed the man in the photo and looked at the woman, his partner, Gabrielle Marlowe, wondering if she had been a victim of Quick's charms or if she were the deadlier of the two.

In each photo they had of her, she'd been wearing variations on the same conservative boxy suit that did nothing for her body.

She was petite; her bio said she was only a few inches over five feet, no weight given, but from the picture and her clothing she appeared slightly thick, no curves, just straight lines in the bland suits she seemed to favor.

Her somber face stared back at him, unsmiling in the picture. Her large, widely set brown eyes were obscured behind a pair of old-fashioned round glasses that seem to dominate her small face. Although her deep golden brown complexion was flawless, that looked to be about the only thing attractive about her.

Then his eyes had gone to her mouth.

Despite the look of untouched innocence that seemed to cling to her, her mouth was pure decadence, ripe and full.

Even without smiling, her lips had a natural curve in the corners that made her otherwise bland appearance reach out and grab him by the balls.

Despite her average looks, he'd found himself drawn to the photograph over and over.

Then, he'd seen her in person.

Damn.

The photograph hadn't come anywhere near to capturing her unique beauty. Although her skin in the photo appeared to be smooth, her features even, there was nothing unique about her, save that decadent mouth of hers.

But in person . . .

In person her skin glowed, shone like rich dark honey. Her eyes, which had been obscured by the old-fashioned glasses in the picture, were large, slightly slanted in the corners, and a deep chocolate brown. Bedroom eyes.

And then his gaze had rested on her lips . . . God. Her lips were so lush and full his imagination had taken flight, with images of suckling her full lower lip into his mouth playing hell with his libido.

Not to mention the woman was nothing but luscious curves.

The first time he'd seen her, she'd been with Adam Quick. It had been easy to spot the pair.

Nightly, at the same time that Nick told him surveillance had shown them coming to the club, he'd stationed himself in a prime position to observe them without being noticed, patiently waiting to get a visual on them since his return from D.C. and his meeting with Nick.

Like most crooks, they followed habitual routines, choosing the same booth when they came to the club, tucked away in a corner of the room.

With animation, the man did most of the talking, and although his tone was too low to hear, Demetri guessed he was talking mostly about his own interests.

Although she feigned attention, Demetri caught the woman's eyes drifting away, usually toward the dance floor, with an almost wistful look on her gamine face.

With an irritated look, Quick would rudely snap his fingers in front of her face to get her attention, and the woman would smilingly murmur something and pretend interest in what he was saying.

He'd been able to continue to observe her without her knowledge. Although Quick hadn't been able to hold her attention, her face, even in repose, was animated, her eyes seeming to sparkle without the glasses obscuring their beauty.

When she'd come into the club tonight, without Quick, Demetri had seized the opportunity.

She'd worn her emotions on her sleeve. She was angry, hurt . . . and, if he his instincts were right, she wanted to prove something.

Yeah, definitely wanted to prove something, as the memory of her opening her legs and giving him a hint of what lay beneath the conservative straight-lined skirt was any indication.

Demetri shook his head. He didn't know what had happened, but he didn't give a shit, not really.

No matter how sweet she looked, how intriguing, how . . . different than what he'd expected, she was nothing but a crook. He'd use everything in his psychological and sexual arsenal to bring her down.

Demetri yanked open the shower door with more force than was necessary and turned on the water. Not bothering to wait until it warmed, he stepped into the stall.

He raised his face toward the multifaceted showerhead, pulling his hands through his hair, allowing the cool water to rain down on his upturned face.

A plan began to form in his head.

"God, what am I doing?" Gaby murmured aloud, worrying her bottom lip with her teeth, clenching and unclenching her clasped hands as she stood in front of the elevator door in the deserted hallway at the back of the club.

She'd been standing there for at least thirty minutes, her mind a chaotic whirl of conflicting emotions.

She unclasped her hands and brushed her fingertips back and forth over the cool metal bars of the antiquated elevator, contemplating what she was about to do with a man she didn't even know.

Ready for whatever, however . . . *any* delicious thing he had in mind, she was game.

In her current state of mind she was down for just about anything.

And she knew that was a dangerous condition for a woman to be in. There was no telling what could happen.

That thought alone sent her heart into overdrive.

She glanced down at herself, wishing she'd worn something more seductive than the navy blue skirt, matching blazer, and sensible shoes.

After she'd come home she'd been tired; the only thing on her mind had been to pull off the itchy hose and crawl into bed, fully clothed.

However, at the time she had no idea her plans would so drastically change.

Instead of crawling into bed with a good book and a glass of wine, she'd walked in and caught her boyfriend in bed with another woman.

And now, here she was about to do something daring, unlike anything she'd ever done before. Intent on allowing a man she didn't know to sex her up like there was no tomorrow. If only for one night. All she wanted was *one* night of selfish pleasure to help her momentarily forget the mess her life was in.

And the man she'd selected for the job was waiting for her upstairs. Sweet. Gaby fervently prayed he could deliver on what his name, his heated eyes, his sensual mouth, promised. She closed her eyes, took a deep breath, and blew out a calming breath before reopening them.

Her face settling into lines of determination, she inserted the brass key into the lock and pulled back the door. The groaning, creaking noise it made as she pushed the iron cage open seemed unnaturally loud to her, despite the booming music filtering into the hall from the club.

She glanced around to see if anyone was watching and shook her head at herself, chastising herself for being so ridiculous.

No one was watching her, and if they were, well . . . who cared? She was a grown woman of thirty years. If she wanted to have anonymous sex with the hottest man she'd seen in a month of Sundays, it was nobody's business but her own. She checked her purse for the condoms she had thrown inside and walked into the elevator.

Once inside the elevator, she pulled the outer doors together and pressed the arrow up button. Her nerves were stretched taut as the elevator lumbered and groaned as it rose.

When the elevator came to a halt and the inner doors opened, she pulled back the wrought-iron door and stepped out. Surprised, she looked around.

She knew he lived above the club, but didn't know it was a loft and that the elevator would take her directly into his home. She walked past the entryway and into the large, open room.

"Hello!" she called out, when she saw no sign of Sweet. "Anybody here?"

Gaby looked around, nervous, but curious about where he lived.

The loft was large, easily spanning the width of the club. She cautiously moved into the room, her gaze wandering over his home.

The design was a continuous flow, one room blending into the next, separated by floor-to-ceiling pillars. From where she stood, she could see a few closed doors that she imagined led to bedrooms, but when her eyes fell on the large four-poster bed in the far corner of the room, raised on a dais, she revised her thoughts.

"Hello, are you here?" Gaby called out, again.

She began to walk farther inside, furtively looking around.

She stepped down a small set of stairs that led her into what must serve as the main living area. The living space dominated the room, simply yet tastefully decorated in muted browns, reds, and cream.

A chocolate-brown suede sofa and matching oversized chair were set in the center of the room, and two crimson occasional chairs flanked a white brick stonewashed fireplace. Gaby's eyes were drawn to a small statue set on the mantel. She walked into the living room, over to the statue, and carefully picked it up.

It was made of what looked to be pure jade. She turned the smooth, cool figurine over in her hand. At first she'd thought it was a statue of a woman, but upon closer inspection, she realized it was a tightly woven male and female, limbs intertwined. It was highly erotic.

"You came," a deep, now-familiar voice murmured.

She had been so caught up in the beauty of the jade statue, she hadn't heard him enter the room.

Spinning around, startled, Gaby almost dropped the statue on the floor. She quickly caught it and replaced on the mantel.

She turned back to face him. He stood several feet away, gazing at her.

Her eyes trailed over his handsome face, to his wet hair that appeared even darker as it lay in thick, wet waves, away from his forehead.

Her gaze ran down the planes of his muscular, bare chest, the light sprinkling of dark hair glistening with moisture, past the low-slung jeans he wore unbuttoned. A thatch of curls was barely visible. Her gaze followed the dusky-haired trail, down to the deep V, lower, until the trail disappeared into his open jeans.

Her tongue snaked out and licked her dry bottom lip, her stomach churning in nervousness. She raised her eyes and met his intent, unblinking stare.

"I-I called your name," the words emerged in a dry whisper. She cleared her throat before continuing. "No one answered."

"I was in the shower," he continued to stare at her, not moving, and Gaby's gut clenched even more.

She began to fiddle with the buttons on her blouse, nervous, not knowing what to do with her hands.

"Take off your clothes."

When he spoke, she jumped. She'd begun to think he would continue to stand there staring at her. She didn't know which she preferred—his intent stare or the demand for her to undress.

"What?"

"You heard me, take them off." His voice was stern, unyielding . . . yet coaxing.

Gaby hesitated.

His gaze raked over her, making her feel exposed even though she was fully clothed; the look in his eyes showed lust, yet she detected a certain cool detachment.

The way he was staring at her was almost calculating.

She shivered, wrapping her arms around herself, more out of self-protection than because she was cold.

When Gaby was a child, whenever her mother was sober and feeling "motherly," she'd take her to the zoo.

Although those times were few and far between, Gaby had looked forward to them. Her favorite animals in the zoo had been the cougars. Even caged as they were, they were bold, sinister, fierce . . . and calculating. As though they were simply waiting for someone to be stupid enough to climb over and enter their lair.

In Sweet's eyes was the same type of look.

The look of an untamed, caged animal with fresh hot meat placed at his feet. *Hot sex on the platter . . .* Gaby repressed a shiver at her own silly analogy.

"You're still dressed." His silky voice deepened.

A moan escaped from her lips.

Although the trips to the zoo had been rare, she still remembered how *she'd* wanted to be that person bold enough to enter the cougar's lair.

Averting her eyes, she glanced down. Her hands began to fumble with the top of her skirt.

"Look at me," he murmured and her eyes flew to meet his. He casually walked over and sat in the chair next to where she stood.

Oh, God, he wanted her to strip for him while he watched.

More than that, she *wanted* to strip for him. Wanted to see the look in his eyes when she shed her clothes.

She wanted to bare her body to him, offer it up for his inspection and for him to do whatever he wanted with her.

Her eyes began to flutter closed until she remembered his demand that she look at him.

She kicked off her heels and reached behind her waist, feeling for the closure before she eased the skirt down her legs.

"Don't step out of your skirt," he instructed, as she was raising her leg.

"What? How will we—" her eyes grew round.

"No questions," he interrupted, one side of his sensual mouth curved, his shuttered eyes lazily surveying her body. "Keep removing your clothes." She looked away and began to unbutton her blouse.

"Don't look away from me," he gently reminded her.

She inhaled a deep breath, and allowed her eyes to drift to his as she slowly unbuttoned her blouse. After she'd unbuttoned the last button, Gaby waited for him to tell her what to do next, surprised at her excitement that she needed to ask his permission before she continued.

His cool eyes assessed her, his smile one of approval.

"First take off your blouse, then your bra. Nice and slow," he instructed.

She slid the blouse from her shoulders, watching him as she did so. The way he watched her so intently made her nipples pearl; the feel of the silk blouse sliding off her skin was unbearably exciting.

She unsnapped the front closure to her bra and allowed it to fall to the floor, joining her blouse. Trembling, she stood before him naked, her skirt pooled at her feet, wondering what he planned to do to her.

"What?" She stopped. Took a deep breath and exhaled, her heart beating a wild rhythm against her chest. "What now?"

Apprehensive but excited, she waited for his next command.

3

Completely nude she faced him.

He sat slouched in the chair, his hooded eyes inspecting her. A shiver ran through her, tightening her nipples, partly from the air-conditioning kissing her skin, but more from his watchful eyes observing her.

He rose from the chair, ambled over, and turned her around, standing behind her. She felt his hands in her hair before he deftly removed the pins that held it in its topknot. Surprised, she felt his strong fingers briefly massage her scalp.

She sighed in appreciation at the unexpected pleasure.

He removed his hands and seconds later her hair tumbled down to her shoulders.

He moved her hair to the side; his cool, spicy breath fanned the hairs at her nape as he brushed the side of her neck with a light, feathery kiss. Her eyes fluttered closed and her lips partially opened. A moan of lust and need escaped.

She felt his smile break across her skin. She could tell he liked the sounds she made.

She found that she liked making them even more.

One of his big palms cupped one of her breasts and her body responded as though on cue; her back bowed in response and she bit the inside of her cheek as anticipated pleasure washed over her heated skin.

He'd told her no questions. Dear God in heaven. Gaby didn't think she could remain silent with what he was doing to her body. With just one kiss . . .

"You don't have anything to fear," he mouthed the words against the back of her neck and goose bumps danced like a million fireflies along her skin.

She remained silent, unsure if he wanted her to speak.

"Von," he murmured and licked a hot path from the back of her ear, down her neck.

Confused, not sure why he said the name, she opened her mouth to ask, promptly closed it, and remained silent, not wanting the pleasure to stop.

He bit down lightly on her earlobe. The slight pain startled her.

"Say it," he demanded, his voice low, hot against her skin.

"Von," Gaby stuttered the word.

He rewarded her by lightly, slowly, stroking his hand over her breast, down the midline of her body, his hand brushing over the springy curls at the juncture of her legs. His hand trailed back up her body, just as slowly.

"If it gets too . . . much . . . for you, that's what you say. When you say 'Von,' I'll stop. I won't do anything you don't want done. But, you have to say it. Can you do that for me?"

She nodded her head, mutely giving him her assent.

Still cupping her breast, he grasped her stiffened nipples between two fingers and squeezed. It wasn't hard enough to hurt, but enough that she felt a sharp sting. She blew out a shaky breath. Surprised at the pleasure the slight sting gave her, her body trembled. The painful pleasure caused an answering wetness to ease from her vagina and run hotly down her inner thigh.

"Hmmm, you like that."

He gave her no time to react. His other hand moved from where it rested on her hip to slip around her waist until he reached her vagina.

Pressing his index finger deep into her moist core, he pumped in and out; the only sounds in the room were her panting breaths and the wet, slurping sound her cream made against his finger. Gaby squirmed against him when he inserted two more of his fingers deep inside her body.

He removed his hand from her breast long enough to pull her head back. As he slanted his hard mouth over hers, they exchanged long, heated kisses. His tongue thrust into her mouth, mimicking the action of his fingers deep inside her pussy.

Her breathing was labored, her body shaking as he continued to play with her breasts and pussy, toying with and gently tugging on her sensitive nipple.

Gaby feverishly bucked against him as she returned his kiss. Their tongues dueled while his fingers screwed deep inside her, his other hand alternating from breast to breast in hot massages. She placed a hand over his, covering her breast.

He released her mouth and nipped the lobe of her ear, chastising her. "No hands. Keep them at your sides. If you touch me, I'll stop what I'm doing. Do you want me to stop?" he breathed the words against her ear.

Gaby shook her head no. She bit the inside of her cheek to prevent the cry of pleasure from erupting from her lips as he began to manipulate her clit.

Although he still wore his jeans, she could feel the steely length of pipe pressing hotly against her back. Her fists clenched and unclenched at her sides as she rolled her hips and bucked against him.

On and on the pleasure spiraled, while his hands and tongue in perfect orchestration manipulated her, holding her body tight against his.

Gaby was mindless, feverish . . . not sure how much longer she could hold back her orgasm.

"Let go," he whispered in a guttural tone, against her lips.

She screamed, and he quickly covered her mouth with his. Her body stiffened and her back arched sharply away from the hard wall of his chest as her orgasm erupted.

She ground her body against his fingers, desperately seeking the sanctuary of his mouth as the first shudders of her release shook her.

He held her. Kissed and caressed her. Allowed her to ride the crest of pleasure until her mewling cries died down to soft whimpers.

When at last her cries ended, he dragged his fingers from her milking walls and wrapped his arms around her waist.

She inhaled breaths of calming air deep into her lungs, the fragrant musky smell of sex thick in the air.

When she felt his arms slip from around her body, her eyes fluttered open. He moved around her, until he was crouched down in front of her spread thighs.

"That was—incredible," she panted the words.

"You smell so damn good," he said, his nostrils flaring as he inhaled.

She gasped when he brushed his fingers over the springy curls. Her body was so sensitive even the light touch was unbearable.

A lone finger dipped between her dew-covered lips and withdrew her cream. Closing his eyes, he brought his finger to his mouth and licked.

"So good," he murmured. "So damn good. I want to taste more of you. But you've got to keep your legs together. If you remove your legs from your skirt, the pleasure stops. You want the pleasure to continue, don't you?"

"Yes," she moaned the words, closing her eyes as her heart beat an erratic rhythm against her breasts in renewed anticipation.

"Good." There was a wealth of satisfaction in the one-word response.

Satisfaction and something more. Gaby chose not to closely analyze anything other than the pleasure he was giving her.

At this point all she wanted was to feel.

By forcing her to keep her legs within the skirt, he'd created a makeshift bind. She could only move her legs so far, forcing her thighs closer together, which increased the steady throb between her thighs.

If she wanted to, she could simply step out of the skirt. But she wouldn't. That would end the pleasure. A pleasure she desperately wanted—*needed*—to continue.

With bated breath she waited to feel his tongue against her.

"Hmm . . . so sweet," when he breathed the words against her inner thigh, Gaby felt a gush of cream ease from her vagina.

She squirmed when two fingers separated her vaginal lips and his tongue lazily stroked her from the back of her entry to the tip of her clit.

His slick tongue lapped along the sides of her crease, darting around her clitoris in a heated playful game, flicking it, but not taking it within the moist cavern of his mouth.

Gaby's hands came out to grab hold of his head, wanting him to take her deeper into his hot mouth.

When he moved his lips away, she wanted to scream in frustration.

"You know the rules. No touching. No talking . . . until it's time," he warned her, the look in his eyes reminding her again of the caged animal in the zoo.

He didn't wait for a response.

Instead, he delved back into her pussy, licking, stroking her in alternating light flicks and long deep strokes, continuing his deadly assault with his tongue until she felt dizzy; her head spun, her limbs shook, her body trembled as she fought against her heralding orgasm.

When he shoved his tongue deep inside, Gaby broke.

"Please!" she cried, unable to hold back.

At that same moment, Sweet applied pressure to a spot directly above her mons and pressed down hard and she screamed. Pleasure slammed into her; her body went up in flames.

She grabbed his head, ignoring his edicts, and ground herself against his face, tears of release streaming from her eyes as his tongue stroked her.

As he laved her creaming portal, he shifted his hands from her pelvic bone and sank his fingers into each rounded buttock cheek and continued to eat her; ravenous in his hunger, her cream saturating his tongue, he mercilessly suckled at her pussy.

Gaby's cries rang out until she was hoarse, depleted, her limbs useless, she slumped forward and would have fallen straight on her face if he hadn't caught her.

"What do you plan to do to me?" she asked, her voice coming out in a choked whisper when she felt him quickly shift her upper body over his shoulder.

"I plan to fuck you senseless."

"Yes," she breathed the word in a barely audible voice. She allowed her eyes to feather closed as he lifted and strode toward the open balcony.

4

With one final shove, deep inside her ass, he groaned harshly and dragged his cock out of her body. Seconds later, she felt his semen spurt on her back before trickling down her spine.

She reached a hand between her legs and frantically worked her clitoris until she spasmed and her own orgasm hit.

"Shit," Adam panted. He sank down on the bed after moving his body away from her.

With his head thrown back on the white, cotton-covered pillows against the headboard, he flung one arm over his eyes, his chest rising and falling sharply with each breath he inhaled.

"It was good for you, then?"

Adam grunted out what sounded like an affirmative, without removing his arm from covering his eyes.

One corner of Marissa's silicone-injected, pouty mouth hitched up in a half grin with satisfaction. With a purely feminine purr of contentment, she reached a slim arm out and withdrew a package of cigarettes from her purse set on the bedside table.

After shaking out a cigarette, she withdrew a gold-plated

lighter encrusted with faux diamonds from her purse, placed the cigarette between her pursed lips, and lit it.

As she sucked the nicotine deeply into her lungs, she closed her eyes and leaned back against the headboard, enjoying the pleasurable buzz that the combination of a good screw—well, a decent screw—coupled with the nicotine gave.

"What?!" Marissa's eyes flew open when her cigarette was snatched out of her mouth.

"What the hell are you thinking about, smoking in here?" Adam grimaced, holding the smoldering cigarette between two fingers and bounding from the bed. He disappeared into the adjoining bathroom and seconds later she heard the toilet flush.

Bare-assed, he strode angrily back into the room, energetically blasting the room with diffusing aroma from an aerosol can of air freshener.

"Are you out of your goddamn mind, bitch? Gaby knows I don't smoke. She hates smoke!"

"Oh, yeah, gotta make sure precious little Gaby doesn't suspect her Prince Charming is getting a little extra pussy on the side," Marissa mumbled, and allowed her eyes to drift down into slits as she observed Adam.

Not that Adam was technically getting pussy from her, Marissa thought. With her he was an ass man, literally. Whenever they had their liaisons, it would take him sodomizing her several times before he'd finally get around to more traditional sex.

She arched her spine and sat up, wincing lightly, as she continued to observe him.

He was handsome in a classic surfer-boy sort of way, with his Nordic good looks—classic aristocratic features; long nose, bright blue eyes, and blond hair.

He wore his thick blond hair slightly long, the ends curling at the nape of his neck and tied back in a small ponytail.

Although he wasn't all that tall, only an inch or two at best taller than she was, at five feet ten inches, he was perfectly proportioned.

She watched his tight, muscled ass and his lean calves flex as he walked around the room spraying. His penis was at odds with the rest of him.

Just like the rest of his body, his cock was lean, average in length, nothing distinct about it, with the exception of the fat, round knob of his dick. It was so round and fat that when she'd first seen it, her reaction had been to laugh. She'd never seen a man's dick that fat at the end, with that funky curve. It reminded her of a warped banana.

She'd swallowed her laughter when he shoved that oddly shaped dick inside her ass.

She hadn't been prepared, hadn't been properly lubricated, and had cried out in pain that first time when he'd flipped her on her stomach, gripped her hips tightly, and shoved his fat-end cock deep.

She'd barely caught her breath from the unexpected backend invasion when he started rooting inside her. In short, staccato thrusts he stabbed into her; the pressure had been painful as hell.

At the same time he'd eased two of his fingers inside her pussy, pressing past her resistance, no gentleness at all. Then he'd added the others, until the bastard had his entire hand jammed inside her, fisting her.

Despite her screaming he'd continued his harsh fucking. She'd breathlessly begged him to stop, telling him that it hurt.

He'd laughed, told her she knew she liked it, ignored her cries, and continued to ply both ends of her.

He continued to screw her with his fist and sodomize her with his oddly shaped dick, rotating it, shoving both deep inside her until she'd surprisingly felt her pussy gush. Her fluids eased over his hand and down her thighs, and within moments she was pumping and grinding, fucking him as wildly as he was fucking her.

When he bit down on her nipple the pain sent a direct zing to her core and within seconds she came so hard, she nearly blacked out.

Despite her dislike of him, his self-absorbtion, his over-confidence, the way he strutted about like a rooster, she'd gotten hooked on his kinky brand of sex.

She'd been his secretary for less than six months. It had taken her all of a few weeks to get him in bed. She'd wondered why he took her up on the offer. Not that she doubted her own attraction, but she knew he was dating that nerdy-ass pharmacist. She also knew he had someone else he was seeing, although he didn't know she knew *that*. After the first few times together, she'd asked him why.

He'd laughed, looking at her as though she were someone to be pitied. With her, he said, he was the one in charge; he was the one calling the shots. She'd thought the answer odd.

At first, when he'd told her he couldn't do the things he did to her to Gaby, his precious Gaby, she'd resented it, even though she had initiated the first encounter with him. Hearing him say that he couldn't get freaky with Gaby like he could with her had made Marissa furious.

He couldn't soil the princess.

For her, he gave his gentle lovemaking. Kissing, eating her pussy, never allowing her to swallow his dick, none of the shit he had Marissa doing, getting her so wrapped up in him, he had her on her knees, begging to suck his cock.

She clenched her teeth in anger. It wasn't supposed to be like that. *She* was the one that was supposed to get him sprung, not the other way around.

As he went about energetically spraying the room, she ran resentful eyes over his body, settling on his pale cock as it swung gently. Her eyes settled over his tight, small, compact ballsack, nestled snugly behind his cock.

Marissa grimaced and slightly adjusted her sore bottom into a more comfortable position. She reached for her purse.

"She's not supposed to come back until tomorrow, anyway. What's the fuss?" she mumbled and defiantly shook out another cigarette.

He spared her only a withering glance from his pale blue eyes, his gaze holding hers for a fraction of a second. Marissa shivered from the expression in his flat eyes, and with shaky hands, returned the cigarette to the package and put it back inside her purse.

Once she'd obeyed his silent edict, he threw her a small, satisfied nod before he turned away and walked back into the bathroom.

"So when *is* she getting back? What time, exactly?" Marissa leaned back against the headboard, pretending a nonchalance she was far from feeling. She heard him open the closet door inside the bathroom, before, minutes later, he emerged.

By the time he reentered the room, he'd pulled on a pair of cream-colored loose-fitting linen slacks, and was in the process of buttoning a matching short-sleeve shirt. After he'd buttoned the last button, he turned his attention back to her.

Marissa plastered a lazy smile on her face, keeping her irritation in check.

As much as she liked to pull his tail, his reactions weren't always predictable. She didn't feel like going through the routine of him having to "discipline" her. The sadistic son of a bitch liked that shit way too much.

He picked up his gold Rolex—fake, Marissa thought with an inner smirk—and fastened it onto his wrist before answering her.

"She's flying in later today. I pick her up at the airport in a few hours. Speaking of which, you'd better get dressed and get out of here. I need to clean up before Gaby gets home," he told her, picking up her discarded underclothes.

As if her clothes were some nasty thing, he held them out for her to take, pinched between three of his fingers, a look of distaste on his angular features.

"Sure, baby, no problem."

Marissa leisurely swung her feet over the side of the bed, stood, and stretched her body, purposely pushing her large impressive breasts forward, and yawned deeply. She took satisfaction in the look of irritation that flashed across his face when she took her time before accepting her clothes from him.

"What's the rush? We have time for one more . . . bit of play, don't we?" she asked, hooking her clothes over her arm. She raked the long acrylic fingernails of her other hand down his chest.

"No, I've got things to do." He reached a hand out and grasped her hand as it stopped at the waistband of his slacks.

A trill of fearful excitement settled in her stomach when he pinned her with his flat stare.

"Did you set up the meeting?" he asked, reminding her of what he wanted her to do for him.

"Yes, uh, I did. I'd better get going," she murmured, and breathed an audible sigh of relief when he released her arm. She barely controlled her trembling legs and stopped herself from stumbling when he abruptly let her go.

"Good," he said in satisfaction as he walked toward the door.

His next words halted her before she could make her escape into the bathroom. "And, Marissa, I won't be in need of your . . . services . . . for a while. I'll call you when I need you. Don't make the mistake of calling me when I'm not at the office again. I don't want Gaby to start asking questions about you. Do I make myself clear?" He didn't bother to look at her as he asked the question.

She nodded her head slowly, even though he wasn't there to see her.

If she played her cards right, went along with what he wanted from her, she would take him away from his princess, as well as the other, she thought, a calculating smile crossing her mouth.

5

Gaby stood in front of Sweet, pillowed against his naked, broad chest, and breathed in the musky scents of the night air.

Her skin tingled when she felt his lips graze down her neck.

"Beautiful," he breathed against her earlobe, the whispered words tickling the fine hairs around the nape of her neck.

"It is," she agreed, hyperaware of her state of undress and his hard body blanketing her back.

"I think we're referring to do two different things." He pulled her even more snugly against his body. Gaby closed her eyes, enjoying the feel of his hard body pressed against hers.

"Although, as beautiful as it is out here, I feel—" she hesitated, unsure how to explain.

"Exposed?" he finished.

She laughed self-consciously and agreed, "Yes—I feel exposed."

When he'd first brought her outside, she'd been too dazed to realize they were on the balcony, with her fully naked, and Sweet still wearing nothing but the low-riding jeans he'd greeted her in. Once she'd come out of her sexually satisfied daze, she also realized she was butt naked in full view of anyone who would chance to walk by the dark alley.

As bold as she was feeling that night, the thought of someone, probably a drunk, walking by and checking out the peep show she was providing wasn't all that appealing. To say the least.

He turned her around to face him.

"Maybe it would make you feel better if you weren't alone . . . and exposed," he murmured and began to undress. Her desire to see him completely naked made her temporarily forget the chance she was taking. Fascinated, hot, needy, she watched him draw his jeans down his long legs and kick them to the side.

His skin was the same light gold all over, with no tan lines to blemish his body. And what a body he had. A lean waist led to thick thighs corded with muscle, long calves, and long, sculpted feet.

Her eyes trailed back up his body and stopped at the juncture of his thighs.

Her tongue snaked out and licked her lips, her eyes drawn, inevitably, toward his cock, nested in the dark curly hair that covered his groin.

He had a beautiful dick.

The skin covering his shaft was just a shade darker than the rest of him. Because of that, it seemed to emphasize its thickness, underlining its sheer masculine beauty.

Fascinated, she stared at it. It was perfectly symmetric in thickness, the blunt end of the shaft's head curving gently against his stomach.

Gabrielle thought of how good it would feel digging inside her, scraping against her spot . . .

"Go ahead, touch it."

Startled, Gaby glanced up at him.

Hesitantly, she reached a hand out and ran her fingers lightly over him. In the moonlight she could make out the blue tracings of his veins that ran like a map around his shaft.

She wrapped around him and squeezed, gently.

"There's no one out here. Just you and me. And no one is going to see us even if they walked by and happened to look up. All they'd see is two shadows in the dark."

"Still . . ." she allowed the words to dangle and reluctantly withdrew her hand.

"Don't think about anyone but me. And the pleasure I'll give you."

He turned her back around, forcing her to face the alley.

Gaby released a small sigh when one of his hands snaked around her waist and rubbed the slight curve of her belly. When the other hand cupped one of her breasts in his hand, softly bouncing the orb in his palm, massaging it, as his thumb rested over her areola and thumbed her nipple, she groaned.

"Sssh. If you make noise, someone *will* notice us. You have to be quiet. Can you do that?"

One hand toyed with and palmed one of her breasts, the roughened pad of his thumb stroking over her nipple. The other hand trailed down her body, over her belly, before reaching the apex of her thighs.

He reached between her legs, his palm stroking the tight curls on her mound, then one thick finger delved between the plump lips of her sex.

In unison, they released moans of satisfaction.

"Yes . . . I . . . I can," she moaned, grinding against his fingers. He had her body pressed flush against his, back to stomach, his mouth against the back of her head. She felt his smile.

"You like that?" he murmured the question.

He moved his head to the side of her neck, pushed her hair to the side, and stroked his tongue along her neck, raising goose bumps over her body.

When he pulled the lobe of her ear into his mouth, suckling hard as both hands continued to play with her, his finger now stroking deep inside her, Gaby felt her cream trickle down, covering his finger and hand.

She bobbed her head up and down in agreement, incapable of speech.

Gaby's heartbeat increased when he added a second finger, easing it inside her vagina in a long glide. When he circled his fingers inside her in clockwise motions, she bit the inside of her cheek to prevent a cry from escaping.

"Widen your legs. I need to get at you better," he released her ear to whisper against her temple.

Nodding her head mutely, Gaby did as he instructed and spread her legs farther apart.

"Good girl, just like that," he praised and continued stroking deep inside her pussy while playing with her breasts.

With her breath escaping in hitched puffs of air, Gaby furtively glanced down; fear of getting caught warred with the thrill of what he was doing to her, what he was forcing her to do.

"No one will see us. This area is secluded and we're too far up. No one will know what we're doing unless you let them know. Can you be a good girl and be quiet?" he whispered against her.

Unable to speak, she remained mute.

"You have to trust me, Gaby," he continued his low-talking barrage against the side of her neck. "Can you do that . . . trust me?"

Gaby swallowed and hesitated before she nodded her head in assent. He lifted her, slightly, his hands on the sides of her waist. She swallowed a sigh of pleasure when his thick shaft rubbed against her ass.

He moved one hand away from her and she glanced over her shoulder far enough to see him reaching into a pocket in his discarded jeans and withdrawing something.

In the dark, she couldn't see what he'd retrieved and palmed in his hand. When his toying fingers inside her pussy hit a particularly good spot, she moaned and turned back around, rolling her hips against him.

Moments later, she felt the broad head of his cock press against her. When his cock feathered around her pussy, seeking entry, Gaby reached a hand back to stall him, twisting her head around to see him better.

"Wait—wait, you have to use a condom! I'm on the pill, but uh, I don't know you, and . . ."

Her words were stopped, mid-sentence.

She clamped her lips tightly shut to prevent the cry from coming from her lips when his fingers pressed deeply into the flesh of her hips and he shoved his thick, turgid cock deep inside her body in one long, hot, thrust, forcing her to her tiptoes.

Helpless, feeling stuffed, so turned on, so hot, her body began to shake. Gaby held out against rooting her body against his thick shaft.

"It's taken care of," he murmured, his lips pressed against her neck.

He opened his mouth and began sucking on her, licking her neck before pulling the fleshy portion of her earlobe into his mouth. Pushing away from her, he grabbed both of her hands and placed them in front of her, forcing her to grasp the railing.

"Keep them there."

With the sight of her rounded bottom slapping against him, her plush breasts jostling with every thrust, Demetri felt his balls tighten, his cock grow thicker inside her slick heat.

He placed one hand on her thigh; he placed the other loosely around the back of her neck to steady her as he plunged inside her tight, moist heat.

"Hmm, yes, yes," she cried out hoarsely with each jostling of her body, her pussy clamping hard on his erection, testing the limits of his control.

He slapped one of the round, brown globes, sharply. The surprise of the sting made her gasp. "You don't want anyone to hear us, do you?"

When she shook her head no, he shafted into her smoothly, forcing her body to lurch forward.

Her smooth brown back glistened with sweat in the moonlight, her body gyrating, grinding against his dick with her head hung down low as she not only accepted his powerful thrust but also gave back as much as she got.

His thrusts became deeper.

He'd given her the directive not to speak, not to cry out. Yet, he had to clamp his mouth tight, grit his teeth together, and close his eyes against the feel of her tight heat clenching and gripping, milking his dick with each glide and retreat of him inside her heat.

He closed his eyes against the sight of her back rising and falling as she panted against his thrusts as he rocked into her.

He'd wanted to draw out the pleasure longer, wanted to get her so strung out, so desperate to come, she'd do anything.

He might have been able to, had she not chosen that moment to reach between her legs and grasp his sac.

The minute her light touch stroked him, his body tightened, and his balls tingled. Sweat dripped down his face and landed on the smooth curve of her waist.

He removed his hand from her neck, where he'd pinned her, to move between her legs. As he pumped inside her in tight rhythmic strokes, his fingers separated the lips of her pussy and stroked her straining bud.

He heard the scream lodged in her throat as her body began to spasm.

She bucked against him, her body jerking and her whimpering cries frantic as she ground herself against him

Demetri waited until the last minute to release. He savored the last delicious moments of her wet heat clamping and releasing his shaft before, with a groan, he could hold back no longer. He placed one hand at the curve of her waist and pulled out of her sweet, hot pussy.

He grasped his cock firmly in his hand and ripped off the

condom. With four short pumps, his cum jetted from his body, landing on the smooth brown curvature of her spine.

The muscles in his neck corded, he felt the veins pulsing as he came on her until he was finally depleted. The last of his cum left his body in painful spurts, landed, slid off her back and down her sides. He rested his chest on her back, gulping in large breaths of air.

After his breath calmed and he'd come out of his haze, he turned her around and lifted her into his arms, carrying her away from the balcony and into the bedroom on unsteady legs.

He placed her in the middle of the bed and fell down behind her. Within minutes, she was asleep.

A satisfied smile lifted the corners of his mouth when he heard her soft snores.

In that moment, she seemed so benign. So innocent. It was hard to imagine her to be the con artist she was thought to be. It was also hard to ignore his gut reaction to her. The one that his mind had to fight against, doubt filling him about his plan to get her to trust him.

To dominate her. She'd responded beautifully, better than he'd thought.

When she'd come into the club without panties and all but begging him to fuck her, he counted himself lucky and had began to devise his plan. Now, his gut was telling him there was more to her than met the eye.

He finally settled down beside her, an uneasy feeling in the pit of his stomach.

He pulled her close to his body, and he, too, drifted off into sleep.

6

When he woke, she was nestled close to him. So close he could see, in the moonlit room, the spattering of freckles across the short bridge of her nose. A small smile lifted one corner of his mouth. She looked so sweet. So innocent.

Demetri sat up in the bed and glanced around, looking for the clock. It was just after two in the morning. He'd been asleep for an hour.

He'd been surprised when he'd drifted off to sleep soon after having sex with her. It was something he hadn't done with a woman in a long time.

Now, awake, he glanced down at her, studying her as she continued to sleep.

One of her small hands was open, palm up, the other tucked beneath her cheek as she lay in peaceful repose. The skin on her face looked incredibly soft.

He moved a hand as though to touch her cheek and caught himself. Instead, he reached around her and grabbed a prophylactic from the nightstand and jerked it onto his shaft.

"Wha-what is it?" she sleepily asked, her eyes shifting open slowly, when he pressed her fully onto her back.

"Nothing . . . just this." He settled between her thighs, nudged them farther apart. Grasping his cock, he pressed past her swollen vaginal lips and eased inside her body until he was fully seated in her. He groaned once he was inside, his dick pressing deeply into her core.

She hissed, her hands coming up to his shoulders to brace herself. "Wait. I, uh—"

He covered her protests with his lips. He earnestly explored the cavern of her mouth with his tongue in deep, carnal strokes that mimicked the strokes he delivered inside her clenching heat.

Placing his hands beneath the bend of her knees, he opened her so that her body cradled his snugly, her knees lying over his forearms, and began to slide in and out of her body. His strokes were short, steady, strong.

He ground against her so that with every stroke he pressed against her tight little clit, rolling his hips to increase the friction, as he adjusted her body along his, aligning them so that he hit her spot with each controlled stroke, until she whimpered and cried out.

No sounds could be heard in the moon-washed room, save their mutual harsh breaths as he stroked into her, digging into her sweetness with fevered attention until she broke.

She screamed into his mouth and with one final thrust he emptied deep inside her, his heart thudding harshly against his chest, his arms, legs, and body violently shaking. He'd fucked her so hard, determined to make it all about the sex.

As his body relaxed, he forced himself to forget the way her tight sweet snatch gloved his dick ferociously in its delicate grip.

Forced himself to ignore the hot little mewling sounds of pleasure she made as he stroked into her. No matter what he did, no matter what deviant demand he made, she willingly accepted.

His cock was finally soft, his hard-on disappearing as he lay nestled between her soft thighs. He moved himself off her, away from the temptation of flipping her around, and lifting her by her pretty round ass, and going another round or two with her. He ignored the need to fuck her until he'd gotten his fill of her.

God, what the hell was wrong with him?

As she lay spent on the pillow, facing him, her soft, curvy little body nestling close, he stared up at the ceiling with sightless eyes.

She was just a job. And this was just a lay.

A way to get her to trust him. Get her to fein for it, for him. She was only a lay: no more, no less.

He reminded himself of this as she placed one small hand in the middle on his chest, her head near his heart. Unconsciously, he lifted her hand, laced it with his as it rested on his chest. She murmured something unintelligible, a smile lifting the generous curve of her mouth, and settled into sleep.

She was so vulnerable. He'd read the vulnerability as the night wore on. With each demand he made of her and which she willingly accepted, she showed him her vulnerability.

And he would use that same vulnerability against her.

He would do whatever it took to get her to open up to him and tell him everything.

If he played his cards right, played *her* right . . . it wouldn't take long.

His gaze ran over her smooth brown back, past the indentation of her waist, past rounded hips and the plump cheeks of her apple-shaped buttocks. He followed the visual journey back, until he reached her face, silhouetted, half in shadow from the moon's glow.

Her face was flushed and her eyes were closed; a small smile lifted the corner of her generous mouth as she lay facing him.

Her wild, mussed hair fanned the pillow she lay on. The

content look on her face, coupled with the relaxed way she lay spread on the bed, presented a picture of a woman completely satisfied, completely at odds with how she looked down at the bar, where her nervousness and anger were easy to discern.

No . . . it shouldn't take him very long at all to get inside her mind, to push past her defenses.

His cock twitched in response to the erotic picture she presented.

Despite his intent to leave her alone, knowing she was exhausted and sore, he placed his hand at the small of her back and ran it over the swell of each rounded butt cheek, before his hand worked its way between her thighs. Her wetness saturated his finger.

She released a quiet moan when he cupped her warm mound and two fingers sliced into her seam, opening her to his probing fingers. Another glided over the stickiness of her residual cream nestled inside the lips of her pussy.

When she winced as he fingered her, he jerked his head up, glancing at her face.

"Sore?"

She opened drowsy eyes to look at him. "Yeah, somewhat," she said and uttered a small, sexy laugh before allowing her eyes to drift closed, again.

"Don't move. Stay just like that," he said and she murmured an assent. "I'll be right back."

With one last lingering caress against her mons, he moved away from her and off the bed. Demetri walked to the kitchen and opened several overhead cabinets until he found what he was looking for and removed the small container of Epsom salts and a bowl.

He filled the bowl with warm water and poured in a generous amount of the salts, twirling it with his fingers to help it dissolve.

On his way to the bathroom, he glanced over at the bed,

where she lay quietly in the same position in which he'd left her. He smiled.

Turning, he went into the bathroom, retrieved a wash towel, and returned to the bed.

Placing the basin on the bedside table, he wrung the water from the small towel and sat down on the edge of the bed.

She lay with one hand under her cheek, the other hugging one of the pillows near her. Demetri felt the corners of his mouth lift at the picture she presented of decadent innocence.

After wringing the water from the towel, he folded it around one hand. With the other hand, he spread her legs farther apart.

"What are you—"

"Sssh, it's okay. I'm just washing you."

She moaned when he began to run the towel over her body in slow swirls, starting at the S curve in the small of her back and working his way down and over each of her rounded butt cheeks.

When he got to the plump underside of one, he trailed his towel-covered hand beneath the crease and moved to her mound, separating the soft lips of her pussy, lightly seaming her crease. He moved the towel away, down her legs, around the bend of her knee, and dipped the towel back into the water.

With her eyes closed, she jerked when she felt the warm, wet towel, touch her again, stroking down her back following the line of her spine. Gaby smiled and turned her face to the side, one arm hugging the pillow closer.

She breathed in his distinct, masculine scent from the pillow, knowing that both the scent and the man were firmly entrenched in her body. She'd probably always associate this unique scent with the man who'd made her feel more alive in the last few hours than she'd felt in a long time.

Gabby felt a ping of shame because she'd made love—scratch that—she'd had *sex* with a man she didn't know from a can of paint. Not only that, but she'd done so while still in a relationship with another.

Even though the man she was involved with obviously had no qualms about sleeping with someone else.

All guilt flew out the window when she remembered the woman's frantic moans and cries of passion and Adam's face, strained and flushed as he held on to the woman's hips while driving into her from behind.

"Do you like this?" the murmured question brought Gaby back to where she was, thoughts of Adam evaporating as strong hands stroked and smoothed over her body.

"Hmm. Yes, I do," she whispered as his hand, wrapped in the warm towel, ran over the rounded cheeks of her buttocks.

"Open your legs for me." When she obliged, he ran the towel along her inner leg, starting at her knees and working up to her thighs, before cupping her mound.

Gaby squirmed around the towel, wincing when his fingers connected with her labia.

"Sore?" he asked, and she nodded.

"I'm sorry. I didn't mean to be so rough with you," he murmured and she heard him dip the towel into the basin of water. He lifted her lower body slightly and touched the throbbing lips of her vagina.

Her breath caught. She closed her eyes and swallowed. Although his touch made her stinging lips ache, it was an ache that felt good, sinfully good.

"Turn over for me," he said and obligingly she turned so that she lay open to him.

"Use your fingers to spread your vagina," Demetri instructed he, and felt his cock stir at the image she presented, splayed out in front of him. He read the instant of hesitation in her eyes and waited.

Her small hands reached down on either side of her mound and opened the lips of her vagina for him.

He offered her a small lift of his lips in satisfaction at her hesitant, yet obedient, compliance.

"You have the sweetest pussy I've ever seen."

He wiped between her lips with the towel and a small trickle of warm water ran between the dark plum-colored inner lips of her vagina.

"I've never had anyone do this to me before," she admitted in a low voice.

He glanced up at her, a question in his eyes. "Not even your man?"

"What do you mean?"

"Your man never does this for you?"

At the question, she bit her lip, worrying it between her teeth. "Wha-what man? Who says I have one?" she stammered out the question. She pushed against him when he pinched the tip of her clit between two towel-wrapped fingers. The sting, he knew, hadn't really hurt.

But it had gotten her attention.

"Don't lie to me."

He ran small circles around her clit with his fingers, massaging the tightening bud, easing the small hurt.

"The one you've been coming to the club with."

He continued to clean her, not making eye contact with her, his attention on his task.

"I've seen the two of you around the Sweet Spot," he said.

The fact that he'd noticed her before tonight gave her a thrill.

After long moments she spoke.

"I, well . . ." She stopped and took a deep breath. "I caught him having sex with his secretary," she finally finished.

At that he glanced up at her. "Not very original, huh?"

He gently inserted a finger, wrapped in the towel, deep inside her body. Her back arched away from the mattress, a hiss of pleasure escaping her lips.

"Not. Not very," she finally managed to say.

"Damn fool," Demetri said and when she laughed breathlessly, it pulled a smile from him as well.

All laughter stopped, replaced by a heartfelt moan, when he

leaned down and kissed her pussy as his finger skewered deep inside her and slowly dragged back out.

"His loss, my gain," he said.

Without waiting for a response, he bumped her thighs apart and leaned down, replacing his fingers and towel with the warmth of his mouth, and finished the task of cleaning her with his lips, tongue, and teeth.

Thoroughly.

7

The cool breeze wafting over her body from the open balcony doors and light filtering into the room wasn't what woke Gaby up. The unfamiliar weight of what could only be a man's—a very large man's—arm was draped loosely across her waist.

That, as well as the big hand attached to the arm clamped between her thighs, cupping her mound, the other lightly resting on her exposed breasts, and a warm, hard chest blanketing her back, was what woke her.

Slowly she opened swollen, gritty eyes, glanced down at her nakedness, and stifled a groan.

She'd hoped—prayed—that last night had all been a dream. A wild, out-of-this-world, don't-wake-me-'til-I-come kind of dream . . . but a dream nonetheless.

She eased a hand down and touched her thigh, feeling the stickiness of her own cum.

"Damn," she whispered when she realized it was, *had been*, all too real. When he mumbled, she clamped her lips shut, not wanting to wake the slumbering man.

Sweet.

The memory of what he'd done to her last night caused a rash of heated memories to flood her mind.

Slowly, carefully, Gaby removed his hand from where it nestled quite comfortably between her thighs and plucked the other from her breast, keeping a wary glance on him to make sure he didn't awake.

Despite their nocturnal excess, his cock was still slightly thickened as it nestled in the crease of her ass.

"Who are you, super damn man?" she whispered and promptly clamped her lips shut when his shaft twitched against her.

She then eased away from him, snaking her body from beneath his arm, and scooted over to the edge of the large, canopied bed. Frantic eyes darted in his direction when he stirred, mumbling; she feared she'd awaken him before she could get the hell out of Dodge.

Her breath caught and held until he wrapped one of his big arms around a pillow, and laid facedown, on the bed, uttering a grunt. With a sigh, Gaby rose from the bed.

She looked back over the man in question, and despite last night's excess, despite the fact that she knew good and well it was only for one night, one part of her played "what if."

What if she stayed lying next to him? What if he woke up and wanted a part two . . . or, considering the number of times they'd had sex, part five or six?

What if . . .

She shook her head at the thought.

No, she'd be best off escaping while she could. The ramifications of what she'd fully participated in weren't something she was ready to deal with. No point in thinking of an encore.

She winced when her legs hit the floor. Her thighs, her backside, dear God, even her breasts—all had the same delicious ache that gave testimony that he'd earned his nickname in spades.

Sweet.

Although what he'd done to her, had her doing to him, had

been anything but *sweet*. It had been the kind of raw, nasty sex she'd never experienced in her life.

And it had fulfilled every one of her fantasies, to the nth power. Exceedingly so.

She winced again when she caught sight of the many used condoms lying spent on the floor.

On tiptoes she walked around the room gathering her clothes, casting furtive glances in his direction every few seconds, making sure he wasn't awake.

Donning her clothes quickly, haphazardly, she dressed. After slipping her heels back on to her feet, she scooped up her purse and slung it over her shoulder as she walked toward the door.

"Damn!" she hissed, as she eased back the cage of the outer elevator.

She glanced over her shoulder to see if the creaking noise had awakened Sweet and breathed a sigh of relief when he slept on, like a baby. A big, sexy, contented baby.

He flipped his large body farther down on the bed and threw the pillow he'd been clutching over his head.

Gaby closed her eyes briefly, sent a thankful prayer to God, and blew out a breath of air before hurrying into the elevator.

She just wanted to get away before he could wake up. If she didn't . . . hell, she didn't know what would happen.

Scurrying into the elevator, she closed the outer door and stabbed the down arrow button repeatedly, trying to hasten the lazy elevator into efficiency. She leaned back against the wall of the elevator with a heartfelt groan of relief when it lumbered to wakefulness and she began to descend.

When Demetri was sure Gabrielle was gone, he opened his eyes and sat up in the bed, pushing the tangled silk sheets away from his body and throwing his legs over the side of the bed.

Glancing over at the clock, he noted the time. Just barely dawn.

As soon as she'd woken, he'd been aware of it, snapping out of sleep as soon as her even breaths of sleep changed.

Both his former military special ops training, and his ... *unique* ... FBI training had been such that his sleep had become light. However, he'd been surprised that after their marathon sex session, he'd actually fallen into a deep enough sleep that she'd woken before him.

He'd also been surprised when he'd wakened to find their limbs twined, with one of his hands cupping her mound and the other palming one of her breasts.

He stared down at himself in disgust. His dick was still partially erect.

He ran a hand over it, from stem to root, his thumb wiping away a gem of his pre-cum with absentminded attention.

He needed to revise his plan.

After last night, he realized that mere sex wasn't going to cut it to get information from her.

He hadn't known anything about her, her bio was sketchy, and he'd only gone on instinct on how to approach the mission. His gut was telling him she was different. That she wasn't just some low-down scam artist. That she was unlike the crooks he used to deal with on a regular basis, that she and her partner— Adam Quick—weren't cut from the same cloth.

Something wasn't right with the picture.

He bounded from the bed, and walked, naked, through the loft until he reached the room he'd designated as his office.

He sat down in the large leather chair, touched the keypad on his computer, and watched it flare to life. He clicked on an icon on his control panel and keyed in a series of numbers and symbols until he gained access to what he needed.

He shook his head. Hacking into government systems that were supposed to be hackproof was too damn easy.

His natural cynicism returned as he typed in her name and seconds later his eyes scanned the information on his screen looking for something, *anything* that might have been missed, something that would clue him in to the woman she really was.

She may not be the same as Adam, her motivation may be different . . . but she was nobody's innocent.

He'd find out what her motivation was, and after that he'd get the information he needed.

He rose and grabbed a pair of shorts and stepped into them before settling down at his desk. He touched the screen and quickly typed in his password and logged on.

His former superior had briefed him on what the department knew about Gabrielle and her partner. What he was searching for now was information on her family members, something about which the intel he'd been given had been sketchy at best. What he did know was that she'd been taken from her mother, due to her mother being an addict and unfit to care for Gabrielle. As a young girl, she'd gone into the system.

And once in the system, a person's information was always there. He just had to pick apart what was available to ferret out anything useful.

He'd already learned more about Gabrielle's personal life than what his superior had briefed him on. The department didn't know about her mother, or Nick hadn't let on what he knew, afraid Demetri would allow it to interfere with his investigation of the woman, afraid he'd feel sympathy for her.

Demetri shook his head as his fingers flew over the keyboard, going in and out of various search engines, private ones as well as government- and military-operated, searching for more information on Gabrielle Marlowe.

"Damn, that doesn't make any sense. Nick knows I'm a professional. Wouldn't allow my own feelings to interfere with my investigation," he murmured. "Something's missing. Something with her mother? Shit . . ." he continued his search, talking out loud as he typed in her mother's name.

After searching for over an hour, he came up with several

references to Gabrielle Marlowe, but it was for the woman he was investigating, and not her mother. It seemed Gabrielle was quite the community activist, volunteering for various organizations helping the homeless and advocating for Medicare and Medicaid reform.

None of her extracurricular activities had been added to the bio he'd been given. Again, he wondered why.

None of it made any damn sense, Demetri thought in frustration. It didn't add up. Nothing he'd learned from her so far. She volunteered and advocated for disenfranchised folks.

And ripped off the government at the same time.

And after one night with her, his knew she wasn't a heartless criminal out to make a quick buck, no matter how hard he tried to deny it.

"Shit," Demetri rubbed the back of his stiff neck, rotating it to massage out the kinks. With a tired sigh, he stood and pushed back from his chair.

He knew where she worked, where she lived. But he couldn't go to her.

All he could do now was chill, sit back, and wait for her to come back to him. And hope that she wouldn't wait long.

Waiting wasn't a concept Demetri mastered very well when on the hunt, he thought, a wicked smile stretching his mouth wide in anticipation.

8

"So, that's about it. I guess I'm still in shock about it all ... don't really know where my head is about the situation."

Gaby methodically twirled the thin stirrer in her coffee. She stared down at the light brown coffee, heavily laced with cream and sugar, swirling within the mug.

She brought the cup to her mouth and took a deep swallow. She winced at the slight burn as the hot liquid slid down her throat.

"Hmmm," the woman across from her murmured and Gaby glanced over the small table at her.

"Hmmm, what?" Gaby asked, raising a brow in question.

Abigail Winters held Gaby's gaze as she took a delicate bite of her sandwich before placing it back down on the gold-rimmed china plate. She dusted her fingertips of crumbs before answering.

"He made a mistake, Gaby. A stupid one, but a mistake. He's human," she replied, bluntly. "And a man," she said and took a small sip of her tea before continuing. "They all make stupid mistakes. I think it's part of their genetic makeup."

Gaby shook her head and looked away, "It hurt. Bad." She replied in a soft voice. "I thought he cared about me."

"And because of this, you don't think he does?" Abigail asked, pinning Gabriel with a stare.

Unable to keep eye contact, Gaby allowed her eyes to drift away.

Abigail reached across the table and placed her hand over Gaby's. The gesture was unexpected. Tears came unbidden to Gaby's eyes.

"I know," the older woman said. "And I understand."

"How can you understand? Hunter would never do something like that to you."

"Don't be too sure. Within the first year of our marriage, Hunter cheated."

Gaby's eyes widened. Abigail's disclosure surprised her.

"Don't look so shocked," she laughed, echoing Gaby's thoughts. Gaby saw the pain flare in Abigail's dark eyes before it quickly receded. "It was after I lost the baby. It was a bad time for us. I withdrew and he . . . well, it was a bad time," she finished.

"I'm sorry." Gaby regretted that she'd said what she did, the pain she'd inadvertently caused her friend. She knew Abigail's history and knew that the baby she lost with Hunter had been the second child Abigail had that hadn't lived.

"It's okay," Abigail said, forcing a smile on her face. "It was a long time ago and we got past it because we loved each other. Maybe you can get past Adam's indiscretion?"

"Yes, well, I don't know that I'm able to forgive that. Maybe I'm not as forgiving a woman as you," she said.

"Nonsense," Abigail said. "You have the biggest heart of anyone I know! And this isn't easy. I know that."

Gaby offered her a half-smile, one she couldn't maintain long before it dropped off her face. "And to be honest, I'm not sure that I love him. I don't know, Abigail. My emotions are jacked up right about now. I really don't know what I feel," she laughed without humor.

"That's fine. Give it time. But, what I do know is that Adam cares about you. I *know* that he does. The few times I've seen the two of you together . . . it shows. He made a mistake." She held up a hand when Gaby's eyes flew to hers, and her mouth opened. "A stupid-assed mistake," she clarified. "But, it was a mistake. At least give the man the chance to explain before you . . ."

Before Abigail could finish, Gaby was already shaking her head no, holding up a hand in entreaty.

"I can't think about all of that. Not right now. I need time," she replied, shaking her head.

In Abigail's eyes was a look of concern and sympathy. She nodded her head.

"Okay, sweetheart. Just give it time. Now, let's talk about the fund-raiser, tonight," she said, briskly changing the subject to Gaby's relief. "And, no, you're not ducking out, before you ask. You need to be there," she said, and Gaby laughed.

Abigail knew her well. Although she'd promised to come to the political fund-raiser, one many would give their soul, or at least a couple of body parts, to attend, it wasn't something Gaby was looking forward to.

But Abigail was right. Gaby needed to be there. And she was grateful to Abigail for using her considerable influence to get her name added to the list.

"Senator Chambers will be there, as well as a few others I want to introduce you to. Powerful men. Men, who if you get them in your corner, can prove to be valuable," she finished raising a perfectly arched, dark brow, smiling around the cup held to her lips.

Gaby ran a fond glance over Abigail Winters.

Abigail was a self-made woman, one who'd pulled herself out of poverty at a young age and risen to the top. She'd shared her story with Gabrielle. Much like Gaby, she'd had a mother who was addicted to drugs and who had left Abigail forgotten, alone in the world at an early age and forced to fend for herself.

She was a woman who had defied societal expectations of what she could accomplish given her earlier life circumstances. She had gone after her goals.

Gaby admired Abigail more than anyone in the world. She'd confided her own life story to Gaby when she'd first became her mentor, fifteen years ago.

At the age of seventeen, nearly thirty years ago, Abigail had run away from the group home she'd been living in and struck out on her own with a boy not much older than she was, running away from the small rural town and heading for the inner city.

She'd run away from the foster home she lived in with the boy who'd gotten her pregnant at the age of seventeen, gladly leaving the foster home, tired of being abused physically and verbally.

However, not too long after she'd run away with the young boy, she'd soon discovered he had a penchant for abuse as well, similar to what she'd suffered at the hands of her foster parents. He'd gotten drunk one night and had beaten her to within an inch of her life. She'd picked up the nearest object and bashed him over the head, knocking him out, and escaped.

She'd told Gaby that then and there she made a decision. She could do bad all by herself. She left the loser before he could even think to lay another hand on her. The second was that she was going to make something of her life.

After that, she'd worked in diners, clubs, fast-food joints, whatever it took to survive, all while finishing her education, earning a GED and later enrolling in the local business college.

A bright woman, she'd quickly caught on to the fine nuances of business and started her own enterprise, supplying other businesses with temporary help. Within five years, her small operation had grown by leaps and bounds, and she'd opened several branches throughout the state and nationwide.

Within that time, she'd met Hunter, fallen in love, and gotten married.

However, Abigail had been determined to be successful in her own right and, at the age of thirty, she was. Deciding to sell her business, she then began to be, what she affectionately called "a helpmate to her husband," as Hunter was CEO of a major pharmaceutical company.

Abigail also became involved in two things that brought her and Gaby together.

Due to her own history, Abigail became involved in sponsoring inner-city girls in business management and she became an advocate for Medicaid.

Knowing what it was like to have no medical care herself as a young woman, it was something she felt strongly about, and having a spouse who worked in the medical arena had given her power to help Gaby with her desire to see a bill passed that would enable the homeless and poor to receive medical benefits that would allow them to get medicine and also allow them to receive outpatient and inpatient rehabilitation for drug addiction.

She'd met Gaby when she'd been in foster care as an adolescent. Gaby had attended the youth center where Abigail had been volunteering. From early on, the two had taken to one another, with Abigail taking an avid interest in Gaby, becoming a mentor for her. Without Abigail . . . Gaby shook her head slightly, and smiled at the woman across from her. She had no idea how her life would have turned out. She owed Abigail more than she could ever repay.

"No, I'm not ducking out. I'll be there," she replied and smiled, even though she felt like doing anything else *but* smiling.

She knew if she wanted to get new sponsors for her community pharmacy, as well as reach those who had the power and influence necessary to support the bill to supply federal monies, she didn't have much of a choice.

Not to mention Abigail was relying on her to be there. Displeasing Abigail wasn't something she wanted to do and it had nothing to do with her own interests. She simply loved the woman.

"Good!" Abigail smiled, and clapped her hands together in satisfaction.

She then gave Gaby detailed information on the power players who would be at the fund-raiser.

"And, for the record, Senator Chambers happens to like women who wear their skirts short and their heels high," she said and winked, laughing when Gaby's eyes widened, the coffee in her mouth nearly spit out at the surprising info.

"Sweetheart, a woman must be fully armed, locked, and loaded, when playing the game," she said, winking.

She grew serious, the smile easing from her carefully madeup, exquisite face. "And I know that I can rely on you. Can't I, Gaby?" she asked, her gaze direct as she looked at Gaby across the table.

"Yes. Of course you can, Abigail," she murmured.

"Good. Now, let's talk strategy!" she said, smiling widely.

Adam's guts were tied up in a twisted ball of knots.

He knew he'd fucked up when he got caught fucking Melinda. Royally fucked up.

And now he'd have to pay for his mistakes.

But, in his defense, he'd had no idea Gaby was coming home early from her convention, he reasoned in his head.

Had he known, he wouldn't have been stupid enough to screw Melinda's ditzy ass in Gaby's bed.

Fuck, what had he been thinking?

It had been so long since he'd been able to have sex and feel like a man . . . so long since he'd been able to have the type of sex where he didn't either have to hold back and be gentle, like he did with Gaby, or be at the complete mercy of another, like he had been with his lover of over ten years.

And the temptation to feel in control was so tantalizing that he hadn't been able to turn away when Melinda had propositioned him. She'd been working for him for just six weeks, but in that time, she'd let him know that she was interested. The first time it happened he'd just come back from being rejected by his lover, told he'd again been a disappointment.

Angry, he'd used Melinda roughly. When she moaned and begged for more of his rough sex, he'd become excited, feeling as though for the first time in a long time, he was the one in control, the one calling the shots.

From then, he'd screwed her in every deviant way he could think of and she'd loved it. Begged him for more, in fact.

With Melinda, he'd felt like a man, a feeling he'd never really had before.

It had been hard to give up that feeling.

Of course, he had made sure that neither Gaby nor his lover knew about it. He'd been so careful. So fucking careful.

When Gaby had gone out of town he'd stayed at her home over the weekend, while his condo had been getting painted. When Melinda called he'd allowed her to come over.

She'd shown up wearing a pair of skintight booty shorts and a midriff-baring T-shirt. His eyes had fixated on her pointy little nipples stabbing against the thin material of her shirt.

Not to mention all that ass hanging out her shorts, just *begging* to be fucked. How was he supposed to resist that?

He hadn't.

No. There'd been no way in *hell* he'd been able to resist.

He blew out an anxious breath as he waited, forcing himself to remain seated, despite his overwhelming desire to bolt the hell out of the room and get away before Lee showed up.

He glanced around the luxurious room, his eyes going over

the Rembrandts, expensive furniture, and overall luxuriousness of the room.

Because of Lee, soon, he, too, would have all of this and more.

It had been easier to act out his need for dominance before he moved to San Antonio, at Lee's request. The times his lover flew in on business, times when the two of them would discuss the latest venture, decide if it was time for Adam to move on or not, were scarce. Yet they were intense. Not just because of the high he got whenever they pulled off or planned their latest scam, but just being around Lee . . . damn, it was a high all of its own.

The first time he'd met Lee he'd been a raggedy kid on the streets, eating out of trash bins and not knowing where his next meal would come from or where he would lay his head that night. Turning tricks to make what little money he could, one step away from being picked up by the cops on more than one occasion.

But, all of that changed. He'd been literally picked up from the streets, given a second chance in life . . . introduced to fine clothes, decent living, and good food.

He'd been loved. For the first time, Adam had been given love. And all he'd had to do was be sexually submissive to Lee and never, *ever* make first contact. And he was always to refer to his lover as Lee. An odd thing, but one Adam understood. Lee loved him, but Adam wasn't the only one in his lover's life.

And Adam loved in return. There was nothing he wouldn't do for his partner.

And that's what he considered Lee; his partner, even though they lived in different cities for most of their relationship, despite Adam's begging that they be together.

"You know I couldn't let you be with me . . . not now, but soon, baby, soon," was the only response Adam ever got whenever he'd asked. Soon, he stopped asking, not wanting to upset his mate.

If the nature of their relationship, their lovemaking, was odd, Adam stifled the need to ask questions.

After the first time, he learned quickly that while Lee was indulgent with him, kept him in a style he'd quickly learned to love, it could quickly turn to something ugly. Unconsciously, his hand went to his back, feathering over the old, nearly invisible welts.

He still carried the scars, although faint, from the first time he'd displeased his lover, the first and only time he'd received the harsh punishment. But now here he was, living in the same town, able to see his lover often as they worked together on the new game.

"You made a stupid mistake, Adam."

Adam jumped, and nearly pissed on himself in fear when he heard the husky voice directly behind him.

"I . . . I—"

"Sssh. No excuses."

Adam swallowed his fear with his heartbeat thudding an erratic rhythm against his chest. He stared down at his hands clenched tightly together, in his lap, forcing himself to remain very, very still.

"Now, I'll have to find a way to clean up your mess. It won't be easy convincing her to take you back."

"I know," Adam whispered the words, his throat nearly closing off as he swallowed the fearful anticipation he felt rolling up from the pit of his gut. "I'm sorry."

Not that he didn't enjoy their encounters. Each time they made love, each time he was at the complete will of his lover, he wanted it more and more. So much that he had become quickly addicted to his lover's way of lovemaking.

Not that it mattered.

In the end Adam submitted like he always did. He knew no other way. He never had.

"Take off your pants."

Obediently, Adam stood and drew his slacks, along with his boxers, down his legs and turned without being told. He grasped the back of the sofa, gripping it tightly, and waited.

He never knew which would come first, the pleasure or the pain. After the first and only lashing, his lover usually found other, unique ways to mete out his punishments, ones that wouldn't leave marks.

So, he waited.

He heard a rustling noise behind him and soon felt a warm breath on his neck.

He drew in a deep breath when a slick tongue stroked down his neck and firm hands grasped him by his hips.

"Do you want me, Adam?"

"Yes . . . yes, please," he begged, breathlessly.

"Tell me how much you want what I have. Tell me how badly you deserve to be punished," Lee demanded. "To be fucked." A pause. "But, which one first?" Adam heard the dark humor in the low voice and shut his eyes, tightly.

"I—I want it. I want—" His words were cut off by a sharp, keening cry when he felt a stinging pain from the thin leather strap against his backside.

So, it was to be pain before the pleasure. Punishment for his indiscretion. And he was being introduced to a new level of punishment.

He bit down on his bottom lip until he drew blood, silencing himself, even as he accepted the painful steady slaps of the leather strap raining down on his ass. The pain became intense, until his body nearly buckled and he nearly passed out.

Yet, he remained still, barely flinching as the belt steadily lashed against him. He felt a tingle in his balls, a near-giddy euphoria engulf him, as the last lash hit his bared buttocks. Then, a soothing hand ran down his back, easing over his stinging flesh.

A cool, soothing kiss preceded a sweet tongue licking away the new welts that now rose sharply on his body.

He had been forgiven.

"Hello?" Gaby snatched up the phone on the fifth ring, slightly out of breath.

"Hello, baby. It's me," the smooth voice on the other end spoke and Gaby wished like hell she'd looked at her caller ID before she'd picked up the phone.

"Am I going to see you tonight?" Adam asked, his voice low, pleading.

Gaby opened her mouth to speak. She promptly shut it; instead, balancing on one foot, she continued to smooth her left stocking up the length of her leg before snapping the band to her garter.

"What are you wearing tonight, beneath your dress? I can't wait to see it," he murmured, speaking in intimate tones, uttering a small, husky laugh. "Wear the pretty pink lace thong and bra set I bought you for Valentine's Day. Your skin looks so beautiful against that color." Gaby wanted to reach into the phone and slap him six ways to Sunday for the sheer balls he must have to call her up as though nothing had happened.

"Gaby . . . baby, are you there?"

"Yes. I'm here," she replied, her tone sharp. "And I told you, I don't want to talk to you, Adam. Not about anything, and most definitely *not* about what I will or *won't* be wearing beneath my clothes. You gave up the right to ask questions like that when you decided to fuck your secretary," she finished, and despite her anger, wanted to laugh when she heard his indrawn breath, knowing she'd surprised him with her bluntness.

"And, you know, you really have a lot of nerve even *thinking* that it's okay for you to make a panty request!"

She snapped the front closure of her lacy demi-bra closed. Pretty lingerie always made her feel sexy. Wanted. Hot. Kind of like erotic armor, whenever she wore it, despite what she was feeling on the inside. No matter how conflicted she felt, the sexy underwear gave her a measure of confidence and strength.

She needed her sexy armor a lot lately.

She cradled the phone between her shoulder and ear and slowly walked back toward her closet, pulling out several dresses, carrying them to her bedroom, and laying them down on her bed.

"Listen, when are you going to talk to me, let me explain? It's been two damn weeks, Gaby! She meant nothing to me, it was just a mistake, please. You have to believe me."

Gaby uttered a rude curse before she drew in a deep breath and stopped. "Look, I can't stop you from coming to the fundraiser tonight. But you can't force me to talk to you. You can't make this right, what you did, by smooth-talking your way out of it, Adam."

She disconnected the phone amid his angry rebuttal and resisted the urge to slam it against the nearest wall in anger.

She stared at the phone nestled in its cradle for long moments.

Screw it.

She snatched up the phone *and* the receiver and, pulling her hand back, threw them with all her might against the wall. The sound and sight of the phone shattering into several pieces temporarily eased the need she felt to do the same to Adam.

When she'd finally distanced herself from the situation long enough, she'd called him to break things off.

It hadn't been easy.

At first he'd tried to lie and say he didn't know what she was talking about. As though she hadn't seen him and his secretary going at it with her own two eyes.

She'd cut him off, hanging the phone up in his face with satisfaction. He'd called back and she'd turned off both the ringer to her home and her cell. Not that any of that had done any good.

He'd come by the school, and, not wanting to embarrass herself, she'd been forced to allow him into her office and closed the door. He'd pleaded and begged for her to forgive him, but she had remained steadfast in her refusal.

He'd then subtly reminded her of their *arrangement.* Before he'd slammed out of her office, he'd said: "If I were you, I would rethink trying to end our relationship. I wonder what the university, your peers, would think, not to mention what would happen to your precious pharmacy if anyone knew what you'd been doing."

Gaby had felt her heart plummet to her stomach.

She sat down on the edge of the bed and stared at her reflection in the mirror in front of her, sightlessly, wondering what in God's name she was going to do to get herself out of the situation now facing her.

9

"Excuse me." She held her drink close against her body and carefully threaded her way through the crowd, trying to keep the smile on her face from slipping.

Gabrielle felt acutely self-conscious at the black-tie event. Although she'd been to the occasional fund-raiser and company event that Abigail had brought her to, nothing compared to this, Gaby thought, looking around at the well-dressed, high-society crowd.

Thankfully she found a place to land, one where she had a nice visual of the crowd, but was not directly in plain view.

She raised the fluted goblet to her lips and took a sip of the expensive wine, wrinkling her nose, wishing she had a Diet Coke instead.

She was no connoisseur of fine wine, had never really acquired a taste for it, despite Abigail's insistence that she at least try. She set the glass down on the linen-covered table in front of her.

She searched the ballroom looking for Abigail and spied her across the room engaged in conversation with a high-profile celebrity couple, laughing comfortably with the pair.

Gaby hated fund-raisers with a passion. The mingling, the bustling crowds, loud talk, and networking she knew were all parts of the game. She was a loner by nature, one who'd learned early in life to keep to herself and who had a natural inclination to make herself as unnoticeable as possible—functions like these were ones she avoided like the plague.

But she had been grateful when Abigail had been able to secure an invitation for her to come to tonight's event, in the hope of cornering Senator Chambers face-to-face, to talk to him alone regarding the bill he was heralding that would cut off funding for the homeless in the city. If it passed, the bill would force her to close down the community pharmacy she'd helped start to serve the homeless and those without medical benefits in the city.

Her glance slid over the room, searching for Adam in the crowded room. She'd arrived less than thirty minutes ago, an hour after the fund-raiser began, and had so far been able to avoid contact with him.

Her eyes flitted over the women draped in jewels that if sold, could feed a small country, past the men in custom tuxes and the waitstaff, who were identifiable as workers only because of the small trays of drinks they carried.

As she scanned the crowed, she spotted Adam making a beeline for her. She jumped up from her seat and briskly walked in the direction opposite from that from which he was coming. She glanced over her shoulder and breathed a sigh of relief when she saw someone touch his arm, stopping him before he could follow her. The look of irritation that flashed across his angular face disappeared instantly; in its place a charming, oily smile appeared.

She felt overwhelmed at the moment. She needed to get away, gather her thoughts. Since coming home from that conference and finding her man in bed with another woman, which led to . . . other events, she wasn't on top of her game.

To say the least.

When she spied the ceiling-to-floor closed gauzy curtains blowing, she swiftly walked across and pushed them aside. She pushed open the glass balcony doors and walked outside, closing the doors behind her with a grateful sigh.

The night air hit her face and blew over her exposed arms and back. She shivered, despite the air's moist warmth. The "real" air felt good.

It was a welcome reprieve from the much cooler, yet artificial air within the ballroom.

She knew she was being ridiculous, but, despite the coolness of the room, the cloying . . . closeness . . . of the rich and powerful people in the room began to close in on her, making her *aware* of the vast differences between her and them.

Her sole purpose for coming had been to help her community pharmacy by talking to anyone who'd be willing to help, particularly the senator.

She shook her head. Foolish of her, she knew. She wondered if a single soul in the room, besides Abigail, gave one damn about anything besides their money, power, and wealth. And how to acquire more.

As she gazed out at the night scene, gazing over the brightly lit city below, her eyes sought something . . . she didn't really know what.

She leaned heavily against the wrought-iron railing and inhaled, dragging into her lungs as much as she could of the warm autumn night air.

"Beautiful night, isn't it?"

She turned and squinted her eyes against the dark until she made out the face of the man who'd asked the question and his voice registered. She relaxed and leaned back against the railing.

Hunter Winter's long, lean body ambled toward her from the corner of the balcony.

"Yes, it is," she agreed and with a small smile turned back toward the scene in front of her.

Once he was close, he, too, leaned into the railing. She felt his eyes on her instead of the skyline and turned toward him.

"I hope I'm not disturbing you? I didn't see you."

"Of course not." He waved a hand, dismissively. "Do you mind?" he asked, pulling a cigar from within the inner pocket of his tux.

She shook her head no. Cigar smoke had never really bothered her. In fact, there was something warm and welcoming about the strongly masculine aroma that had always appealed to her.

She watched him clamp the cigar firmly between his strong white teeth and take a long drag after lighting it.

"Want one?" he asked, a twinkle in his eye as though he *knew* she'd say no.

Gaby began to shake her head no, then, watching the gleam in his eyes, nodded her head yes instead. She laughed at the surprised look in his dark eyes.

In all honesty, Gaby don't know which one of them was more surprised, him or her.

Seems as though she'd been doing a lot of things out of the ordinary lately, she thought, and shrugged.

Proud that she only coughed a little, she took a small puff, inhaling enough to fill her mouth and allowing it to fill her lungs. She blew the smoke out between pursed lips. The smoke instantly gave her a light-headed feeling.

She watched in fascination as the curling smoke danced and rolled around her before blowing away along the wind.

"You're an interesting woman, Gaby," Hunter said, after he had taken a second deep inhalation of his own cigar.

She turned to him.

"In what way? Because of the cigar? I've always wanted to know what they tasted like," she replied, taking another inhalation, this one deeper. She exhaled and mentally patted herself on the back when she didn't choke. Not that she planned on making it a habit, she thought.

He narrowed his eyes against the twining smoke and continue to stare at her. She grew uncomfortable beneath his intense gaze.

"Well, the cigar, too. But—" he stopped, took a deep pull from the cigar. He turned his head away from her, and slowly blew out the smoke.

"Although, that's not what I'm talking about. There're a lot of . . . layers . . . to you."

Her brows drew together, "Layers?" she laughed, an embarrassed kind of sound, unsure if he was complimenting her or not.

"Yes. Layers *just* below the surface," he said. When he reached out and drew a finger along her jawline, she flinched. He dropped his finger.

He stared at her. In the darkness, his eyes seem to bore a hole directly into her soul. Again, she shivered, despite the warm night air.

"These events can be stifling. I always try and escape at least once or twice in the evening," he said, grimacing. Much like she felt when escaping Adam, Gabrielle felt a momentary reprieve when he switched subjects.

"I thought you and Abigail loved them," Gaby returned, her surprise making her forget her temporary unease.

A look of disgust graced his lean face.

"*Abigail* loves them. I'd rather be at home reading the latest *BusinessWeek* and smoking a good cigar."

"I know. I feel the same. Give me the latest issue of *Bio-Pharm*, a grande chocolate mocha with extra whipped topping, and I'm a happy woman."

They both laughed, and Gaby was once again at ease with Hunter, glad the discomfort of the moment before had been dispelled.

After their laughter subsided, he continued.

"But, like I said, Abigail enjoys them. So . . ." his voice

trailed off and he lifted a Gaelic shoulder, a small smile lifting the corner of his mouth. "A man can do stupid things when he's in love," he replied, a strange look crossing his face. He glanced away from her and took another deep breath from the cigar.

He smiled down at her. "Well, we'd better go back. Don't want Abigail to come looking for us, now do we?" He asked, and Gaby nodded her head no, chuckling.

He took her arm, and she willingly allowed him to bring her back inside, wondering why she'd allowed the moment of tension to have her feeling crazy.

She shrugged it off and put it all down to the crazy turns her life had taken over the last few weeks.

With a tired sigh, Gabrielle sat down on the edge of her bed, opened the tin container, scooped out a handful of the creamy ointment, and began to anoint her arms with the mixture.

She closed her eyes, inhaled a deep cleansing breath, and exhaled, moving her neck side to side, trying to ease the sore muscles in her neck.

The smell of the cocoa butter/shea butter mixture, mixed with a variety of sweet-smelling essential oils and herbs, put a pleasant smile on her face as she massaged the cream over her tired body.

Truth be told, her mind was tired, more so than her body. Her world had been turned upside down, inside out, and every which way but loose.

And she'd only complicated matters more by going to bed with Sweet.

It had been nearly three weeks since her encounter with him, and she hadn't been able to get him out of her mind.

She and Hunter had returned to the ballroom. She'd spied Adam coming after her, and her body had tensed. Hunter glanced down at her, a frown between his brows, and without a word, gave her a wink and walked toward Adam, guiding him in another direction.

After Hunter had given her the help she'd needed by distracting Adam, she'd quickly hunted down Senator Chambers. As she spoke with him, he'd listened to her, his attention, to her surprise, solely on her. He didn't get that glazed look in his eyes she'd expected as she'd gone in to her well-practiced spiel. She knew the surprise showed on her face when he invited her to come to his office to go over particulars of her program.

"Abigail has done nothing but sing your praises," he told her as she'd shaken his hand. "And if Abigail feels it's a good program, I trust her. Come by my office Monday."

Although she hadn't gotten to discuss the reform bill, she'd been so happy that he seemed interested in her program she'd been on cloud nine, and her pleasure hadn't diminished when she'd finished speaking to the senator and turned and found herself face-to-face with Adam.

Not far behind him she'd seen Hunter, with Abigail next to him. He'd shrugged his shoulders, shooting Gaby an apologetic smile, and turned away with his wife.

She turned toward him and braced herself, physically and mentally.

"Gaby, sweetheart, please talk to me," he'd said, his voice breaking, a pleading look on his face.

Right there, in the middle of the crowded room, he pulled her close, running a shaky hand over her upswept hair. He hugged her tightly to his body and placed a light kiss on the side of her face.

It was the first time Adam showed her affection, publicly. Shaken and surprised, she'd been too stunned to break away from him.

She finally disengaged herself from him, looking around, self-conscious because of his openly intimate gesture.

"Please, Adam . . . not here."

He looked down into her eyes, a wealth of sorrow in his. "I know I fucked up, baby. Just don't shut me out," he begged.

Gaby had never seen this expression of insecurity on his face. She'd always been the one, she knew, who was insecure in the relationship. She was the one who wondered why he'd even had interest in her in the first place. To see him so obviously shaken was new to her.

And to her shame, it pleased her.

"Okay, okay, not here. But, tonight, after this is over. I'll come over and we—"

"No. You won't come over. I have a lot to do over the next few days, at work and the pharmacy. When I get from under some of this work we can meet," she inserted before he could finish.

He nodded his head and stepped away from her. His normal look of confidence stole over his face as he ran a finger down the side of her face. Gaby turned her head. The look fell from his face, his jaw tightening.

"Okay, we'll play this your way. But you won't leave me, Gaby. We have too much . . . invested . . . in this relationship for me to let you go," he promised.

A troubling chill ran through Gaby at his wording.

He smiled, a look of satisfaction stealing over his features. Boldly, he leaned down and kissed the corner of her mouth. Gaby drew back when she felt the biting sting of his teeth nip her lower lip.

"I'll be . . . *waiting* . . . for your call."

With that, he'd turned from her and within seconds had weaved his way through the crowd, disappearing from her sight.

Gaby sighed and forced all thoughts of Adam and his slightly threatening tone from her mind, hoping that's all there was to it, just in her mind. Instead, she thought of the debt she owed Abigail for introducing her to Senator Chambers.

Gabrielle knew she owed Abigail a lot. She bit her lip, thinking of her mentor. Gaby worked during the day at the university, teaching pharmacology to graduate students, a job that Abigail and Hunter had helped her to get after graduation. She'd worked hard and took over classes when another instructor was unable, and had made tenure, quickly. Not only did she want to impress the university with her work ethic, but the extra money she used to buy over-the-counter medication as well as other medications was needed to open her small community pharmacy.

Relying on charitable contributions and eventually small government subsidy money, she'd opened her South Side clinic, a clinic that provided both over-the-counter and prescription drugs.

During the day she taught, and as soon as her day was over, she went to her clinic, in the late afternoon as well as weekends.

From the referrals from the free clinic, she then provided over-the-counter and prescription medication to those who couldn't afford their medicines any other way.

Mostly, her clients were indigent folks, the homeless and working poor, as well as elders whose Medicaid didn't cover all the money for the many medications they were on.

She'd felt needed . . . necessary . . . as she provided for those who otherwise wouldn't get what they needed.

To get the word out about her pharmacy, Gaby had also—during the day—gone into the lower-income neighborhoods. She had gone places no one else would dare go, and given out her free medications.

Always in the back of her mind, she had been searching for her mother.

Growing up the daughter of a drug-addicted mother, Gaby knew what it was like, up close and personal, to be disenfranchised—living on the fringe of society.

It had been in the dead of winter, and a particularly cold one for the typically warm climate of San Antonio when she'd found her mother.

It had been over ten years since she'd seen her mother, and despite the low skullcap that covered her kinky white hair, and the harsh lines that bracketed a once-beautiful face, she'd known it was her.

Catherine Marlowe had been sitting on a bent, turned-over metal garbage can, her frail arm exposed, wrapped in a rubber hose, while a shaky hand was in the process of stabbing the end of a dirty hypodermic deep into her veins.

Stunned, Gaby had stood, staring as her mother depressed the end of the needle and the drug shot into her vein.

"Mama?"

When she spoke, Catherine hastily yanked out the needle and Gaby's eyes trained on the thin stream of blood that ran unchecked down her arm, before she glanced at her mother's face.

Her bloodshot eyes had flown to meet Gaby's.

Catherine had jumped up and quickly turned, knocking the can over in her stumbling haste to get away.

Gaby had run the short distance and grabbed her by the shoulder, forcing her around to meet her gaze.

"Mama . . . it's me. Gaby," she'd said, running her eyes over her mother's hunched form.

It had taken several moments for recognition to set in. When it did, tears slipped down the woman's haggard face.

"Is that really you, Gaby?"

Gaby had pulled her into her arms and hugged her mother fiercely. Despite the thick bulky coat Catherine had been wearing, Gaby had felt the fragility of her mother's bones beneath her fingers.

She'd begged Catherine to come into the clinic, that she could refer her to a clinic that could help her kick her addiction. Catherine had cast furtive eyes up and down the alley, as though afraid someone would hear her in the deserted alley, and had asked that Gaby help her instead.

Gaby had been momentarily confused by the request. Then it dawned on her what her mother wanted her to do.

Catherine had been adamant that she wasn't going to "no damn clinic," that all they did was lock her up like some caged animal, she'd said, her words running together.

"Besides, it ain't never helped none," she'd mumbled. "But, baby, I'm tired," she said, her shoulders slumping even more.

"I'm tired of living like this," she waved an arm toward the overturned trash can. "But, I got to do this my way. And you can help me. I heard about you and that pharmacy you have. You can help your mama, baby . . ." she turned her bloodshot, pleading eyes on Gabrielle and Gaby's breath caught, tears burning the back of her throat as her gaze went over her mother's body, the ragged clothes, the frailness of her bones . . .

Fearing she'd never see her mother again if she didn't bring the methadone, Gaby had reluctantly agreed when her mother made the suggestion. She'd gone to the clinic and retrieved the methadone, and come back to the same location the next day.

It hadn't stopped at the one time. In her desire to see her mother and her belief, one she held on to although in the back of her mind she knew it was wrong, that her mother really wanted help, she'd continued to give her mother the drugs. She'd altered her books so that she could skim what she needed without any detection.

In exchange for her giving her mother the drugs, Gaby convinced her to go into a homeless shelter she was familiar with. The shelter had strict rules on drug usage. One instance of being caught and the resident would have to leave.

Catherine had promised that, as long as Gaby helped her, she would abide by the rules.

Although she alone ran her clinic, with the help from her intern, she was still very much aware that she could get caught, subject to all the same accountability as any other pharmacy, particularly as she received government subsidy money.

Then she'd met Adam.

Adam was a pharmaceutical supplier and although he was higher in management, he'd come to her pharmacy one day to speak to her, as Elaina, her normal rep, had been unavailable.

She'd been flattered, and if she were honest, overwhelmed. He'd gone out of his way to let her know of his interest in her on a personal level. She was floored that a man who looked like Adam—handsome, so sophisticated—would be interested in her like that.

She'd shyly agreed to go out with him and the two had become involved.

It hadn't taken long for Adam to discover what she'd been doing. At first, afraid of his reaction, she hadn't known what he would do, what he would think of her if he knew. She'd tried to keep it secret. But, when he happened to look over her books and asked about a discrepancy, she'd told him everything—about her mother's addiction, how Gaby was skimming from her own supplies to help her. How her mother promised to try and stay clean, would stay at the shelter as long as Gaby provided the treatments.

The entire time she spoke, he sat there, holding her hands, occasionally murmuring his sympathy to her. She didn't stop at telling him about the drug addiction.

She told him about her life growing up with an addict and never knowing where she would lay her head, as they moved from apartment to apartment, kicked out when her mother had used the money for rent.

When she'd finished she looked at him. In his eyes was sympathy and understanding and something more.

He then shared with Gaby how he'd grown up on the streets, and knew what that life was like. Had it not been for a friend he, too, would have probably ended up just like her mother. He understood.

She'd closed her eyes, allowing the tears to slip down her cheeks.

Then he'd offered to help, outlining how he could, in such a casual way she'd been stunned. He could manipulate his records; there was always a surplus, he'd told her, of various drugs. He could supply her with what she needed to help her mother.

"I don't know what to say," Gabrielle had said, overwhelmed that he'd help her. She turned toward him, holding on to his hands. "It won't be for long, I promise. She's getting better. Just a little while longer, with me helping her . . . I think she can kick the habit this time," she'd said, holding back the tears. "I don't know how to thank you."

He smiled and brought her hands to his, kissing the palms.

"There is one small thing," he said.

"Anything," Gaby had eagerly replied.

He'd smiled that charming smile of his and said it wasn't much. That like the one who helped him long ago, he longed to help others. Then he'd laughed softly. The two of them could be a kind of Robin Hood for addicts.

Her smile had slipped as she wondered what he meant. He'd said they could help others like her mother, by "holding" on to other medications, storing them for him at the clinic.

"How?" she'd asked.

He'd said that he knew of others who for one reason or other couldn't get the medications they needed. People who needed help but no one was able to help them. Together, the two of them would be able to help.

Gaby had been torn. Yes, she wanted to help her mother, but to actually purposely steal . . .

"Darling," he'd said, gathering her close. "What do you think you're doing now, by giving your mother the methadone?" he'd asked gently.

"I know, but—"

"It won't be much. And the people we're helping, they need it, Gaby. Just like your mother. And, like your mother, it won't be for long. Just long enough for them to get better. To get medications they wouldn't be able to afford otherwise. And it won't be much. A small skimming, one no one will notice," he'd promised.

Gaby had reluctantly agreed. From there, Adam had come in to help her. The two had spent several evenings together at her free clinic. Adam had volunteered to help her with her books, and she'd been grateful for the help.

It had been gradual at first. But, eventually he'd completely taken care of the books for her, documenting the supplies and ordering new ones.

God, what a fool she'd been . . .

She forced the thoughts that had been running in her mind, that she'd been beyond stupid, and that Adam had been running a horrid game on her. One that she was now thoroughly involved in and had no way of getting out of without going to jail, right along with him.

She ran her hands down over her breasts, cupping them in her hands. This time, thoughts of Sweet's big hands doing the same thing, the rough pads of his thumbs flicking across her nipples, stole their way into her mind, diminishing her thoughts of Adam.

She stared down at her breasts. Her nipples were growing fat, stiffening into rigid peaks as she mimicked Sweet's caresses.

God, she ached.

She released her breasts, scooped up another generous portion of the scented cream, and smoothed it over her stomach in small, tight circles, messaging it deeply into her skin.

Gaby sat back on the bed and placed one bent leg on the mattress, and allowed the other to dangle over the side, bracing her thighs farther apart.

Her fingers trailed, as though with a mind of their own, along the sensitive skin of her inner thigh. She closed her eyes, a smile of remembered pleasure crossing her full lips.

Sweet.

Her chest rose and fell and her lips opened; a small sigh of pleasure escaped when she allowed her fingers to trail toward her mound.

Her touch grew bolder. She placed the fingers of each hand alongside the outer lips of her vagina and spread them. Her breath hitched, her chest moved in and out as a finger feathered over her clit in a back-and-forth seesawing motion.

She struck a finger into her mouth and laved the digit and inserted it into her now-moist opening. Her thumb scraped against her hypersensitive bud as she continued to plunge her fingers in and out of her slit, her hips rolling against her fingers.

Remembering what he'd done to her, she pressed the heel of her hand just above her mound, hard, and her hips bucked.

A moan escaped and she bit her inner lip, silencing herself.

Just as he had.

She ground herself against her hand, rolling and bucking her hips until she felt her orgasm hovering.

She moaned and withdrew her hand from above her mound and grasped one of her breasts. Twirling the now-thickened, elongated nipple between her thumb and forefinger, she squeezed so hard she felt a sting of pain. The pain and pleasure was so good, so damn good.

Her movements became frantic as she bucked her hips, her head tossing against the padded headboard until she felt the beginnings of her orgasm unfurl low, strumming in her lower belly.

"Oh God, yes . . . oh yes," she panted, eyes shut tight as she reached for climax.

The image of Sweet's darkly handsome face was superimposed over images of Adam's much fairer face as he slammed into her over and over, her hands bound behind her as he stroked into her, controlling her passion until she felt as though she would die if she didn't release.

"Oh God, yes, yes . . . *yes* . . ." she breathed the chant over and over as the sweet tingling sensation of release took over.

After her breathing calmed enough, she opened her eyes. She raised shaky fingers and brushed errant strands of hair back into place in the low ponytail.

She turned, a sound alerting her that she was no longer alone in her bedroom, no longer having her private party.

And came into eye-to-eye contact with Adam.

10

"God, you're beautiful."

Adam walked farther into Gaby's bedroom until he stood less than a foot away from her.

"What are you doing here? How did you get in?"

Her embarrassment at being caught pleasuring herself warred with her anger that he had stood there, for God knows how long, watching her.

He held out a key between two fingers, the corners of his mouth lifting in a small, lustful smile. "I still have a key, baby."

She jumped up, crawled to the edge of the bed, and tried to snatch the dangling key chain from his fingers.

As soon as she made contact, his hand enclosed around hers and he pulled her tight against him, bringing her flush against his hard body.

"Not so fast, Gaby."

He drew his nose slowly down the length of her neck, and back up just as slowly. Gaby inhaled a shaky breath when his tongue snaked out and trailed the same path, down and back up, until he reached her earlobe and lightly bit down.

"What—what are you doing, Adam?" she grunted the words, struggling to get away from him, her breath now coming out in strangled, shallow gasps.

"What you want. What you crave," he answered and continued to stroke his tongue down the side of her neck.

"No! I don't want this!" She struggled to move away from him, but he only laughed and took an exaggerated breath.

"From the distinct smell of pussy in the room," he paused and took another deep whiff, his thin nostrils flaring, "I would have to call you a bald-faced liar on that one, Gaby," he finished and laughed, low.

"I told you, I don't want you." Angry, Gaby shoved him away from her as hard as she could.

As he stumbled away a surprised look flickered on Adam's face, quickly followed by a dark flush of anger.

Taking satisfaction in his expression, Gaby rose from the bed and in short, precise movements, tied the sash of her robe closed. She advanced toward him, stopping several feet away.

"Give me my key, Adam." She placed one hand on her hip, the other one held out, palm opened. Anger coursed through her.

"Gaby, let's talk. Please—"

"Are you serious? What do we have to discuss?" Gaby shook her head, amazed at his insistence there was anything for them to discuss. "I mean, really, do you really think there is *anything* for us to talk about? Dear God, Adam, I *saw* you! You had that bitch bound and gagged while you did things with her you never did with . . ." she stopped, her body flushing as images of Adam and his secretary flashed in her mind.

She turned around to face him.

He blinked, eyes narrowing. Slowly, he began to advance on her. Gaby shot her hand out to stop him.

"I've been so careful with you, Gaby. I never dreamed you'd want it like that, baby. If I'd known . . ."

An incredulous look crossed her face. "What? You think that's what this is about? Why I'm angry? God, how could you be so obtuse?" She turned to move away when he caught her hand, flipping her back around to face him. Her chest began to heave, anger, resentment, and hurt caused her heart to thump wildly against her chest.

When he ran a hand down the side of her face, she flinched and moved her head to the side.

"I made a mistake, Gaby. Please. I have other . . . needs, sometimes."

At that she spun her head around so fast she felt like she nearly gave herself whiplash. "Yeah, obviously," she returned, sarcasm dripping from her tone. "And obviously I'm not the woman to satisfy those other . . . *needs.*"

"But, you can be." He leaned down and grazed the corner of her lips with a small, biting kiss. He drew away from her. "Give me another chance. Please. I won't fuck up this time."

Hearing the curse and Adam's tone of frustration made Gaby stop her struggling and look up at him. She rarely heard such emotion or language from him. He'd always been coolly detached, and rarely had she heard him curse.

He pulled her back, close to his body, wrapping his arms around her waist.

"I'll do right by you. I promise. I won't have to go looking anywhere else." He trailed his face down against the side of her neck, again. Goose bumps feathered down her arms. "I got rid of her. She doesn't mean a damn thing to me. She was just a means. That's all."

Slowly Adam pushed her away enough so that he could place his hands between them. He unknotted the ties and peeled back the robe, his hot, lustful gaze on her exposed body.

"Let me show you."

With her body so close to his, she felt the ridge of his cock, thick, against her mound and opened her mouth to speak.

"I won't take off my clothes," he promised, correctly interpreting the look she gave him.

"This is just for you, Gaby. Trust me," the pleading words were spoken low, with such urgency and desire, they insidiously worked her emotions into a confusing tangle, and zeroed in on her heart with the accuracy of a well-flung arrow. She barely registered when he pushed her backward, until she felt the edge of the mattress bump the back of her knees. Before she knew his intent, she was lying flat on her back with him crawling up her body.

With both of her hands held within one of his, he lifted them above her head and used the ties to wrap her wrists together, before looping them between the bars on her headboard.

"Adam—"

He silenced her, slanting his mouth over hers. "Please," he whispered against the corner of her mouth. "Let me do this for you."

He then licked a path with the flat of his tongue down her body. Panting, Gaby tightly clenched her eyes shut.

He lifted one of her breasts into his hand and laved her nipple, a nipple that now spiked, blood-filled and eager. She felt more than heard his small, masculine laughter against her breasts before he opened his mouth wide and began to suckle her.

The feel of his hot tongue on her breasts curled a lustful path of desire through her body, making her nerves strum in a feverish need to be fulfilled. As he pulled on her, with her eyes shut, instantly her mind was filled with images not of the two of them, but of her and Sweet.

He dragged his mouth away from her breasts, the sound of her nipple popping out of his mouth audible in the quiet room. When he licked between the valley of her breasts and latched on to the other eager nipple, the image of Sweet licking and devouring her as he pounded into her was so real, so vivid, that she cried out.

"Yes . . ." she whispered to the man in her mind.

Adam released her nipple and slid his tongue down her body, before stopping at the nest of tight curls between her thighs.

She felt his warm breath on her inner thigh. Two long fingers separated the lips of her vagina. When a tongue snaked into the seam of her pussy her body arched off the bed from the electric flames that shot through her body.

Her eyes flashed open, her breath coming out in harsh pants, and glanced down.

Instead of the dark head between her legs, there was a blond head, instead.

"No!" With renewed strength and resolve, she bucked her body, dislodging him from between her legs. So strong was her shove that Adam fell off the bed.

"Untie me," Gabrielle said, bitterly angry at Adam as well as herself.

"Now, damn it!" she said, between tightly clenched teeth when he looked as though he was going to ignore her.

She was holding on, trying to keep it together, only by a thread.

His eyes narrowed as he stared at her. Expressions flashed across his face too fast to catalog. Gaby held her breath and waited, her face set.

In the position she'd allowed herself to be put in, she knew she was vulnerable to whatever he wanted to do to her. She felt angry tears burn the back of her eyes, yet refused to look away from him, glaring at him, as he looked at her.

When he walked toward her, she held her breath and only released it when he leaned over and untied the belt from the headboard, releasing her.

Once she was untied, she rolled away from him and stood

on the other side of the bed. She didn't look at him, couldn't, keeping her face down as she retied the ends of her belt. "You need to go."

She expected an argument. When she heard nothing, she looked up and they stared at each other across the expanse of the bed.

"I'll go. For now."

He turned on his heels and left the room. Gaby followed him out and watched, warily, until he reached her front door.

He turned back to face her, his hand on the doorknob.

"You're in this as deep as I am," he said. The look in his light eyes, even from that distance, sent a shiver of fear through her body. His meaning was clear to her. "Don't forget that, Gaby. And this is *far* from over."

"Just go, Adam." She turned away.

He said nothing, and, for a minute, Gaby thought he'd challenge her. That he would refuse to go.

When she heard the door open and close she breathed a sigh of relief and turned back around.

Quickly she walked toward the front door. Shoving aside the sheer curtains of the long narrow window next to the door, she peered outside and watched as his long strides took him to his Mercedes parked in her driveway.

As soon as she heard the powerful purr of his vehicle flaring to life, and saw him peel out of her driveway, she shut her eyes and leaned against the door.

"God, what in hell am I going to do now?" she asked out loud, throwing her head back against the door.

"I . . . I have to go. I have a meeting," Adam breathed the words, completely wrung out. His breath hissed behind his clenched teeth as he felt his lover slowly drag the thick unyielding shaft from his body.

Once the last hard inch had come out, he had to grab the edge of the desk so that he didn't fall face forward.

"Get dressed. They're waiting for you," Lee spoke against his neck. Adam nearly wept when he felt a soft, sweet kiss on the back of his neck.

He closed his eyes, briefly, a smile of relief on his face. Again, he'd been forgiven. This time for not being able to convince Gabrielle into taking him back.

He straightened his body and with shaky hands righted his clothes.

He turned to face Lee. "Will you be here when I get back?" he asked, hesitantly.

"I have somewhere to be." Lee said, with distraction in the normally husky voice, smoothing unseen wrinkles from the classic navy suit that draped his lover's tall, thin body. Adam ran an assessing eye over Lee.

When Lee noticed his stare and raised a brow, Adam quickly averted his gaze and bobbed his head up and down. "Okay. I-I'll see you later then? Tonight?" he knew he was pleading, begging to see his lover again, but he was desperate. He had to make sure he was forgiven, had to be sure he was still loved. He'd do anything to make sure of it.

"I need to use your phone to make a call." There was no promise of a visit, but Adam nodded his head slowly as Lee crossed the room and sat behind Adam's desk.

"Of course. Feel free," Adam replied, even though as he looked across at his lover, he knew Lee's mind was no longer with him, that Lee was already focused on other things, other people.

It was one of the things Adam loved about Lee, the utter focus on doing what it took to succeed. And Adam knew Lee would bring him to the top as well. As long as he did everything Lee told him and didn't make any more dumb-ass mistakes.

He turned away and quickly crossed the room to leave. "I'd better go," he said again, and with one long glance, left.

As he walked out of the door, he missed the calculating way Lee looked at him. He also missed the small book his lover placed inside one of the desk drawers.

11

"I think that's about it, Rosario. Everything has been inventoried. All meds accounted for," Gaby said, stretching her back.

She massaged her temples in an effort to rid herself of the ache that had been hovering, threatening to break through, despite her migraine medicine.

"I have one more set of books to go through," Gaby's intern, Rosario, replied without looking up from her task of checking the physical spreadsheets laid out on her desk against the Excel documents on her computer screen.

Gaby glanced at the clock. "Uh uh . . . It's late, time for you to get home, Ms. Rosey," she said, smiling affectionately over at the older woman who sat on the floor, boxes scattered around her. If she allowed her to, Rosario wouldn't leave until she was satisfied she'd completed the task.

Although Rosario had no idea the reason for the meticulous inventory, she had been invaluable in helping Gaby with the daunting task of going over the books. Gaby had been careful to only allow her intern to go over the books from before Adam took over, not only because she didn't want her to realize the discrepancies, but, if worse came to worst, she didn't want her to get caught in the scam. To unwittingly gain knowledge that could be used against her, if Gaby turned herself in.

Something she'd been thinking more and more about, over the last weeks.

"Late?" Rosario glanced at her watch. "It's only six o'clock. I don't mind staying to help you finish," she insisted. "Besides, I don't have any other exciting plans." She laughed and pushed her wire-rimmed frames up the short length of her round nose.

"Thanks, but, I think I'm going to call it quits myself, in a few," Gaby said, smiling. When Rosario looked at her, doubt in her dark eyes, Gaby laughed. "Seriously!"

After Gaby convinced her intern she could handle the rest, the woman finally reluctantly left.

Although Gaby had been happy for her intern's assistance, when she left, she breathed a sigh of relief. She needed to be alone for the next part of her investigation.

She rose from her desk, retrieved her bag, and lifted a small key from within. Going back over to her desk, she fitted the key in the lock and lifted out a small, leather-bound ledger from inside.

She opened the book with a deep, troubled sigh. She hadn't opened the book since she'd stolen it from Adam a few days ago, the day after he'd come into her house. She'd gone to his work to demand her key back and his secretary—a new one— had allowed her to enter his office while he was in a meeting.

Just like Adam, everything was neat, in order, and pristine. The office was beautifully—and expensively—furnished. Her fingers ran over the top of the small butter-soft leather loveseat in the center of the office, as she walked throughout the room.

In front of the loveseat was a smoked-glass and chrome table, which sat on a geometric-print Persian rug.

On the taupe-painted walls were what Gaby thought to be two original Warhol prints, signed, as well as a few other expensive prints. She didn't know the price of art, as she had only knockoffs and reprints in her home and office, but, on close inspection, the prints seemed to be originals.

His desk was large, ostentatious, actually, Gaby thought. She'd never given much thought to how much of what Adam owned was rare, expensive.

She'd once made an offhand comment after seeing both his home and office, asking how he could afford the beautiful and expensive things he owned. He'd turned to her, his ice-blue eyes staring a hole in her for so long Gaby had felt goose bumps of fear run down her spine.

She'd flinched when he'd raised a hand, unable to control her reaction. She felt an odd sense of shame, yet stood there still as she could. There had always been something about Adam that Gaby felt uncomfortable with.

She'd relaxed, slightly, when the cold look dropped from his face as though it had never been there. He smiled, slightly, and ran a finger down the side of her cheek, an odd expression on his face.

If her body hadn't reacted so harshly, she would have thought she imagined his look.

He'd stared down at her neck and the fear returned and replied, his tone cool, that if she *must* know, the art in both his condo and office were simply reprints. The furnishings he'd bought from a friend in the business who'd given him a good deal, substantially lower than retail.

Duly chastened, Gaby had profusely apologized, even though Adam assured her no harm, no foul. He'd stepped away from her and continued to show her around. She'd never brought the subject back up again, but had filed the incident in the back of her mind.

Alone in his office for the first time, Gaby was overtaken by curiosity or something more.

With furtive glances toward the door, she'd quickly crossed

to his desk, sat down in the supple leather chair and begun to open drawers and glance over the contents, careful to replace the things she shifted around.

When she discovered nothing out of the ordinary, she'd felt foolish, stopped her search, and closed all the drawers. She'd shaken her head, chastising herself for what she'd been doing, and had been about to rise from the chair when the hard-edged corner of a small, leather-bound book caught her eye; the book was stuck in between the grooves of one drawer.

After a short tussle, she'd been able to pull the book out. She opened it, and her eyes widened as her glance ran over Adam's neatly handwritten script. There were two columns of figures and names of various drugs. One column held one set of numbers, the other a second figure. Her eyes scanned down the list, and her brain began to catalog what it all meant.

She'd heard a noise outside the door, snapped the ledger closed and stuffed it in her oversized bag. She leapt from the chair, quickly crossing the room and sitting down in one of the guest chairs seconds before Adam entered.

He'd been happy but surprised to see her there. Flustered and wanting to get the hell out of there as soon as she could, Gaby hadn't asked for her key back to her apartment, and, due to her extreme nervousness, had agreed to have dinner with him later in the week when he asked.

She'd seen the surprise and then satisfaction cross his face at her quick agreement, and with an excuse that she had to return to work, had fled his office.

She opened the book and settled back against her chair. Beginning at the first page, she methodically went through every page, a horrid feeling settling in the pit of her stomach as what she was seeing began to register in her brain, and she learned just how stupid she'd been in not realizing that he had been using her all along. Blinding rage welled. She felt violated. Raped.

After her brain registered that what she'd taken from Adam's office had been a very detailed account of his duplicity, a dual set of numbers boldly documenting how for over a year he'd been stealing a select amount of drugs from the supplier he worked for. She'd retrieved her own books, and compared them.

Her heart felt like it had plummeted to her stomach as she read.

Like a fool, for six months she'd allowed him to fuck her literally, and, she realized as her eyes flew over each page, figuratively.

12

Demetri'd waited for Gabrielle Marlowe to come back, was in fact surprised when she hadn't, and had had to reassess the situation, as well as the intriguing woman whom he hadn't figured out to save his damn life.

He ran a hand through his hair in frustration. It was time to make a move.

Besides getting the investigation rolling, he hadn't been able to get the woman out of his mind, and it wasn't just the thought of catching her and getting to the heart of the scam. It was her.

He hadn't been able to get the image out of his mind of what it had been like to be with her, to hear her mewling cries as he gave her pleasure.

It had been nearly two weeks since he'd seen her, nearly two weeks since the night she'd come into the Sweet Spot, looking for sex.

Looking for him.

Two weeks of him being confident that she'd return, that she would be feinin' for another erotic episode the likes of which he'd never had with anyone else, even during the time he and

Siobhan had spent undercover during their last mission to-gether.

Their chemistry had been off the fucking charts; there was no use lying to himself, pretending otherwise. He doubted that the prim and proper Gabrielle Marlowe had ever experienced that type of sex, either. No way in hell.

He'd sat back and waited. When one day led to another, to a week, and now, nearly two weeks later . . . his anger and his lust for her began a slow burn, boiling, until he knew he could no longer wait. He had to have her.

He placed a hand over his dick. It was hard as a fucking rock whenever he thought about her, which had been constantly.

"Shit!" he bit out the expletive, running a hand over his un-ruly cock.

Just one more time, one long, hot night of having her be-neath him, crying and panting beneath him, one more time . . . that's all it would take to exorcise the images from his mind of her wrapped around him crying, begging for more. One more time stroking, pounding into that sweet pussy, and he could get his shit straight, get his mind right, focus on the investigation.

"Boss . . . anything else before I leave? I thought I'd head out. Brandon just clocked in."

He looked up, so caught up in his thoughts of the woman that it took his brain a few seconds to register that one of his employees was standing in his doorway.

Sherri smiled at him as she leaned her body against the door frame.

"Uh, no, I'm fine, Sherri. Thanks."

"You sure I can't get you *anything?*" a seductive, inviting smile stretched her pouty lips invitingly.

She arched her upper body, drawing his attention to the way the buttons on her starched white uniform seemed to be beg-ging to be freed, before he met her eyes.

"No, I need to go take care of something. Maybe some other

time." A look of irritation crossed her pretty face before she made a small pout and advanced into his office, unasked.

Sherri had been working for him for months, and, before he'd flown to D.C. to meet Nick, he had led her to believe there would be more to their relationship than mere boss/employee.

Hell, she was the type of woman he normally went for. Tall and leggy with a banging body.

Sherri was the kind of woman who knew the score; she was looking for a good time, good sex, and no complications.

Particularly the uncomplicated part.

Yeah, the uncomplicated part of her personality was one of the most attractive.

"You know, Sweet, I'm not the kind of woman who's used to waiting around."

"I don't recall asking you to wait, Sherri." He raised a brow and sat back in his seat, his lids dropped low, watching her as she turned and closed the door and he heard the sound of the lock clicking into place.

She walked farther into the room. Once she reached his desk she perched her round bottom on the edge and licked her top lip.

"No, you haven't," she agreed with a carefree laugh before leaning over closer to him. "But you, well, you're worth the wait." She leaned over and pressed her pouty lips against his.

Her soft lips caressed his and the end of her tongue licked across the seam, silently asking to enter.

When a long, manicured fingernail trailed down his chest and began to unzip his fly, he placed a hand over hers and gently pushed her away.

"Sorry, Sherri, but I have to be somewhere. We'll have to pick this up another time," he promised, lying.

She only smiled and shoved his hand away, continuing to unzip his fly. With quick dexterity she had him unzipped, his cock in her soft hand, stroking him.

"Are you sure you don't have time for a little play? Seems to me you want to."

In her hands his cock began to grow, thickening as she stroked him in soft, lazy caresses.

A month ago, he would have said to hell with it and given the woman what she wanted, what his unruly cock wanted.

But now, although one part of him wanted to flip her around and spread her legs and fuck her until neither one of them could stand straight, Gabrielle's pretty face flashed in his mind. He held onto the image of flipping *her* over instead, her sweet cries of pleasure ringing in the recess of his mind. She was too prominent in his thoughts for him to think of bedding another woman.

Gently, but firmly, he pushed Sherri away and stuffed his cock back in his pants.

"Another time, Sherri," he said, again lying

A hard look crossed her face. "Fine. But I won't be here forever," she said and strolled slowly toward the door.

"Like I said . . . I don't remember asking you to be," he said and saw her shoulders stiffen. She opened the door and slammed it shut behind her.

He made a mental note to tell his manager, Brandon, to look for another bartender. He had no intention of taking Sherri up on her offer.

At least not until he rid himself of his need for a sweet little con artist named Gabrielle Marlow.

Demetri pushed away from his desk and grabbed his keys, his thoughts already leaving his employee, his cock swelling in anticipation of seeing Gabrielle.

"Hello—anybody there?" A very deep, masculine voice called out.

Gaby had been so immersed in her ruminations that when she heard the call, she abruptly sat up and promptly banged her head on the edge of her desk.

She uttered a curse, rubbing the side of her head as she struggled to get off the floor. "One minute, please," she yelled out.

She glanced over at the clock, surprised at the time. She'd been sitting on the floor for over two hours, documents spread out in front of her.

She got to her feet after gathering the documents and quickly putting them all away, safely, and walked from behind the glassed-in area and out the door.

As soon as she stepped out, she stopped. Her eyes widened and her heartbeat slammed against her chest, as she stared at the face, the body, of the man who had been a constant companion in her mind, her dreams, over the last weeks.

"Wha-what are you doing here?" She stammered, staring at him as though he were an apparition from one of her nightly erotic dreams.

One side of his lips curved up. It was the same one-sided half-grin that had appeared in more sweat-inducing, wake-up feeling-hot-and-achy-all-over kind of dreams that had invaded Gaby's sleep repeatedly.

Just thinking of the dreams, along with the things they'd done together that night, deep into the early morning hours until dawn broke, made her feel that same tingling *sweet* ache between her thighs.

Her attention was drawn from the small dimple in one cheek, to his mouth and the hint of his perfect white teeth— God, even the man's teeth got her hot and bothered—to his soulful eyes.

Eyes that were staring at her as though he *knew* what was going on in her mind. That he knew every kinky, hot little scene she had replayed, scenes that she'd had go over and over in her head, like a lyric to a favorite song.

That he *knew* the dreams he'd inspired had left her feeling out of sorts and desperate to see him again. Desperate to feel his body shifting over hers, stroking into her, making her come so many times she lost count.

That he knew that the dreams she'd had, nightly, had her wondering if the memories of their night together had been blown up in her mind, a figment of her imagination.

Or had they all been amazingly true?

She swiped at the corner of her dry lips with her tongue and felt a trickle of sweat bead against her forehead.

She turned away, walked toward him, and stopped a few feet away. She brought her fingers to her brow and wiped the sweat away.

"Do you think it's smart to leave the door unlocked with you alone, this time of night?" he asked.

"I thought I'd locked the door. I got caught up in paperwork," Gaby replied, hyperaware of their aloneness.

"I wouldn't think that's safe to do in this neighborhood," he replied bluntly, continuing to stare at her.

Gaby felt like a deer in the headlights, unable to look away from him.

"Like I said, I got caught up in paperwork. Time slipped away from me."

His presence, the way he was looking at her, made her nervous. A hell of a lot more nervous than she would have felt had she known she hadn't locked the door.

Her eyes moved over his large, hard-packed body as he stood in front of her, arms crossed, his muscles bulging behind the worn Levi's molding his thick thighs.

"That wouldn't have helped you if someone had come in wanting something more than aspirin."

"All the prescription drugs are kept behind the glass," she nodded her head toward the glassed-in area. "The glass is bullet-proof, and the door leading to my area is locked, *and* I have a phone back there, as well. No one could have come inside. And help was only a phone call away if I needed it."

"Even so, you should be more careful. Anyone could have walked in and you could have gotten hurt. Especially in an area like this." Like a dog with a bone, he wasn't going to let it go. Gabrielle struggled to keep her irritation in check.

She was tempted to show him just how well she could protect herself, thinking of the small but powerful .25 caliber that lay under her counter behind the partition.

Abigail had given it to her weeks ago, and reluctantly Gaby had accepted it and instruction on how to use it. Abigail, too, often warned Gabrielle about her tendency to work late hours at the pharmacy and said she worried about her safety.

She opened her mouth to tell him she wasn't helpless and promptly closed it. It was none of his business.

"I can protect myself. I grew up in *areas like this*," was her only reply, instead.

"I didn't mean to offend you."

Gaby shook her head and drew in a deep breath. She was overreacting.

She knew it.

Both to his presence as well as his references to her not being safe.

He was right; the area wasn't the most secure, and she had been stupid leaving the door unlocked when she was all alone this late at night.

"I'm a little hypersensitive about some things lately, two of them being the pharmacy and this particular community. You didn't offend me." She didn't know why she told him that last bit. She doubted he cared one way or another about her community either. She placed a nonchalant smile on her face.

"I'm sure you didn't come all the way down here to give me a public service announcement on safety." She saw his eyes narrow slightly, at her sarcasm. "Wait—how *did* you know I was here? I didn't even tell you my name, much less where I worked."

"Wasn't too hard to find you when you left this," he said reaching in his back pocket.

When he pulled out his wallet and withdrew a card, she walked toward him, curious.

"You dropped this at my place the night we were together," Between two fingers he held her pharmacy license.

"God, I wondered what I'd done with that." She reached a hand out to take the wallet version of her pharmacy license away from him. When she did, their fingers touched and he drew her hand into his and held on to it.

Her startled gaze flew to his. "Thank you," she murmured. She again tried to take the card, but his hold tightened on hers, unyielding when she tried to withdraw.

"You have beautiful hands," he murmured. "Long fingers."

He ran his fingers over each one of hers, gently pulling on them, caressing them. The simple action gave an answering pull-and-tug reaction between her legs.

"Sensual hands."

He turned her hands over in his.

Four fingers held the back of her hand, and his index finger traced along the lines within her palm, down over her rapidly beating pulse that she could feel fluttering against his fingers.

The soft touch was oddly erotic.

"Has anyone ever told you that?"

Gaby's eyes darted back and forth between glancing up in to his eyes and back to his finger feathering down the palm of her hand.

She withdrew a sharp breath and her nipples spiked against her silk blouse.

"No. I can't say that anyone has."

When she tugged her hand away, he allowed it.

Gaby didn't delude herself. She knew he had allowed it. The reprieve, although slight, was welcomed.

"Well, thanks. I wondered what I did with that." She said,

referring to her license. "I alerted the state board. No one could have used my license. It would have been denied, an alert set on it in case anyone did. Not that anyone would know how to use it. I guess." Gaby knew her nerves were making her babble, and stopped.

"Anyway, thanks for returning it." She drew her bottom rim of her lip fully into her mouth and worried it back and forth, something she did whenever she was nervous. And Sweet made her about as nervous as anyone ever had.

Sweet brought his thumb up and stroked over her bottom rim, forcing her to release her hold.

"Thanks," she replied in a husky voice and stepped away.

She expelled a long breath she hadn't been aware she was holding and strode away from him, quickly, toward the counter.

Lifting her bag, she busied herself with fishing out her wallet, chastising herself for the way her hands shook as she placed the card inside.

Demetri felt her nervousness. She was so easy to read. She couldn't keep eye contact with him, and had been about to chew her bottom lip off if she wasn't careful, as she worked the full rim between her two top teeth.

When he'd held her hand, he'd felt the fine tremble in them and the race of her pulse had been strong against his fingers.

He smiled with anticipation and quietly walked behind her.

He placed his hands on her shoulders, and she jumped.

"You don't have anything to be nervous about with me. I won't do anything to you. Unless you want me to . . ." he allowed the sentence to dangle.

He moved aside the fine silk of her blouse and placed his hands on the smooth, silky skin covering the tops of her shoulders, feeling the way her muscles bunched beneath them, tense, applying slight pressure in a calculated gesture to soothe her.

She turned her head slightly to the side, glancing at him from the corner of her eyes as he moved his hands down the front of her blouse.

She withdrew a sharp breath when he slowly slipped the buttons open one by one, until her blouse was fully opened.

"What are you doing?"

He moved the strands of hair that had escaped the tight bun in the center of her head to the side and kissed the side of her neck.

"What you've wanted me to do since I came in," he whispered the words against her neck. "What you've wanted me to do since the first time we fucked three weeks ago. There's nothing to be ashamed of, Gaby. And there's nothing to be afraid of, either."

"I'm not—" she stopped speaking when he deftly unhooked the small clasp in the center of her bra, raking his thumbs across her dark brown nipples and cupping her breasts in both palms.

Fascinated, he watched her nipples, a darker color than the rest of her honey-colored breasts, elongate as he stroked them.

"I'm not ashamed." She said the words, yet her heart was racing, the beat heavy against his hands as he cupped and molded her big pretty breasts in his hands. "And, I'm not ashamed."

One of his hands released a breast to lift her skirt. He stroked his hand over the round, firm globes of her buttocks, over the matching pale blue silk panties.

He released the other breast. His hand trailed down the valley between her breasts and cupped her mound. He fondled her through the silk, his lips curling up in a smile of anticipation when her cream dampened her panties.

"No?" he asked, biting down on the delicate lobe of her ear.

He slipped a finger past the lacy edge and fingered one side of her creaming, slick lips.

She clamped her legs together tight and bucked her body against him. "No."

He was close to her. He could smell her arousal as his body crowded against her, his finger delving farther into her panties.

He nudged her legs apart, enough so he could press a finger deep inside her. She moaned, pressing her upper body away until she was nearly prone on the counter.

"Please," she cried, her body straining away from him.

Demetri could feel her desperation to both come and get away from him. The heady mixture had his dick hard, his excitement rising as she squirmed against his body and hands.

He stamped down his rising need to get inside her, ruthlessly clamping down his almost painful, escalating lust. This had to go right. She had to beg for it, want it so bad she lay aside her inhibitions and just gave in to him. He peeled her panties down until they reached her knees and bent her completely over the counter so she had no choice but to lay her head down.

He ran his fingers down the line of her back and watched in pleasure as her breasts pressed down on the counter, and her bottom arched back. In the position she was in, the lips of her pussy peeked out, swollen and quivering, her cream trickling down the inside of her thighs.

"Please what, Gaby?"

The way he said her name was pure sin.

When she tried to move away, to get away from him, his hold tightened, preventing any further movement. He fenced her in between the counter and his hard body.

She felt deliciously exposed, with her ass out, panties bunched around her ankles, utterly at his mercy. The feeling was as unwanted as it was delicious in its sheer eroticism.

"Why didn't you come back to me?"

The question threw her off balance, even as sweat began to trickle down her forehead, between her breasts, and between her legs.

Between her thighs she felt another moisture ease from her

pussy, drip slowly down, as his warm breath fanned against the skin of her exposed neck, his back pressing her deeper into the counter.

"Why . . . why would I do that?"

She knew what he wanted her to say. What he wanted her to admit. She knew because it was the same thing she wanted.

"Because of this." He lifted her by the hips until she was on tiptoe and dragged her ass up and down, grinding her against his cock.

She pulled away from his raunchy cock as it poked insistently against her ass.

She heard the rasp of his zipper, and seconds later his naked shaft was pressing against her.

"Are you saying you don't want this . . . that you haven't been thinking of it, of us, for the last two weeks?" A finger dipped inside the center of her pussy, and he withdrew evidence of her lie.

"No," she said, not ready to give in to what his touch was demanding.

"Yes," he countered, the one-word demand spoken hotly against her neck.

When his tongue darted out and licked her, she moaned.

"Oh yes," he laughed huskily against her skin. "You want it."

There was no use denying the truth of his words. Especially when a second finger joined the one dragging in and out of her heat, stroking her as he ground against her buttocks. The evidence of how much Gaby was enjoying what he was doing was there for him to see . . . to feel.

"You've been dreaming of it."

She opened her mouth to deny his words and clamped them shut when a third finger sank deep inside her core.

He stroked her, scooping out a measure of her cream, withdrew his fingers, and spread her cream over her throbbing clit.

In small, tight swirls he circled her clit.

"Does that feel good?"

"Yes," the words were choked from her. "God, yes."

It was too much, what he was doing to her. Behind her tightly closed lids, stars danced and shimmered as her body tightened.

As one hand stroked and prodded inside her, the other tugged her shirt from the waistband of her skirt. Smoothly, he slid the blouse down her arms.

"I'm going to make you come, Gaby. With my mouth," he whispered against my neck. "The first time." His promise sent a fresh stream of cream from her pussy

"Is that okay?"

Before she could speak, he dragged his fingers from within her body and she felt him kneel behind her.

Bumping her legs farther apart, he ripped the panties from her body in one sure pull.

She drew a swift breath when his head nudged between her thighs, forcing her to widen her stance.

With his big hands gripping on either side of her thighs, he held her securely within his grasp and tilted her, bringing her flush against his face.

And licked her pussy.

The first stroke from his tongue nearly had her coming and her breaths became desperate, her body on fire as he licked her like a big cat eating cream, slowly, his tongue rasping over her pulsing lips, his tongue flickering, darting in and out of her in a deadly assault that made her gut clench and release. Beyond her control, she rolled and ground against him, helplessly.

Demetri breathed in deeply, inhaling her scent. His dick swelled, uncomfortably engorged, as he suckled her, but he ignored it.

God, she smelled so fucking good.

He hadn't forgotten how unique, how sweet and spicy her natural smell was.

He stroked a finger deep inside her pussy and spread it around the plump tight bud of her clit as he laved her cunt. She whimpered, yet ground back against him. Her need to come, he knew, was too much to allow her to do anything but.

So damn responsive. He hadn't forgotten how responsive she was to him, either. It had played hell with his mind, his libido.

He pressed a finger deep inside her pussy, pumping it in and out as her sweet ass bucked against him. The little moans of delight she gave as he played with her heightened his own pleasure. His dick thumped in agitation and anticipation.

He ignored it.

Separating the lips of her pussy, in fascination he watched as with every drag and pull of his finger she clenched and gripped his finger, her cream, white and thick, now ran freely down his finger, coating his hand.

"God, I've got to taste you," the words were torn from his throat.

Eagerly he leaned in and licked her again. She reared back so strongly against him, he had to again place his hands on her hips or she would have bucked him off her.

He leaned back in and nosed inside her moist folds. He swept his tongue from the tip of her engorged clit, swirling and mouthing the hard little nub, inside her sweet hole, and out in short stabbing flicks, feeling her body tremble against his hands and face.

He drew his tongue back out and suckled her flowing cream before following the soft line that separated her pussy from her plump bottom.

He held her still with one hand, so still she couldn't move, could only accept the oral fucking he was giving her. With his mouth, lips, tongue, and the fingers of one hand he screwed her, until the pressure built and she was dizzy.

"So fucking good," he mouthed the words against her, before his tongue darted, along with his fingers deep inside her clenching heat.

Gaby was ready to explode. He was suckling her like her pussy was manna from heaven.

"Do you want me inside you?"

"Yes—" she stopped speaking when he shoved his tongue deep inside her. She took deep, calming breaths. "Please . . ." she felt no shame begging for it, she wanted him, wanted to feel him deep inside her, wanted him to fuck her hard, long, deep. Wanted him to make her feel needed, wanted.

Instead of withdrawing from her, he continued to hold her, kiss and lap at her.

On and on he ate, sucked, and prodded her pussy. Gaby let go. She squeezed her eyes shut, grimacing as she held on tightly to the counter, helplessly rotating her hips, pushing back as she ground against his face.

As he sucked her, he'd inserted several fingers inside her pussy. Knuckles-deep inside her, he ground his fingers in a tight corkscrew motion, screwing relentlessly as waves of pleasure pounded into her as harshly as his strokes of tongue and fingers.

"Tell me you want it. You want me. Now!" he demanded in a voice rough with arousal.

"Yes!" she cried out. "Please, please, please . . ." she chanted, lost in the orgasm that caused her body to shake, her mind numb with pleasure.

He lifted from behind her and she cried out in denial. She heard the rip of foil and seconds later he deftly eased her into position, his shaft pushing deeply into her body. With one sure shove, he was balls-deep inside her.

The orgasm slammed into her, intensified, multiplied a hundred times. He held on to her, one hand holding the back of her neck, holding her head down, as the other bit into the side of her waist.

In harsh, sure strokes he pounded her pussy, his thrust controlled. His strokes were so strong, one part of Gaby's mind, the part that was still able to think, was glad he held her down. If not, she knew he'd fuck her into the wall.

As she came, Gaby screamed, her toes off the floor as she rolled her hips against him, wanting to feel every inch of that hard pounding rod slamming in and out of her.

"Fuck!" he grunted, his tone harsh.

When he leaned down, his big body slamming over her back, blanketing her, he shoved aside her hair and bit down on the side of her neck.

"Oh God . . . yes, yes, yes, yes . . ." Her words blended into one long keening cry as he pummeled her pussy.

One orgasm rolled into another, until she came so hard, she grew faint. She fell onto the counter, her body one big bundle of oversensitive nerves as he held on to her, his hips jackknifing, his unrelenting cock stroking in and out of her.

He thrust into her two more times. "Yes," she heard him shout from behind her before he gave in to his own release.

Seconds later, his hard, moist chest covered her as she lay on the counter, their breathing labored and harsh after their tumultuous climax.

13

Gaby followed Sweet as he navigated the nearly empty back-streets that led to the Sweet Spot.

After they'd recovered from their lovemaking at the pharmacy, she'd uneasily glanced at him after getting her clothes together.

She'd tried to run, tried to escape what he'd done to her, what she'd allowed him to do, but he wouldn't stand for it.

"Come home with me," he'd said.

Her eyes had flown to his, startled.

"Please."

And just like that, she had agreed.

No overthinking. No hesitation. He'd said please. His voice, his eyes, the way he looked at her . . . all of it had overwhelmed her. She wanted this. She wanted this man. And, God help her, she was going to take what his eyes were promising he'd give her.

Another night of erotic pleasure.

As she'd gone about locking up, gathering her things, several times she'd had to pick up things that had fallen from her grasp, her nerves stretched taut.

She'd glance over at him and her heart seemed to stutter at the intense way he was silently watching her, and she would drop yet another object. The last time she'd done it, he'd come over and taken it from her, and finished stuffing the folders into her bag. With a murmured word of thanks, she'd finally gotten her act together, locked up, and with him behind her, silent, left the pharmacy.

When he turned into the parking lot of the Sweet Spot, Gaby followed. Instead of turning into the overfilled lot, he went down a short alley directly behind the club. She pulled her small Camry beside his truck, cut the engine, and pulled her bag into her lap.

She sat behind the wheel, hands tightly gripping the wheel until her knuckles ached, and watched him ease his long legs out of the cab of his truck.

When he reached her, she opened the door, allowing him to help her out, and glanced at him from the corner of her eye as she matched her steps to his longer strides.

"We'll go through the back entrance," he said and she expelled a thankful sigh.

Even though the club was packed, and she doubted anyone would pay them any attention, the thought of prancing through the club and up to his loft wasn't something she was looking forward to.

She knew she'd feel as though everyone in the club was watching her, knowing she was coming there for one reason and one reason alone.

To get another sampling of the Sweet Spot.

Once they reached his loft, he went about turning on a few lights. Uncertain what to do, Gaby stood in the middle of the living room, looking at everything but him. She felt his eyes on her and turned around.

He placed a finger beneath her chin, forcing her to look up at him. When she turned her face away, to avoid his avid stare, he added more pressure, again forcing her to look at him.

"Now, tell me." Her eyes focused on the sensual curve of his lips as he spoke.

"Tell you . . . what?" she asked, yet knew what he wanted to hear.

He wanted her to admit how much she'd thought about him. He wanted her to admit how badly she wanted him.

As he stood staring down at her, his face tightened, his eyes hot with need, the finger beneath her chin slid down, and his hand opened and closed, his fingers wrapping loosely around her throat.

"Give in to me." The demand, like the man, was boldly possessive. Primal.

"I want you."

Their gazes locked. She *felt* his anger.

She felt an answering anger in return. Confused, angry, wondering what he had done to her, to get her so sprung, to get her to wake up late nights with him on her mind, resentful yet desperate to feel him above her, stroking into her, making her feel like she'd never felt before.

Making her hot, desperate, and achy, but at the same time, making her feel really wanted. *Needed.* Just as she read the anger, she read his need blazing hotly in his gold-flecked eyes.

"No one has ever done this. Made me feel so—"

"Needed," he finished the sentence and they stared at one another.

"Yes."

She saw the slight flare of his nostrils, the way his gaze seemed to focus on her lips as she choked out the admission.

The admission had been ripped from somewhere deep inside, a place where she couldn't lie or deny the truth.

A place she'd purposely placed at the back of her mind, to try and forget.

As she'd gone about her daily activities, barely a moment had gone by when she hadn't thought about him.

The hold he had on her mind had been close to frightening in its intensity, the way she hadn't been able to get what they did far from her thoughts at all times.

She ran a glance down his body, skirting her eyes away from the large bulge between his thighs, the way it brushed against her mound, causing the lips of her vagina to pulse and swell beneath her skirt, just from proximity.

Her body responded as though he hadn't just screwed her six ways to Sunday less than an hour before.

She swallowed down her lust when he leaned just the smallest inch closer, his denim-covered cock now brushing against her, and nodded her head.

That was all he needed. He took enough time to unzip his pants and pull out his cock, before he lifted her, pulled her legs around his waist, and slanted his mouth over hers. With a cry she accepted him.

He backed her up to the nearest wall and wrapped her legs higher around his waist.

"Wait, please, I—" she broke away from his kiss, her breathing erratic.

"No. No more waiting. No more lying. Just this. This is what you want. This is why you avoided me," he bit the words out from behind clenched teeth, the muscles in his neck bulging.

She fought against him, yet he knew that the fists beating his chest were aimed at herself as well, fighting against the desire that drove her into his arms from the beginning.

His hands were hard at work, shoving her skirt up her legs, exposing her naked pussy to his searching hands. The more she fought him, the more he wanted her.

He felt completely out of fucking control.

Sweet pressed a thick finger inside her pussy and withdrew the evidence that she did want him. He held his finger, wet with her cream, between them. Her eyes went back and forth between his finger and his eyes, her chest heaving, anger and desire glistening brightly in her beautiful chocolate-brown eyes as she glared at him.

"Stop fighting me, goddamn it," he grunted, and traced his cream-coated finger over the succulent, full, lower rim of her lip. "Give in to me. To us," he murmured. She closed her eyes.

When her tongue snaked out and licked her own cream away, before drawing the digit fully into her mouth to suck, Demetri felt a bead of cum drip from the tip of his dick.

"Fuck," he groaned and dragged his finger from her mouth. She licked her bottom lip, her eyes hot, staring into his. He felt the heat of her lust sear him, making his body strum with an answering need to fill her, to give her what her eyes and body were begging for.

He dipped his finger back, deep, into her well and withdrew more of her moisture. He kept his gaze on hers, brought his finger to his mouth, and sucked her cum from it.

"So damn good," his voice hitched. Giving her no time to react, Demetri pushed her against the wall, grasped his cock in his hand, and entered her.

Her body melted around him, her legs wrapped tighter, higher, around his hips, and he began to stroke into her.

Although his body was on fire for her, he was careful, not wanting to hurt her on the hard wall, and simply ground against her, rotating his hips, skewering her into the wall with each painfully slow rotation.

The position of her body on his, the slow grind, coupled with the kittenish little noises she made, all played hell with him as he battled against the need to pound into her sweet, tender flesh.

"Harder," she panted, her nails scoring his back, her eyes tightly shut.

"No, I can't . . . I'll hurt you," he panted. Holding back

from taking her in the way he wanted made his body shake. His body wet with lust and sweat, he lay his forehead against her. She was so damn sweet and responsive, so hot for him, it made him crazy.

He'd bedded more than enough women to know her responses were real. He'd seen her sensuality below the surface, even in the photo, untouched sensuality that held innocence at odds with the passionate woman hovering beneath the surface.

She cupped his face in both of her small hands, her full lips apart, panting. "Harder, please . . . I need it. I need *you,*" she begged, her voice tight.

He buried his head against her neck and dragged out of her heat. When she moaned and clenched down tightly on his cock with her hands balled into fists, striking against him, he laughed, a painful sound.

"Vixen," he grunted, his harsh breath matching hers.

He turned around with her in his arms and strode through the dark room until he reached the raised platform in the far corner and laid her on the bed.

He spread her legs, settled between them, and reentered her, embedding himself in her until his balls slapped against her plush round buttocks. His groans matched hers and he stayed in that position, luxuriating in the feel of her warm heat wrapped around his shaft.

But, soon, it wasn't enough. He began to stroke inside her, long drawn-out slides of his cock in and out. He stuffed her with his cock, only to drag it out, and groaned along with her at the hot sweet glide.

Her moans of satisfaction matched his.

As he screwed her, he sucked one of her luscious breasts, suckling as much of the large orb as he could fit into his mouth. She made noises of delight when he tugged on one extended nipple.

He rolled his tongue over the sharp, erect bud, drawing it

back into his mouth before releasing it to latch on to the other breast.

"God, please, Sweet . . . please, I need to come," she begged as he banged her pussy, mercilessly. She knotted the sheet in her hands and tossed her head back and forth on the pillow.

That was what he needed to hear. He didn't know how much longer he'd be able to hold off.

He pressed into her as far as he could, her walls clamping down on him, clenching and gripping him, like a thousand fingers along his cock.

He grabbed her legs and pressed them far apart so that she had to take all of him, all of his seed, his need to mark her making him feel like an animal.

His plan had been to dominate her, make her beg for it, but damned if it'd worked out that way. Just like at the pharmacy, he'd lost control and he'd been the one to demand . . . to beg.

Fuck!

When he knew he couldn't take it anymore, the tight clamp of her gripping and milking his dick, he reached between them and sought out her tight little bud. He pressed against it until she screamed, her body jackknifing off the bed as her orgasm released.

Just in time.

He was barely able to wait until she completed her release before he pulled out.

Grasping his shaft, he pumped his hand over its hardness once and his seed came spitting out.

In satisfaction he watched his cum land in hot steamy jets on her creamy brown skin, the difference between the color of his cum and her skin an erotic sight beyond anything he'd ever seen, as it ran down her breast, down the middle of her body, and trailed off the side.

Once he finished, his heart slamming against his chest, he shut his eyes against the sight of her, satiated, with her eyes closed, sighing breaths coming out of her full, kiss-swollen mouth.

And even now, it wasn't enough. God, he needed more.

A lazy smile of contentment curved Gaby's mouth when she felt a warm towel run over her breasts and down her body. She opened sleepy eyes to see Sweet perched on the side of the bed cleaning her.

"You're so damn beautiful," the words were spoken in a hoarse whisper. He leaned down to claim her lips.

"You're not so bad yourself," she whispered against his mouth, once he released her. He placed the towel on the table beside them.

He turned to face her. "If I hadn't come to find you, would you have returned, Gabrielle?"

"I . . . I don't know. I've never done anything like that." When she saw the blank look on his face, she clarified, "Picked up a man," she said and felt her cheeks flush. She turned away. "And, honestly, I thought it would be less embarrassing for you that way."

"What do you mean?"

"Look, I know about you, your reputation . . ."

"What about my reputation?"

"How you got your nickname," she laughed, embarrassed, but tried to brazen it out. "I didn't want you to think I thought it was more than it was."

"And what was that?"

"We both know what it was. You don't have to pretend, play games. I'm a big girl, I know the score," she said, infusing pseudosophistication she was far from feeling into her voice. When he turned her around, she stared into his handsome face, forcing a smile on hers. "So, the answer to your question is, no. I probably wouldn't have."

"But, did you want to? Did you want me? Want it to be more than a one-night affair?"

She licked a tongue over her lower rim. "Yes," she replied simply.

She read satisfaction in his eyes before he turned away from her.

Deftly, he reached across and blindly opened the side drawer and withdrew a foil package. When she saw what was in his hand, her eyes flew to his.

"Again?"

Her eyes widened and her gaze went to his shaft. Hard, thick, and curved, it lay against his stomach and she felt the dormant desire within her curl in her stomach. She bit a corner of her bottom lip.

"Yeah. Again." His lips curled into a seductive smile before he ripped open the package with his teeth and sheathed his erection.

He drew a finger between the lips of her vagina and withdrew her moisture. He brought his finger to his mouth and, with his eyes trained on hers, licked her cream from his finger.

"God, you're so damn responsive," he groaned.

She hissed, her back arched sharply, pushing her breasts forward. The temptation to kiss her breasts was one he couldn't ignore.

"Tell me you want me, Gaby."

He stared down at her intently, his shaft poised at her now-dampening folds.

When she turned her head away, avoiding his eyes, he placed two fingers alongside her jaw, forcing her to look at him.

"I have to hear it this time. I have to hear you say it." He wanted to be the one she wanted. The only one. "I don't play second string."

"Wha-what do you mean?"

"I don't want your mind on anyone else. Just me . . . just us. Just this." He grasped his shaft again and rubbed it against her mound, along the seam of her pussy.

One part of his brain recognized his anger was irrational.

The other part of his brain's only concern was getting inside her and having her admit his dick was the only one she craved.

Just like her pussy was the only one he wanted to be inside. The only one that had him waking up in the middle of the night, cum on his sheets, having the kind of dreams he hadn't had since he was a fucking kid.

He ignored the taunting voice that mocked him, telling him it was more than what was between her thighs that had him feinin' like an addict without his daily fix.

Her mouth tightened, an expression of doubt settling over his face as she stared up at him, silently refusing to give in to him.

Their eyes locked in a battle of wills, even as desire and lust were a twin, hazy cloud engulfing them.

"It's just sex."

At her words the cloud of lust and desire changed, grew. It darkened, until it was pure black, a thundercloud.

He slanted his mouth over hers, angrily at first, demanding. She bit into his lip, her small teeth sharp. Surprised, he drew back.

"You don't . . ." she stopped, her breathing labored, before finishing. "You have no rights over me. No claims," she finally finished, defiantly staring at him.

"No?" he lifted a brow, challenging her denial.

He grasped her hands between both of his, shackling them with one of his hands. Her chest was now heaving, the breath coming out in short, quick, puffs of air from between her partially opened lips.

He brought her breasts to his mouth and nursed her, drawing her into his mouth deeply, withdrawing slowly.

When her nipple popped out of his mouth, he swiped his tongue across and blew softly on it, and watched it elongate, spike. He released her hands and flipped her body so that she was on all fours in front of him.

"Tell me you're mine," he demanded harshly. He burrowed his face into her neck, and bit down sharply on the side of her neck, even as his fingers continued to work in and out of her quivering, clenching pussy. "Tell me this pussy is mine."

He added two more fingers into her, screwing into her in short, rapid turns until she cried out, keening sharply. She grabbed him by the back of the head as her body rose from the bed and pulled his mouth to hers.

Their mouths met in a tangle, tongues desperately seeking each other, as her climax claimed her.

"Yes!" she yelled, rolling her hips against his fingers, grinding and mashing her pussy against his fingers.

With her admission that she wanted him, needed him, he withdrew his fingers and adjusted her on his dick, breaking past her walls, physical and mental.

As he stroked inside her, Sweet was going crazy, so caught up in the sweet smell of her cum that rose sharply, surrounding their entwined bodies.

"Oh, God, I can't take it . . . I . . . oh," she moaned, sharply, when he stroked downward.

"Yes . . ." he agreed, unable to say more.

Through the red haze of lust and sweat that clouded his vision, he watched her with his eyes narrowed against the sweat that ran down his face.

He was struck with the beauty of her sensuality. Her head was thrown back, eyes shut tight, her heavy breasts heaving, her body slowly rolling upward, meeting him stroke for stroke.

Her words and the way her small hands gripped and tightened on his ass sent his lust into overdrive. Grunting, unable to speak coherently, Sweet shoved his hands beneath her, grasping the round fleshy globes of her buttocks, and pulled her roughly against him.

She fell back against the pillow, her head rolling back and forth.

"Oh God, oh God, please, please . . ." Gaby begged, her words blending, merging into one melodious cry as another orgasm raced through her.

She gave in and screamed her release. As she came, in the background roar of blood filling her head, she heard him give a responding cry of release, before he pumped into her once more, before his hard body fell on top of hers.

Once she came down, her breath and body calming, Gaby went completely limp, beyond satiated. Her muscles felt loose, languid.

When she felt the now familiar heat of his body behind her, she willingly went into his arms and within seconds she slept.

14

"Mama, I need money for school lunch. Miss Woods said she can't let me eat for free no more."

"What the hell you talking 'bout girl? Get on out of here!" her mother mumbled, turning her back to Gaby, as Gaby stood hesitantly in the doorway to her mother's room.

But her mother had not turned fast enough. Gaby caught a glimpse of the familiar yellow tube wrapped around her arm.

"Mama, I'm hungry. If I don't pay—" she pressed on, the grumblings in her stomach giving her the courage to walk farther into the room.

Her mother whipped her body around and glared at Gaby, her eyes red and wild, screaming, "I told you to get the hell out of here!"

Tears ran unchecked down Gaby's small face as she stared at her mother as she tied off with one hand and her teeth, in her other hand she held a needle, poised over her vein.

"Bu-but, Mama, I'm hungry." As much as she didn't want to incur her mother's wrath, Gaby continued, desperately.

"You hard of hearing, girl? I said get out! Wake your sister up and tell her to get you something to eat," Catherine muttered and turned back around.

Gaby stood, shifting from foot to foot, uncertain what to do.

She didn't want to make her mama mad, but the teacher said if she didn't bring money for lunch, she wouldn't get to eat.

At that moment, her stomach growled again, reminding her that she hadn't had much to eat since school lunch the previous day.

And if she didn't pay the past-due amount, Ms. Woods already told her she wouldn't eat.

"Mama . . ." she gave one final entreaty. When her mother continued to ignore her, with her small shoulders slumped, Gaby turned away.

She knew her sister wasn't at home, and even if she was, she wouldn't care if she had money for lunch or not. Like her mother, her sister's only concern was getting the next high. And having sex with a bunch of different boys, Gaby thought.

Late last night she had woken to the steady thump against her wall, the wall that connected her sister's room to hers. Tabitha had one of her men in there with her; Gaby had known it from hearing her sister's giggles and accompanying male laughter. Sighing, she'd turned over, thrown her pillow over her head, forced herself to ignore the grumbling in her stomach, and tried to go to sleep.

Once the sounds died down, she'd heard her sister and her current "boyfriend" leave the house and she doubted she'd see her sister for a long time. So, no, her sister didn't care about Gaby any more than her mother did.

Gaby went into the kitchen, her stomach growling so hard she felt nauseated, and scoured the kitchen looking for something to ease the pain.

She found a couple of pieces of old, dried bread, a jar of mayonnaise, and some curled-up bologna.

"I'm so hungry," she whispered and grimaced, yet she quickly devoured the nasty sandwich, drank a glass of water, and went back to bed.

"I'll never be like them. Never," the young Gaby whispered, "I'll never let drugs . . . a man, make me like them."

With a tear slipping down her cheek, Gaby turned restlessly in the bed.

Demetri's heart clenched when he listened to the childlike voice asking her mother for money for food.

He sat up in bed propped against the headboard, and listened as Gaby spoke in her sleep, in an oddly childlike voice. In her sleep, she was asking her mother for money for lunch, telling her mother she was hungry.

As he listened he realized she was dreaming, and the longer he listened his shock grew into anger for the child she had been, long ago. When she began to cry, softly, he pulled her into the safety of his arms.

He turned her around so that she faced him. Leaning close, he kissed her softly, kissing away the tears and the long-ago pain.

Her soft cries soon died out, replaced by an occasional sniff as he ran soothing hands over her back.

"Shhh, it's okay, baby. It's okay. I'm here," he continued whispering nonsense words, soothing her until she finally quieted down.

When her arms crept around his waist, hugging him tight, he drew in a deep breath. Softly releasing it, he pulled her soft, pliant body closer, until there was no space separating them.

With his head lying gently on top of her soft hair, he ran his hands over her back for a long time. Even when she'd settled back into sleep, his mind puzzled over the woman lying so trustingly in his arms.

15

Gaby woke with her body wrapped around Sweet's, just as the sun was creeping through the sheer curtains covering the balcony.

She peered down and saw one big, hard, male thigh lying over her legs, her face close to his chest, and her arms wrapped around his.

Confused and embarrassed that she'd wrapped herself around the man like a boa constrictor, she carefully unwound her arms and nudged her legs from between his.

When he didn't open his eyes, she scooted away until she reached the far side of the bed.

She tiptoed around the large bedroom, looking for her clothes. When she couldn't find them, she grew frantic. "Where the hell did they go? Damn it!" she mumbled, casting furtive glances toward the bed and the big man sprawled naked in the center.

He hadn't moved since she got up. He'd only rolled over, flat on his back.

One arm was flung out beside his body. The other was bent at the elbow, above his head.

Her eyes traveled south. With the sun slanting through the room, it was her first time seeing his body in the light of day. His lightly tanned skin seemed to shimmer, catching the early morning rays of sunlight.

The sheet had come down when she'd eased away, and now rested on the upper part of his thighs. Her eyes went to the light sprinkling of hair that formed a V around his groin.

Even in sleep, his cock was thick, curving upward, laying against his stomach.

He moved, and Gaby's eyes flew to his face. When his eyes remained closed, she breathed a sigh of relief and quickly renewed her search for clothing.

"Here I go again," Gaby murmured, realizing she was doing the same thing she'd done weeks ago when they'd had their first encounter.

Again she glanced over his sleeping form, a small smile of appreciation forming on her lips.

She'd slept soundly last night. For the first time in longer than she remembered.

She surpressed a laugh, knowing that one of the main reasons she'd slept so well had been because of sheer exhaustion.

The man had helped her come more times than she had in her entire lifetime, yet that wasn't the only reason she'd slept so well.

She pulled at her bottom lip, considering the man who lay so peacefully, and walked back to the side of the bed.

In sleep he appeared . . . younger, somehow. The stern expression that normally graced his handsome face was missing, the faint lines scoring the side of his mouth softer as he slept.

"Maybe you have as many things on your mind as I do, Sweet . . ." she whispered the words.

Her fingers ached to reach out and touch him. Yet, she held back.

She glanced over at the bedside clock and noticed that, although the sun had begun to rise, it was just barely six o'clock. Maybe she could stay for a little longer.

With one last look at him as he lay peacefully sleeping, she left the bedroom.

Sweet waited until Gaby left before opening his eyes.

He leaned over and glanced down, seeing her scattered clothing still on the floor. His attention to detail noted that although her clothes remained on the floor where they'd dropped them in their haste to make love last night, his shirt was missing.

A smile curved his lips upward. She was wearing his shirt and nothing else. She wasn't going anywhere.

Deciding that the time came that she had to show *him* that she trusted him. She had to make the decision to stay, and in doing so, admit that she was beginning to trust him.

He lay back down and closed his eyes. Secure in his knowledge that she was where he wanted her to be, he drifted off to sleep.

"I wondered where you went."

Startled, Gaby spun around, quickly placing her hands on the kitchen counter to right herself.

"I didn't see you," she coughed, cleared her throat. Her voice emerged rough, nearly gone. She felt as though she'd said that same thing to him more times than she could count.

She carefully stepped down from the stool and turned to face him.

"I thought maybe you'd left again. Without telling me." The reproach was mild, yet she blushed.

"No. I, uh, was looking for something to drink. I'm sorry, I should have asked."

She tugged his shirt down where it had ridden up her thighs.

"Have a seat. Let me make you something to drink," he volunteered, walking farther into the room.

As he came closer, Gaby glanced over his body.

He hadn't bothered putting on a shirt and only wore a pair of jeans. Her eyes rolled over his hard, naked chest, down to the flat planes of his abs, and landed at the top of his waistband, where he'd left his fly undone. She could make out the dark sprinkling of hair.

"I just wanted some milk," she admitted.

"Milk?" he asked, turning away from the counter.

"Yes, I uh, like warm milk. Acquired a taste for it when I was a teenager. I haven't managed to kick the habit."

When an answering smile lifted the corner of his lips, she laughed, self-consciously.

"Hey, there are much worse addictions," he said and winked. His lightheartedness put her at ease.

"Go on, have a seat, I'll warm it up for you," he said and Gaby nodded, and sat down.

"I can make you something to eat if you're hungry," he volunteered.

"No, just the milk is fine. I don't eat much in the mornings."

The mild, casual exchange erased some of the tension she had felt when he first entered the room.

He poured milk into a small kettle and placed it over the stove. The play of muscles along his sculpted back fascinated her as he performed the simple tasks.

"It's not the same heated in the microwave." He winked. The gesture was unexpected, and Gaby felt the remaining tension ease away.

He leaned against the counter and folded his big arms over his chest, intently watching her. "The best things have to be warmed up slowly, carefully. When it comes to a gentle boil, the result is pure nirvana," he finished, his gaze so intent, so focused on her, that Gaby flushed.

"The other secret to good warm milk is a secret recipe, one handed down from my grandmother," he said, turning and opening an overhead cabinet. She craned her neck to see and smiled when he pulled down a bear-shaped container of honey and a small shaker of a spice.

"Oh yeah, and what would that be?"

When the whistle trilled from the kettle, he poured the milk in two mugs, walked over, and sat down to join her.

"I wouldn't take you for a man who drinks milk," she said and took a careful sip of the milk.

"Not just any milk, you gotta do it right," he said and poured a dollop of honey into the mug.

"Honey?"

"Hmmm, nothing beats it," he said and winked. "Wanna try?" he asked, grinning. She nodded her head eagerly and allowed him to add the sweetener to her drink, along with a dash of cinnamon.

"Hmmm, you're right," she said after taking a sip of the doctored mixture. "It *is* good."

"Old family secret, but, I guess I can let you know," he said and she laughed.

"Well, I don't really have any family recipes to share, not unless you count Colonel Sanders, but I think everyone knows that secret," she said and laughed lightly.

She glanced up. "What?" she asked, feeling self-conscious beneath his stare.

"Nothing. You talk in your sleep, you know."

She took a careful sip of the milk and avoided his stare.

"So, what did I say?"

Demetri sensed her discomfort.

"You were talking to your mother, I think. But you seemed sad. You cried." He didn't want to tell her how much she'd said, didn't want to embarrass her more than she already was, yet the memory of her childlike voice begging her mother for money for food still rang in his mind.

"Oh," she answered quietly.

He changed the subject. "Why don't I make us something to eat? You must be hungry?" he asked, and noted the small blush that stained her cheeks.

Damn. The minute the words came out, he wanted to kick his own ass. In her dream, she'd cried because she was hungry.

"After last night, I could use a bit of sustenance. I'm a growing boy," he said, purposely lewd, waggling his brows up and down in an attempt to lighten the moment.

When her eyes flirted to his groin, and she saw the way his cock, always at the ready, strained against his zipper, he bit back an answering grin when she unexpectedly laughed.

"God, don't you ever get tired?"

"Not until I'm dead, I hope," he quipped and rose.

Demetri breathed a sigh of relief at her laughter, the tension easing from the room as she leaned back, brought the mug of milk to her mouth, and drank.

He grabbed what he needed and went about making breakfast.

"Wanna talk about it?" He asked, cracking eggs in a big bowl. "About your dream, that is," he said, nonchalantly. He buttered the pan. Once it began to sizzle, he added his mixture.

"I'm told I'm a pretty good listener."

Gaby carefully placed the mug of milk down on the tabletop when he spoke.

"Yeah?" she asked, huskily, her eyes wary.

"Goes with the job . . . bartending."

She smiled. "I thought you owned the bar."

"Same difference," he said, shrugging one shoulder.

When she didn't speak for a long time, he shrugged again. "It's up to you. But sometimes talking about it can help," he deftly flipped the large omelet.

"I . . . well, when I'm anxious; worried, I do that sometimes," she replied carefully, her voice hesitant. "Talk in my sleep, that is."

Sweet remained silent, allowing her to speak freely, without any comments from him, sensing that what she was going to say wasn't going to be easy for her.

"What did I say?" she asked. Demetri read the casualness she purposely infused in her tone.

"Actually, you cried," he replied just as casually, just as nonchalantly. He flipped the omelet on a large plate, took out two forks, and walked back over to the table.

"Hope you don't mind sharing." She shook her head no.

Gaby wasn't sure how to respond, although she cringed inwardly. She distantly remembered her dream, one of her as a child, on one of the frequent occasions when her mother had neglected her, all but forgetting Gaby's existence during one of her manic stages.

"It wasn't long. Just seemed like you were having a bad dream."

She haltingly began to speak, telling him about her mother, her addiction to drugs, and how if she didn't have the money she'd resort to prostitution. He heard—felt—her shame. She told him, her eyes with a faraway expression in them as she relived what was a painful past, related to him how often they moved—her mother, her older sister and herself—once the rent had become too past due and they were kicked out. She told him how there was never enough food, how her mother, in her lucid moments, would cry and promise to do better, be better . . .

"She really tried," she turned pleading eyes toward him, as though begging him to understand.

She stopped. "And when my sister left, it didn't get any better. Eventually I ended up in foster care."

Demetri took the empty plate to the sink and rinsed it. He knew there were large gaps in her story, knew from the halting, painful way she spoke that there was much more. When she didn't continue, he returned to the table and sat back down facing her.

"You were taken from your mother?"

"Yes. That was the last time I saw her." From the final way she said it, Demetri ventured a guess that her mother had died.

Despite the lack of expression on her face, in her eyes, Demetri read her sadness.

After she finished, she looked away, out the window, a pensive look on her face, before she turned back to face him. Her lips curved upward in a smile tinged with sadness.

"I bet you think I'm pitiful."

He shook his head, replying softly. "No, the exact opposite. Nothing you say is going to change the way I feel about you."

"And how do you feel about me?" The question was direct, as piercing as the way she looked at him, her expression completely open, yet he read her vulnerability. A vulnerability he'd originally seen in her, one he had hoped to exploit.

But, not now.

He brought his hand out to run softly down her face. He leaned over, capturing her lips with his. "I care about you, Gabrielle. I think you know that already," he murmured once he released her lips.

The truth of his words hit him right in the heart the minute he said them.

He lifted her in his arms and strode with her though the loft and laid her on the bed, covering her tear-stained face with soft kisses, while in the back of his mind he knew he was in deep-shit trouble.

The rules of the game had changed and he didn't have the fucking playbook and was now running on pure instinct, he thought as he covered her body with his own.

16

Demetri parked his truck across the street from the South Side Mission, tugged his baseball cap on his head, brought the brim of his cap low, and killed the engine of his truck.

"Are you able to talk?"

"Yes."

"Everything okay?" Nick asked.

Although his voice hadn't risen, changed much in inflection, Demetri caught the fine nuance of reproof that flavored Nick's voice. He hadn't had much in the way of communication with his former commander lately.

Glancing around, he noted there were several other old cars parked near him, some in better shape than his own '76 Chevy pickup, so he knew that he didn't stick out as different.

He lifted the small binoculars from the passenger seat and after adjusting them, from his vantage point, he could clearly see inside the mission.

He gave a short laugh. "Everything's peachy," he replied, distractedly. He didn't ask why Nick was questioning how the investigation was going; he already knew the answer.

Since he and Gabrielle had reconnected, he'd had little communication with his former commander over the last two weeks.

During his tenure under Nick's command, if an operative didn't touch base with his unit commander, there was immediate concern that something had gone awry.

But, he was no longer operating under any agency or bureau's suffocating, long-armed embrace.

He scanned the room and caught sight of Gabrielle, surrounded by what appeared to be the residents of the mission.

He reported in as needed, when he had information to give that he thought important. Otherwise he went alone, feeling no need for communication.

Those days were long past, and he damned sure had no intention to revisit them. After this investigation was over and his last ties were severed, Nick, as he promised, would try and locate his partner.

Right now, he'd spend as much time with Gabrielle as possible.

During one of their conversations she'd shared with him her commitment to the homeless and the amount of time she spent with them astounded Demetri.

When she left earlier that morning, after a night spent together, kissing him, she'd promised she'd return later tonight. He'd casually mentioned accompanying her on one of her visits, and she'd been surprised, he could tell.

"I want to see this other side of you. You're a complex woman. One I want to know more about," he'd answered the unasked question, stroking a caressing hand down the side of her face. With an almost shy nod, she'd agreed for him to accompany her the following week. However, as soon as she had left, he'd followed.

He told himself his intentions were purely because of the investigation, to find out what her connection was, and how she was using it for her criminal activities.

But that was a damn lie and he knew it.

"You have anything new? Have you gotten any . . . closer . . . to her?"

"When I do, I'll let you know," he said, not apprising Nick of the change in their relationship.

There was a short pause. Demetri could tell he was pissed off.

Fuck it. He wasn't under anyone's command.

"Okay. Get back to me when you have something," was Nick's only reply.

"What about you . . . anything new?" Demetri asked, knowing Nick wouldn't have called just to check in on him.

"I've uncovered a few things."

"Such as . . ."

"Such as, for one, Hunter Winters has a kid."

Demetri was surprised. It wasn't something he'd uncovered yet about the man.

"He's not a kid anymore. Actually, he should be about thirty or so, give or take a year. Gabrielle's mentor's husband," he clarified, although there was no need. Demetri had become intimately acquainted with all the key players in Gabrielle's life.

"Seems he had a kid roughly thirty years or so ago," he said and at this piece of news, Demetri perked up, paying close attention.

"It doesn't appear he's had any communication with the kid. At least, there's no paper trail. No child support, no communication with the mother."

Demetri asked, "I'm assuming the birth mother wasn't his current wife?"

"No. The kid was a product of an affair."

"How'd he show up? How do you know he's the father?"

"Like everyone else, once you're in the system, eventually you can be found."

"No mother?"

"She died when he was fifteen."

"No other family?"

"Doesn't appear to be. Mother was a runaway. When she died, he was left alone."

"Except for his father."

"Yeah. A father he never knew. The mother," he paused, "never told him about his father. But, on his birth certificate she gave him his father's last name."

"You'd think she would have hit Winters up for money for the kid. It's not like he couldn't afford it."

Although Hunter had made his own money, he came from a rich family.

"Hmmm. Not sure why. But, she did try and reach out to the guy less than six months before she died."

The news made Demetri pause. Instantly, his gut told him there was more to the death.

"Cause of death?" Demetri asked automatically.

"Overdose," Nick supplied, smoothly, and continued. Demetri filed the information away for later examination.

"Convenient," was his only comment.

"Kid went into the system, but it wasn't until after they'd located the man the kid was told by his mother was his father."

"And that man was Hunter Winters."

"The one and only. But, seems like Winters claimed the kid wasn't his. Cold son of a bitch, didn't even have the decency to fly down to see the kid and find out for sure. Just had his solicitor set up money for the kid."

"What he do?"

"Same thing most rich guys do when they unexpectedly find out they're a reluctant papa, faced with a kid they don't want to claim."

"Tried to pay the woman off?"

"Appears that way. Only thing is, she died before the money came through. Kid went into the system and that's all she wrote. At least, until he turned eighteen. He cut out after that, that's all we have." Nick finished.

"Nothing else? He didn't show up on the radar anywhere else?"

"I did a bit of snooping. It seems like he was anxious to cut out of the small town. His last foster parents had no knowledge of where he went."

"He never claimed the money?" Demetri asked.

"Guess not. Not even sure if he ever knew about it."

"Any record of where he went from there?"

Nick paused, Demetri could almost see him scrolling down the screen of his computer, scanning the information quickly.

"Went in and out of juvy hall . . . petty crimes," Nick mumbled. "After that, I got nothing."

"What was the kid's name?" Demetri asked, although his gut already told him who it was.

"Says here, Adam Winter."

"Quick . . . he changed his last name," Demetri stated, rather than asked.

"Appears so," a short pause before he continued. "From the records, the last seen pictures, he's Adam Quick. Gabrielle's lover," he finished.

Demetri stopped himself in time from cussing Nick out when he said Gaby was Adam's lover. If he knew of his growing feelings for her, Demetri doubted he'd keep him on, thinking he'd compromise the case.

In the way he had the last time.

The self-admission stung, but he didn't lie to himself.

Before he severed the connection, Nick made one last comment. "And stand by; make sure you have your phone on, in case I need to contact you."

Demetri yanked the earbud from his ear and tossed it in the passenger seat. He flipped open his phone, and turned it off.

He put the conversation, as well as his former commander, out of his mind, and picked up the binoculars again.

During the time he'd spent with Gaby, he'd focused on getting her to open up to him. The process had been slow. Damn slow. She had begun to share more of herself with him, bit by small fucking bit. Yet, she maintained a certain distance from him, one he was determined to break through.

His attention focused back on the small woman inside the shelter. Within minutes she was coming back out and he quickly slid back against the seat of his truck and placed the binoculars to the side.

Strapped to her back was a large satchel as she briskly began to walk down the streets. When she turned in to one of the alleys farther down the street, Demetri quickly flipped on the engine, rolled out of his parking space.

Luckily, he found a spot. By the time he'd followed her, she was quickly surrounded by a bevy of homeless people. Taking a chance, he rolled down the window of his truck and picked up the binoculars, again, wondering what she was doing.

Her animated, pretty face came into view, and, for a moment, Demetri was transfixed by the gentle smile that transformed her face into something beautiful.

He forced the binoculars away from her face and zeroed in on her hands. She was handing out pamphlets as well as small brown paper bags. Many of the homeless people grabbed the bags and held them tight, as though someone would try and steal them from them.

"What the hell is she giving them?" Demetri voiced out loud.

Every possibility ran through his mind. Was she involved in some kind of illegal distribution of trial medications? Using the homeless as guinea pigs for test drugs?

Demetri knew the possibility was there.

Money and greed were alive and thriving in any big business. And the pharmaceutical business had many tentacles that reached beyond the buying and selling of medication.

She turned her head and tilted it, her eyes squinting as though she *knew* she was being watched.

Demetri quickly turned away, rolled up his window, and started his truck. Seconds later, he pulled out of his spot and drove away, wondering what the hell his pretty little crook was up to.

Demetri had driven so fast back to the club and his loft he knew he'd been damn lucky he hadn't gotten pulled over. It was a Sunday afternoon. In the Bible Belt of Texas, even the cops took a day of rest on Sunday, it appeared.

Pulling out a dark skullcap and long trench from his closet, he'd swiftly donned a change of clothes.

He needed to fit in, his plan being to return to the south side of town, and in particular, the heavily populated homeless area.

Wearing the old coat and skullcap among the homeless people wouldn't look odd, even during this time of year, when it was still very warm, as most of them wore multiple layers of clothing, despite the weather.

He kicked off the Nike running shoes he'd been wearing and scouted out in the back of his closet for something more suitable, satisfied when he unearthed a pair of beat-up Converse with a multitude of holes, and quickly laced them on his feet.

A look in the large bathroom mirror and he was satisfied with his appearance.

He went to his kitchen and withdrew a couple of bottles of whisky. Uncapping one of the bottles, he'd poured a small amount on his hands, and using it as he would cologne, he'd patted it on his cheeks, over his body, before taking a swallow.

That done, he rode his private elevator straight down to the back entry of the Sweet Spot, not wanting to come across any of his employees, and drove back to the south side of town, where he'd seen Gaby.

As he drove through the streets, he searched for her, hoping she hadn't left.

His luck held out as he spotted her and he again parked the truck, this time a distance away, and waited. When she left he jumped out of his truck, and concealing the bottles of whisky in the deep pockets of his trench, walked toward the alley.

The men in the alley looked him over warily, their watery glazed red eyes running over him with deep suspicion. He avoided direct eye contact with them, shuffling his feet as he walked, purposely stumbling before righting himself.

Eventually, they'd turned away, their interest in the new-comer quickly fading. He approached one of the derelicts, sat down, pulled out the half-empty bottle of whisky, and took a long deep swallow.

In his peripheral vision, he noted the drunk eyeing him, his eyes on the bottle tipped to Demetri's lips, as his tongue swept out to wipe the lower rim of his full lips.

Demetri turned to him. He lifted the bottle, silently offering the man a drink.

The man took the bottle and threw his head back, greedily drinking before Demetri nudged him.

With a grunt, the man handed him back the bottle with a mumbled "thanks."

"Who's that woman who comes 'round here?" Demetri asked, casually, after taking another drink of the whisky, wiping his mouth with the back of his hand.

The man turned bleary eyes back toward Demetri, his eyes darting to the now nearly empty bottle in Demetri's hand.

Demetri handed him the bottle again. After draining the last of the whisky, the man handed it back, empty.

"What woman?"

"The one that was here 'bout twenty minutes ago. She was giving out stuff. What I miss?"

The drunk laughed. "Oh. Her. The doc." The old man reached with a gloved hand into his pocket. He withdrew a beat-up package of generic cigarettes. He offered Demetri one, and although Demetri didn't smoke, he accepted the cigarette, knowing the old man was repaying him for the alcohol.

"Doc?" he said, after taking an exaggerated pull off the cigarette.

"Yeah, she been coming around for the last year or so. You ain't from 'round here, huh?" the old man asked, taking a deep pull off his own.

"Nah, just moved down from Dallas. They're not too cool toward the homeless," he said, lifting a shoulder in a shrug. "Man can't even find a place to sleep out without being fucked with."

The old man nodded. "Yeah, I heard that," he said, nodding his head sagely. "The doc, she comes around every week just 'bout. Gives away a bunch of brochures about medicine and stuff. Clinics we can go to."

"That all she does? I thought I saw her giving away something else."

"Yeah. She gives away stuff like aspirin, small shit. Nothing that can get you high."

Demetri was disappointed, hoping he'd find something, anything, to clue him into Gabrielle's connection with the scam.

"Can I see?" he asked.

The old man reached into the cart at his side and handed him the flyers. " 'S all yours."

"Thanks," Demetri said, taking a cursory look at the flyers, before bunching them in his hand and stuffing them inside one of the inner pockets of his trench.

After a few moments more, puffing his cigarette, the old man had ambled away, leaving him still wondering what secrets Gabrielle Marlowe held hidden, and what he needed to do to get her to trust him, open up to him in a way he was desperate for her to do.

For the investigation. It was time to end it, wrap it up, find out what, who, she and Adam were in league with. No more, no less.

He ignored the mocking laughter in his head calling him a damn liar.

Demetri opened the door of the shelter and spotted Gabrielle immediately. Even in a crowded room he was able to zero in on her. She stuck out like a bright peacock against the dull drab of the dining hall.

As soon as he'd returned home, he grew restless, and instead of going to his office and doing paperwork, he'd changed clothes and headed back to the mission, to Gabrielle.

As he walked farther inside, he took a look around.

Obviously, the staff tried their best to cheer the place up. The large room he'd entered still held a lingering odor of fresh paint, yet somehow it only served to highlight the overall drabness of the room. Cheap, dollar-store prints hung on the walls. A large, white government-issue clock hung above the kitchen counter in the far corner of the room.

The mingled smell of food mixed in with the faint smell of paint assaulted his nose, nearly made him nauseous. Lunch was soon to be served, as was evident from the smells as well as the men and women who began to fill the room.

He saw Gaby, talking to a small group of people.

He walked closer and stopped, leaning against one of the columns to observe her when she wasn't aware he was there.

He smiled at the difference in her appearance. Gone was the sedate, boxy suit she normally wore; in its place she wore a short skirt that barely reached her knees and a butter-colored silk blouse that softly molded her large, firm breasts.

Her hair, normally worn upswept in a tight bun, securely pinned in place, was loose, thick strands framing her heart-shaped face, the ends curling around the tops of her shoulders.

She turned from speaking to someone, as though she felt his

presence. He gave her a small smile. She shyly returned the smile and his smile grew, unconsciously, when he noted the small blush stain her cheeks.

She mouthed "hi" and despite feeling silly, he had a wild need to go up to her and kiss the shy smile off her face. When she blushed more brightly, accurately reading his expression, he let out a chuckle.

Their private, silly moment was interrupted when an old man tapped her shoulder. She raised a finger, motioning that she'd be with him in a minute, and spoke to the man.

Demetri pushed away from the wall and strode closer to her so he could hear what she was saying.

"Sí, Mr. Rodriguez," she said, patting the old man's shoulder. "There is a bed for you at the shelter. I called for you. Ms. Ortega is holding the bed. But," she cautioned when the little man's head bobbed up and down, a grin cracking his lips wide, showing a gap-toothed yellowed, missing-teeth smile.

"Pero, usted can' rotura de te las reglas otra vez. Ésta es su última oportunida," she spoke gently, yet sternly. Demetri was impressed with the thread of steel in her voice. Although his Spanish was rudimental at best, he understood she was warning him he couldn't screw up again.

"No, no, I don't mess up, Señora. *Haré major.* I promise," he replied hastily, in broken English.

She smiled one of her bright smiles and the little man's solemn face broke into a happy grin. When he reached over and quickly kissed her cheek in gratitude, she stumbled back, surprise showing on her face.

Not threatened by the old man's gesture, Demetri suppressed a laugh. She was completely unaware of how she affected those around her. How people responded to her.

Seeing this side put into place another piece of the puzzle of who Gabrielle Marlowe was.

The sensual side of her he knew well, but he found that with each day that passed, the more time he spent with her, the more he wanted to know everything about her.

As much as he initially tried to deny it, he no longer could. His interest had nothing to do with his investigation of her, and everything to do with the woman and his growing feelings for her.

Yet, he knew that because of the investigation their relationship would change dramatically, once she knew the truth.

Fuck . . . that was putting it mildly, he thought.

She glanced his way, catching him looking at her. They stood staring at one another; the sounds of the busy shelter receded, as if the two of them were all alone.

She tilted her head to the side, a question on her face, her brows drawn together in a frown, as though she read his thoughts.

She'd begun to read him as well as he read her.

He crooked his finger at her, telling her to come over. She was moving toward him when the homeless man tapped her shoulder again, seeking her attention.

She broke the connection, and turned her attention toward the man in front of her.

But not before he saw the small womanly smile tug the corners of her full lips upward.

So much untapped sensuality.

As soon as she finished speaking with the old man and he ambled away, Demetri walked over to her.

"Hi. I wasn't sure if you were coming today," she said.

"Yes," he said. He leaned down and kissed her.

Instead of turning away from him, as he half expected she would, she moved farther into his arms and returned the kiss.

When he broke the kiss, he ran a hand over her hair.

"I like it," he said.

"Oh, thank you," she said, a pleased smile on her face. "I, uh, decided to do something different with it."

"I came early today. I was hoping to meet with someone, but she didn't show," Gabrielle said, and her shoulders slumped just enough to show her disappointment, the smile on her face slipping.

He walked alongside her and glanced down at her from the corner of his eyes.

"Someone important?" he asked, casually.

"I suppose you could say that. It was my mother."

Demetri stopped walking and turned her around to face him. "Your mother?" he asked, turning her to face him. "I thought you said your mother was dead," he said.

When he'd asked her about family, she'd told him she was alone in the world and left it at that. Although he suspected she had family, neither he nor Nick and his formidable government search engines had been able to unearth any information on her parents. The best they'd been able to find had been her sister.

Records showed her sister had been in and out of the system, for petty crimes, drug possession, prostitution, petty theft, larceny . . . the list had been long, dating back from when the girl was no older than fourteen.

The last record of her was at the age of eighteen, when she'd been picked up for dealing. The charge hadn't stuck, because of police mishandling, and she'd gotten off.

"I guess I didn't really know how to tell you about my family," she admitted and Demetri heard the doubt in her voice. "Not exactly something you tell the guy you're dating. My mother's a drug addict, my sister is a whore and a drug addict."

"I think we're past the dating stage, don't you?" he asked.

"I don't know what to call what we are, to be honest, Demetri."

"Why don't we—" his words came to a halt when someone called Gabrielle's name.

Gabrielle turned away, and her face lost some of its animation, her cocoa-brown skin blanching as her eyes widened.

"Excuse me, I . . . need to . . ." her eyes were frantic as she stepped away from his embrace.

Demetri turned toward the voice and the minute he did, he felt like punching the nearest wall.

Adam Quick stood in the entry, his eyes narrowing, glancing at the possessive hold Demetri had on Gabrielle.

Gabrielle glanced back and forth, between the two men, the tension so thick, so palpable, it was as though it were a living, breathing entity.

"Um, this won't take long," Gabrielle broke the thick silence and smiled a shaky smile.

She turned toward Demetri, her eyes pleading with him not to ask any questions.

He saw the desperation in her eyes. Although it took everything in him not to go over and punch the grinning asshole's perfect teeth out, he nodded his head shortly.

He held back. Barely.

"No problem," he infused a light tone in his voice. "I can wait for you. I parked in front."

She nodded her head, gave him a relieved smile, and turned.

He stopped her, pulling her back around to face him. He leaned down and kissed her, taking his time. When he released her, she stumbled and he righted her. "Don't be long," he said and with a nod in Quick's direction, strode away.

17

"What are you doing here, Adam?" Gaby asked, angrily, keeping her voice low.

Although Demetri had left, she had no desire to have the staff overhear her conversation. They were familiar with Adam, as he'd occasionally come by the shelter with her.

She snatched her arm away when he reached for her.

"Is *he* the reason you haven't been answering my calls?"

"If he is, it's none of your damn business, Adam. You gave that up when you decided to screw around on me." She clenched her teeth to keep herself from adding, *and when you stole from me and Tricom.*

"Damn, aren't you going to let that shit go? I told you that bitch didn't mean anything to—"

"Lower your voice," she cut in with a hiss, turning her head slightly to see if Sweet had returned, or anyone else heard him.

"Come with me," she said and quickly led Adam down a narrow hallway that led to the small office she kept at the shelter.

Once they entered, she closed the door behind them and turned to face him.

"Listen, I didn't come here to have a fight. I miss you, Gaby. I'm sorry. What else do I have to do to convince you of that?" If she didn't know him for the lying bastard he really was, his look of hurt would have fooled her into thinking he really cared.

Those days were long past.

"And I've told you, we're over. You need to get that through your head, Adam. We're over."

Adam's jaw tightened and a dark red flush ran along his lower jaw.

He grasped her elbow, tightly, his fingers biting painfully into her skin.

"And I told *you*—" As he spoke his eyes bore into hers, the look in them filled with fear and desperation despite his bold words. "This is over when I say it's over. Don't forget you still owe me, Gaby—"

"Owe you for what? I don't owe you one damn thing, Adam!"

She stared into his angry red face, fascinated, despite her fear, with the near-maniacal look in his eyes.

"You're the one who's been stealing from Tricom," she bit out, in a low, angry voice. "And you've been using me to do it!"

When she realized her blunder, she clamped her mouth shut. But it was too late.

He grabbed her roughly by the arm and hauled her close.

"What the hell are you talking about?" His eyes narrowed. "What do you know about Tricom, Gaby?" he demanded and pulled her so close against his side, less than an inch of space separated them.

"I-I know what you've been doing. I know how you've been using me," she stammered out the answer. As soon as she said it, his hold on her tightened painfully as his fingers dug into her upper arm.

She nearly threw up in fear. Now that he knew she was

aware of what he'd been doing, there was no telling what he would do.

His hold on her loosened, and a calculating look entered his eyes.

"Yes, I guessed you had figured it all out. I wondered how long it would take," he murmured. "But, it doesn't have to change anything," he said, the corner of his thin lips lifting in a slight smile.

"You think you using me to hide what you've been doing—using me, my pharmacy, to hide that you're stealing from Tricom—won't affect our relationship?" she yelled the words at him, her face contorted with anger at the balls he had to think she'd continue having a relationship with him.

"It doesn't have to be like this, Gaby. We can move past this, we can make it work."

The words were spoken against her neck.

The heat from his body reached out and nearly suffocated her.

"How, Adam? How are we supposed to get 'past' this?"

She knew she was all kinds of a fool for tipping her hand, and letting him know she knew what he'd been doing. But damned if she had been able to hold back the words, anger and betrayal beat too strongly in her to allow that.

Was there no one in her life who wasn't using her? Was there anyone who could just love her for her, and not what they could get from her? she wondered, and ground her teeth together, fighting back angry tears.

"Let me go," she hissed, shoving against him.

"Not until I'm good and damn ready. Now listen, bitch—"

"No, *you* listen."

They both spun around to see that Demetri had silently come up next to them. His approach had been so silent, so quick, so . . . deadly, that a shiver ran through Gabrielle.

Although he and Adam were of similar height, Demetri

seemed to tower over the blond man; his body, his sheer presence, was commanding and dominated the entire room.

"Get your hands off her," he stated calmly.

Adam's eyes widened as he stared at the man in front of him. Despite the doubt in his eyes, he kept his hand tight on Gabrielle.

When he showed no signs of releasing her, Demetri yanked Adam's hand away from the hold he had on Gabrielle, crushing Adam's hand within his fist.

With the other hand, he grabbed Adam by the lapels of his expensive Ralph Lauren blazer. Calmly, as though he were picking up someone who weighed no more than a child, he lifted him a good six inches off the floor.

"Let me go," Adam grunted his face red and flushed with embarrassment as he flailed uselessly in Demetri's grip.

Demetri ignored him and turned to Gaby, his face mild as though he wasn't holding a 175-pound man suspended in midair.

"I'm going to take this out," he said.

Despite the fear and acute embarrassment, Gaby wanted to laugh hysterically at his referring to Adam as though he were an inanimate object, announcing his intent as though he were telling her he was taking out the trash.

She nodded her head, and he turned and left, tugging a blustering Adam along in his wake like an errant toddler.

Gabrielle rubbed her elbow, easing the ache she had from Adam's tight hold as she watched Demetri remove Adam from the center.

"Is everything okay, Dr. Gaby?"

Gabrielle turned at the voice, and smiled when she saw Mr. Rodriguez standing in front of her, wringing his small hands together in agitation. "I was coming back to your office to ask a question and heard the man fighting with you. I went and brought your man here to help."

"I'm fine, Mr. Rodriquez. But thank you. Everything's okay. You'd better go inside. I don't want you to miss lunch," she said and encouraged the old man to go inside the dining hall.

"I will wait until your man returns. Just in case," he said firmly, and a reluctant smile eased over her mouth.

"Thank you, sir. I'll take it from here."

Gaby spun around and cast a wary glance over Demetri, looking for signs that he'd made good on the promise in his eyes when he'd hauled Adam away.

Nothing was out of place; he looked as put together as when he left. Except for the look in his eyes. To describe it best, it was a look of unleashed rage.

She shivered and turned toward Mr. Rodriquez.

"I'm fine. You can go now," she sought to reassure him. However, the look in Demetri's eyes didn't seem to cause alarm for the old man. With a short nod, he turned and left.

Left alone, Gaby nervously bit into her lip, until she felt a tang of blood stain her tongue.

"Let's go. You and I need to talk. And no bullshit this time, Gaby. I want to know what the hell is going on," he said, his words echoing Adam's.

Cupping her beneath the elbow, he escorted her out of the shelter.

Her day of reckoning had come at last, she thought, allowing him to lead her out of the shelter.

18

Demetri walked inside her small house, following her closely. "It looks like you," he said, and she turned after placing her bag on the kitchen counter.

She watched him walk around the living room. She'd bought the house soon after graduating from pharmacy school for a low price, knowing that she'd have to renovate it, as it still had some of the original fixtures in place from over thirty years ago.

She'd begun to renovate it, bit by bit, updating the kitchen and bath areas first, updating fixtures and countertops, before tackling the bedrooms and living room. After combining two of the small bedrooms into one large master suite and joining bath, she'd then had the third bedroom opened up and joined to the living space, creating a comfortable living space, complete with built-in bookshelves.

Recently, she'd been able to add a small breakfast nook to the kitchen, the large windows left bare to allow the sun to stream through the kitchen and living area, giving the small home an air of brightness.

Not wanting to overwhelm the area, and make it look

smaller than it was, Gaby had opted for minimalism in furnishing. Three large overstuffed chairs instead of a traditional sofa and loveseat for seating were strategically placed around the room, to maximize the space and allow guests to enjoy each other's company while not being cramped.

"It's beautiful," he said after completing a small, self-given tour.

"Thank you," she said softly, fear and anxiety twisting her guts in knots replaced the pride she felt in her home.

"Can I get you anything?" she asked.

"The truth," he replied bluntly and turned to face her. "What's the deal, Gaby? What does that asshole have on you?"

The tingling pit in her stomach grew. Her own day of reckoning staring her in the face, in the form of six foot plus of an angry lover demanding she come clean.

She began to bite her lip and clasped her hands together, nervously running her thumb over and over the palm of her hand.

When Demetri strode over to her and grasped her hands, his face set in an angry scowl, Gabrielle wanted to run far and fast, get the hell away from him.

He stopped a hairbreadth away from her. The scowl lifted from his face and he sighed. He drew her hands within his much bigger ones.

"Stop that. You don't have to be afraid with me, baby. Never that." He brought her hands to his, gently kissed the center of her palm, and led her over to one of the oversized chairs in the corner.

Sitting down, he pulled her down with him. She released a nervous laugh. "God, you scared the hell out of me, Demetri," she laughed, nervously.

"Whenever you start biting your lip and wringing your hands, I know you're anxious. Afraid," he murmured, looking into her eyes. The intent way he was gazing at her was unnerving. She looked away.

"How do you know I do that when I'm . . . nervous?" she asked.

He turned her back around, to face him, his thumb caressing the curvature of her chin. "I notice everything about you. Like when you're grading papers, you get this really intense look on your face. Your forehead gets all wrinkly. Especially right here," he said, the pad of his thumb going between her eyebrows.

"And when you're worried, you gnaw your lip so bad, I'm always afraid you're going to chew your own damn mouth off." He pulled her down and suckled her lip before releasing it. "And that would *really* piss me off. I lay claim to those beautiful lips of yours." The comment startled a laugh from her. "And, when you're upset, or uncertain, you wring your hands."

Gaby marveled at how well he read her.

"And how do I feel now? What is my body telling you?"

One side of his mouth hitched in a smile. His glance fell away from her face and down to her breasts.

His hands trailed between her breasts and over each one. Immediately her nipples responded, beading beneath his caress.

"I think that's pretty obvious," he said. A slow grin spread his lips wide.

"Pervert," she laughed, punching him in the chest.

He caught her hand in his and pulled her closer. "But that'll have to wait. I want some answers, Gaby. I know who Adam is. I've known for a long time."

"What . . . *how* do you know who he is, and how did you know his name?"

Demetri considered his next words carefully. He intended to get Gabrielle to open up to him, completely. He was tired of her hiding the truth from him, and he was determined that she was going to be the one to confide in him. He wasn't going to have to dig up any more dirt about her past. She was going to tell him, freely.

After she opened up to him about her mother, he wouldn't settle for anything less than her telling him the complete truth. Starting with Adam.

He'd wanted to rip the asshole's arm from its socket when he'd seen him grab her, and in that moment, without a shadow of doubt, Demetri knew she was his. No two ways about it.

He'd also realized she was innocent. Somehow, some way, she wasn't the criminal the Bureau painted her to be. But, he'd known that from the beginning.

He'd seen too much of the real Gaby.

A woman who was as untapped, as innocent of her own sensuality the way she was, no way in hell was she some slick professional, out to con the government and taxpayers out of millions by scamming medical supplies.

And they way she cared for her homeless . . . hell, no. None of that was fake. She was as real as they came. And unless she told him the truth, she would go to prison, and that wasn't something he would ever allow to happen.

"Tell me, baby. Please," he pleaded. The plea was as real as it got as well. No longer was he an ex-FBI special agent trying to capture a thief, if he ever had been, which, he knew, after being with her for a short time, he had not.

He was a man trying to find a way to help the woman he . . . cared about . . . out of the shitty web she'd somehow gotten herself tangled in.

"Well, how do you know his name?" she asked again.

He had to come up with something quick. If he told her who he really was at this point, he knew she'd run like hell in the opposite direction and never look back.

But she was nobody's fool. He had to give her a semblance of the truth.

"I used to work security, before I opened the Sweet Spot, seven years ago. I have a few friends with access to information. I wanted to know more about you. So, I had an old buddy find out who the guy was you used to come into the Sweet Spot with," he said, and watched her eyes widen, then narrow.

"You'd seen me in the club before? With Adam?"

"Yes, a few times. I watched you. I thought you were beautiful. Too beautiful to be with a self-absorbed asshole like the one you were with," he added. The admission seemed to give her pause, as though she wasn't sure how to respond.

She confirmed his thoughts with her next words. "I don't know if I should be flattered at the compliment, or creeped the hell out that you had me checked out," she said, the wary look still in her eyes.

"Understandable. But, *you* have to understand that it's in my nature. What's mine, I take care of. In that, I need to know if there's anything standing in the way of taking care of what's mine."

Her eyes widened. She'd heard the hard edge in his voice, but it couldn't be helped. He was trying to be as honest with her as he could given the circumstances.

"But you can trust me, Gaby. I promise you that," he hoped she read the sincerity behind his words.

She settled more comfortably in his lap and turned around, facing the opposite direction.

He smiled behind her back and breathed a sigh of relief when her hands settled over his, crossed at her midsection. She must have. Her hands stroked his, and though she wasn't facing him, he read her trust as she leaned her back against him.

"I met Adam six months ago," she began, only to stop. "No, actually I met him a year ago. We started dating six months ago. I met him at a fund-raiser Hunter and Abigail were helping to sponsor, for one of Abigail's causes."

"He was so handsome I couldn't stop staring at him, wondering who he was. When Abigail introduced me to him, I made a complete fool out of myself."

"How so?"

"I was so tongue-tied I could barely speak." She laughed lightly, but the laugh was hollow. "I wasn't even able to talk to him. I felt like I'd made a complete ass of myself."

"I doubt that," he murmured, holding her close.

"Maybe I should back up in the story. I led you to believe my mother was dead for a reason."

Demetri kept silent, allowing her to speak freely.

"I never tell anyone about my mother. Like I told you, she's an addict. After I hadn't heard from her when I was taken away, well, it just seemed easier to say she was dead than to say she didn't care enough to try and find me."

"I'm sorry," he murmured, stroking her hand lightly with his.

"It's okay. Anyway, growing up with my mother wasn't easy for me or my sister. At first my sister tried to take care of me. Although she was a few years older than me, she was too young for that kind of responsibility."

Demetri continued to hold her. "My sister tried at first. She really did," she said and his heart ached when he heard the earnestness he heard in her voice. As though she were trying to convince him. Or, more likely, convince herself.

"But, like my mother, she started taking drugs. And, like my mother, she soon got caught up in it."

"Drugs?"

"That and prostitution. We didn't have any money. Grew up in an area where a beautiful woman could easily get money for drugs if she were willing to turn tricks."

Demetri wanted to ask her how she escaped going down the same path—*if* she'd escaped—but didn't. It was her story to tell.

"Eventually my sister left. She was about sixteen or so. She left town, and Momma didn't realize it until she had one of her rare sober days. When she did, she at least had the fortitude to realize that with my sister gone, there was no one to take care of me. I tried to help her. I tried to take care of myself, but . . ." Her voice trailed off.

He heard the tears in her voice. It always amazed him when he'd hear victims of abuse blame themselves and try and protect the abuser. Her mother, through negligence, was no better than someone who physically abused her child.

He remembered how Gaby had cried in her sleep. The words she'd said, telling her mother she was hungry.

"How old were you when you were taken from your mother?"

She sighed. "I was ten years old. At the time, I begged them to let me stay with her. Told them that I could take care of myself."

"Baby, you were so young. Didn't anyone see you were neglected?" he asked.

She sighed. "Yes. The school social workers called the state. I was always hungry, and badly underweight for my age." She stopped, and gave a lopsided grin. "Not that you would know that now," she said and he laughed with her unexpected humor.

"I love a woman with curves. No man wants a bone unless he's a dog," he said and bent down, nipped her ear.

She giggled, the light laughter easing some of the sadness she wore like a blanket around her shoulders.

She went on to tell him how she was in foster care, and for the first year, her mother tried to come in see her, as she was in drug rehab and was trying to salvage her life. Once out of the clinic, though, her mother had been unable to resist the lure of the streets and the drugs and quickly fell back into her same routine.

"It hurt, but by that time I'd met Abigail," she said, and there was a new lightness that entered her voice, dispelling the sadness.

"Your mentor," he murmured. He knew who the woman was, Gaby had mentioned her several times and he knew how much she meant to her.

"Yes. If it hadn't been for Abigail, I don't know how my life would have turned out."

Gaby had already told Demetri that the woman had been responsible for her going to school, that she'd been the recipient of a yearly grant Abigail and her husband Hunter Winters gave to needy girls.

"She became the mother I never had, in a way. I could tell her anything," she said. She paused. "She was the one who introduced me to Adam. She and Hunter, her husband."

Demetri remained silent, processing all that she was telling him.

She paused, took in a deep breath.

"And Adam? What does he have on you?" he prodded.

"It all has to do with my mother. I hadn't seen her in years, and when I did . . ."

She told Demetri how she'd come across her mother in the alley and how her mother had begged Gaby to help her, that she wanted to come clean, was tired of living the way she had for so long. Demetri heard the self-doubt in her voice, the struggle, when she considered what her mother wanted her to do to help. In the end, she hadn't been able to tell her mother no.

"It wasn't too long after that when I met Adam."

"Did you tell anyone?" he asked.

She sighed. "No, not at first, how could I? I wouldn't have until I met Adam," she paused. "He said he could help me. That he loved me and that he would help. I was so stupid," she admitted in a voice filled with self-loathing. "But it wasn't me he was trying to help. All along he'd been setting me up."

At this point in the story, Demetri paid even closer attention to everything she said.

"I think it'll be easier if I show you," she said and scooted off his lap. He sat forward on the chair and watched as she bent over and retrieved her pack from the floor. She opened it and withdrew a leather-bound ledger, which she handed over to him.

He accepted the book and opened it.

His eyes narrowed as he scanned the pages. Soon, it became obvious what Adam had been doing.

He closed the book, but held on to it. He turned to her, his eyes narrowing. "How did you get this?"

She bit her lip, and at his look, one side of her lips curved upward. "Sorry, old habits and all that."

He held out a hand to her, drawing her back to his lap. Settling back against him, she told him how she'd come across the book. When he asked if Adam was aware she had it, again, she paused and nodded her head.

"He does now. At the shelter . . . I told him." She turned and buried her head against his shoulder. "What am I going to do, Demetri? If anyone finds out, I'll go to prison," she cried, her tears muffled against his chest.

He stroked a hand over her hair.

"It's going to be okay, Gaby. I promise you. We'll figure this out," he spoke the reassuring words even as his mind puzzled over what he had to do to get her out of this mess.

What started out as a simple case to catch a thief had slowly turned into something a lot more complex, he thought, holding her close.

19

Before Gaby could push open the entry door to the Sweet Spot, the booming sound system with its deep, hard pounding bass greeted her and she grinned in anticipation.

Although she and Sweet had spent most of their free time together, and had shared meals, and gone out, not to mention all the incredible sex, this was the first time they'd been to his club, despite the fact that he owned and lived above it.

When he'd invited her to come, telling her she needed something to get her mind off Adam and everything else that was going on for a while, she'd happily agreed.

And the way he'd invited her . . . a sensual, happy grin flirted her lips, dispelling the constant state of fear she'd been in over the last few days, waiting for the hammer to fall.

"I bought something for you," he'd said, watching her as she dressed, getting ready for work, as he lounged naked on the bed.

She looked at him from the mirror as she put the back on her earrings. "Oh yeah? What?"

He bounded from the bed, naked, with his dick swinging, and she shook her head at his next-to-nothing modesty.

Yet she admired the way the muscled cheeks in his ass flexed as he walked over to the large, walk-in closet near the bathroom.

Curious, she'd turned to follow him.

"I thought it was time for me to show you off in public. We've gone out a few times, but I thought you might like to accompany me to the hottest club in Texas."

"Oh yeah, and which just might that be?"

He grinned. "You wound me," he replied, theatrically placing a hand over his chest. "Is there any other better than the Sweet Spot?" he asked and she laughed. "I have something I want you to wear for me. I saw it, and knew you'd look sexy as hell in it. It was made for you." He pulled out a dress bag and handed it to her.

She took the dress bag from him and unzipped it, withdrawing a short black dress . . . the perfect "little black dress," the kind that most women had in their closets. The kind she'd never dared wear.

Her eyes widened as she took the dress out. It was gorgeous.

"Do you like it?" Despite the casual tone, she saw the way he was carefully looking at her, his expression unreadable.

She held the dress up to her body and glanced over at him. "How did you know my size?"

"I make it a point to know everything about the woman I'm . . . with," he said, the slight pause making her look at him.

She smiled. "It's beautiful."

"Go try it on," he encouraged, his lips curving up.

She quickly took off the clothes she'd just put on, slipped the dress on, and ran to the bathroom to look at herself in the full-length mirror.

He came up behind her and smiled at their twin images in the mirror.

"Just like I thought . . . sexy as hell," he whispered, kissing the side of her neck as she examined herself, critically.

The dress was daring, no two ways about it. The front was

cut low in a V, folded over so that the ends wrapped her breasts, providing only peek-a-boo images of them, strategically cut so that only a hint of the swell of her breasts showed.

She turned her head and looked at the back. It, too, was cut low, so low that there was no way in hell she could wear panties with it, just like the top, she would have to go sans underwear in the outfit.

"Well?" he prompted when she stood there, staring at her image.

She licked her lips. She'd never worn anything nearly as provocative and daring as this dress. In it, she didn't feel like a pharmacist/university professor. She felt like a complete tramp.

And she loved it.

"Oh . . . and I forgot these," he said and spun around, and ran back into the closet.

He returned with a shoebox. She opened it and took out a pair of the highest, most delicate, open-toed, strappy red stilettos she'd ever seen.

"Sit down, try them on. I want to see the full effect," he said and pressed her down on the bed. Taking her foot in his hand, he'd put one and then the other on, slowly wrapping the ties up and around her leg, tying the ends in a neat, perfect bow.

"Just like a Christmas present," he said.

He brought one daintily clad foot to his mouth, turned it around, and kissed her instep.

Pulling her to her feet, Demetri turned her back around so that she saw herself in the mirror, him standing close behind her.

With their gazes locked, he'd withdrawn the large black bobby pins she'd used to meticulously pin up her hair, allowing it to tumble wild and free to her shoulders.

The woman that stared back at her looked . . . wild. Wanton.

"Beautiful," his voice had been a deep husky whisper against the side of her neck, tickling her skin.

He turned her around and led her back to the bed.

"Time for me to unwrap my gift . . ."

Yes, she was definitely going to be late, she'd thought allowing him to draw her down to the bed.

"Miss . . . can I take your wrap?"

Gaby shook her head, coming out of the delicious memory of just how well he'd "unwrapped" her, and gave the attendant her wrap.

Looking around, she didn't see Demetri, and walked to the bar instead.

She ordered an apple martini from the bartender, thankful it wasn't the female bartender she'd met the first time.

The bartender gave her a once-over, appreciation gleaming in his eyes, before he reluctantly turned around and took the order of a couple standing a few feet farther down the bar.

After ordering, she turned around, scanning the room for signs of Demetri.

"Ummm, you smell as good as you look." A deep voice spoke directly behind her, pulling her snugly against his chest. Gaby smiled and leaned her head to the side when he brushed a familiar kiss along the side of her neck.

"And from the looks of it, I'm not the only one who thinks so. Should I be jealous?" Demetri asked, his warm breath fanning the sensitive skin beneath her earlobe. He took the lobe into his mouth, biting down lightly before licking the small injury.

She turned in his arms, a smile on her face. "I don't think you have anything to worry about," she said, her eyes going over him.

He, too, was dressed up, looking good enough to eat, wearing a deep hazel brown blazer that exactly matched his eyes, over a close-fitting black shirt. Dark dress slacks clung to his well-shaped, big thighs, and on his feet he wore black leather cowboy boots.

She pushed away from him and did a small pirouette, asking, "You like?" grasping the ends of the handkerchief-bottom skirt in her hands as she spun around for him.

"Hmmm, yeah. I like. A lot." He claimed her lips in a slow, seductive caress. "Good enough to eat. And daddy's feeling particularly hungry tonight," he finished, huskily.

The way he spoke the words, in his deep chocolate voice, sent waves of desire through her body.

If any other man had referred to himself as "daddy," Gaby would have laughed in his face. But damn . . . the way he said it, in his take-me-there voice . . . yeah, he could be her daddy anytime, she thought with a shiver.

At that moment, a man brushed past them, giving her a very interested once-over, and Demetri pulled her possessively closer.

When she laughed and gave the man a wink, mainly to piss Demetri off, he swatted her on the backend.

"Ow!" she cried out in pretend pain.

"No flirting with that outfit you're wearing. Don't make me have to spank you," he said, and swatted her lightly on the ass, again, and kept his hand cupped beneath one round, firm globe.

She giggled and clamped a hand over her mouth, surprised at her reaction.

Good Lord.

The man was turning her into a flirtatious giggling wannabe siren, instead of the serious professional woman she was.

Instead of embarrassing her, filling her with shame, the thought that she was a siren, one who men found attractive, was strangely appealing.

And if she was a bad girl and needed to be spanked . . . the image of her over his lap, her ass raised with his big hand spanking her, then caressing her, made her breath catch in her throat. Yeah, she'd play the bad-girl role anytime, she thought.

He glanced down at her, and cocked his head to the side, as though he were reading her thoughts.

Despite herself, she blushed.

"I think I'd better find us a table before you get me in trouble."

"Get you in trouble?" she asked as he guided her to a table with a reserved sign in the center.

"Yeah, the next man that eyeballs you like you're dessert on the menu, I'm likely to knock his teeth down his damn throat," he groused, and as another inappropriate giggle escaped, she allowed him to pull back her chair.

"You look beautiful tonight," he murmured, taking her hand and placing a small kiss in the palm. "As though you don't already know that."

She smiled happily. When a waitress came by, Demetri ordered for the two of them, and Gaby glanced around the already filling club.

It was only eight o'clock, and already the place was crowded. She wasn't one to really go out. Nonetheless, on the few occasions she allowed a colleague to coerce her into going clubbing, she knew that things didn't really get started in most clubs until around ten or later.

Not so at the Sweet Spot. The music, although loud, wasn't so deafening you couldn't have a conversation, as the club was divided in two split levels. On the main level, the one they were on, was the bar, and although there was a small dance floor, the area was mainly occupied with tables where those who weren't interested in dancing could come for a drink and conversation.

On the upper level there was a small bar as well, and the larger dance floor. That was where the patrons who came to dance mainly went.

He'd told her that he'd gone to quite an expense in soundproofing the walls in the dancing floor, as well as adding soundproofing to the paneling in the loft, so that little noise filtered through from the club.

"Would you like to dance?" he asked and she turned to him.

"Um, well, maybe later."

"Come on, they're playing our song," he said and pulled back his chair, placing his hand out for her to take.

"Our song?" she asked, lifting a brow.

"Any song is our song, as long as it allows me to feel you moving against me," he replied with a purposeful leer.

With a shake of her head and a laugh tumbling from her lips, she placed her hand in his and allowed him to lead her to the dance floor.

The beat was a fast R&B hit, mixed with rap, and Gaby gave in to the excitement and fun. Smiling, she popped and dropped it low with the best of them, and wanted to laugh as Demetri, with his eyes wide, smiled at her as she danced.

She might not get out much and dance, but when she was all alone in her house, she often danced as a way of exercise.

As she moved she loved the way her body felt, sensual, sexy, as she rolled her hips and snapped her fingers. She drew close to him, and slowly ground her body on his, her legs on either side of one of his, as she danced, simulating riding his thigh.

When he tried to pull her close, she laughingly darted away and got behind him, dancing close, wrapping her hands around his waist.

Demetri loved the sheer exuberance in Gabrielle. As she played and teased him, dancing better than any of the women in the latest hip-hop videos, he marveled again at yet another side of her.

She was so full of life, so damn sensual, his head spun. When she let go, she was a force to be reckoned with.

And he saw that, from the admiring glances she was getting, he wasn't the only one who thought so.

He motioned to the D.J. in the glassed-off booth high above the dance floor, and seconds later the music changed.

When the music changed, slowed down to a sweet slow song,

the deep, husky voice of the popular female singer singing of finally finding love at last, he pulled her into his embrace.

"Hey . . . what you do?" she asked, casting suspicious eyes
his way, her chest heaving, sweat beading on her forehead.

"Ownership has its privileges," he said and laughed at the
pout on her face. "What? I couldn't take it anymore. Feel what
the way you were moving has done to me."

He pulled her closer against him, his cock, hard, erect, nudg-
ing against her.

Her eyes widened and her mouth formed a perfect O.

"Later . . ." he promised, wrapping his arms securely around
her waist.

She placed her arms around his neck. In the stiletto heels she
wore, their height difference was reduced, and she fit perfectly
in his arms.

"Is that a threat . . . or a promise?"

Just as he was ready to respond by taking her off the floor
and dragging her upstairs to show her which, someone tapped
him on the shoulder.

He turned his head, looking behind him with a scowl on his
face.

"Hey boss . . . you got a call in the office," the man said,
grinning despite the evil look Demetri was giving him, at the
woman in his arms.

"Hell, take a message, Marcus," he said and turned back
around. His scowl deepened when the man tapped him again
on the shoulder.

"Sorry, but it's from a supplier who says he's canceling the
shipment if you don't come and talk to him."

At that, Demetri paused.

Shit.

It was Nick.

He knew it without a doubt. It was his former commander's
way of letting him know who he was.

He turned back to Gabrielle. "Baby, hold that thought. I've

got to take this. Go order another drink. I'll be back as fast as I can," he said, and kissed her swiftly on the mouth. With a regretful last glance at her as she stood on the dance floor, a look of disappointment on her pretty face, he leaned down and captured her lips with his again before releasing her.

"I promise, this won't take long."

With that he turned and left, swiftly walking toward his office.

Gaby glanced at her watch.

Demetri had been gone close to an hour and still hadn't returned.

Instead of ordering another drink, she'd spent the time dancing and had been having a ball. But, no matter how much fun she had flirting and dancing, enjoying the attention, she longed to be with Demetri.

With a sigh, she rose and decided to visit the restroom.

She smiled at the men who touched her arm as she weaved her way through the crowd, shaking her head no at the request to dance.

When she finally reached the end of the room, she paused, looking for the bathroom.

"Ah, there it is," she said and grimaced when she saw the long line.

She really had to go, badly.

Although she'd only had two martinis, she'd drunk several tall glasses of water, her thirst high as she danced back-to-back dances the last hour as she waited for Demetri to return.

She fished inside her bag for the key to Demetri's loft and decided to use his.

Inserting the key into the lock, she walked inside and waited for what seemed like forever for the elevator to ascend.

When she stepped out, she had only taken a few steps inside before she heard Demetri's voice, raised.

Cautiously, forgetting her nearly full bladder, she walked

farther inside and curiosity brought her to the semiclosed door to the room she knew was his office.

In all the time she'd been in his home, he normally had the door closed. Once the door had been opened and she'd tried to peer inside. He'd come up behind her and closed it, saying it was his office, and although he hadn't been rude, she'd taken the hint that it was off limits.

Now, with the door partially opened and his voice angry and clipped, she crept closer and listened.

"I don't give a shit what you *think* you know, she's not—"

"No, you listen. It sounds to me as though you have gotten too close to the subject. I brought you in because I thought you could do the job. If you no longer feel as though you have distance on this—"

"I can do my job," Demetri broke in, grimly.

Fuck.

At this point he knew that if he were pulled off the case, and an actual agent was assigned, Gaby would go to prison.

When he'd taken the call, he'd come to the loft, thinking Nick had called to give him new information. Instead, his former commander informed him that he needed answers. Now.

Nick told Demetri that *his* superiors were breathing down his neck to end the case. They knew Adam and Gabrielle were involved, and were no longer interested investing federal money in financing any further investigation.

They wanted someone to hang the rap on and the two were the ones to get it. Although, there was something in Nick's voice, something barely detectable, that made Demetri wonder what the hell was really going on.

"I thought the reason you wanted me to take this case was to get all the answers. Find out who is at the top of the food chain."

There was a pause before Nick spoke again. This time Demetri was sure of it, there was something else going on. Just what the hell he needed, yet another bullshit twist.

"Look, this needs to wrap up. The agency needs it to do so. We need this finished, now. Or . . .

"Or?" Demetri prompted.

"Let's just say a lot is riding on this. The least of it being my ability to find Siobhan," was his cryptic reply.

Demetri considered his words—both what Nick said and what he didn't say. He walked over to the window and stared out the floor-to-ceiling windows, a pensive look on his face.

"Give me more time. I'll get all the evidence you need to bring them down. Not just Adam and Marlowe, but whoever is at the top. But, you gotta give me more time."

There was another significant pause, before Nick finally answered.

"You have two weeks. That's as much time as I can buy you. In two weeks, I need this case to come to an end, Agent Mylonas," he said and ended the call before Demetri could call him out on referring to him by his former title.

"Shit!" he cursed, closing his eyes and rubbing his temples.

When he heard a gasp and spun around, he saw Gabrielle at the door.

He knew he'd never forget the look of pain and betrayal on her face. It would be sketched in his mind forever.

20

"When are you going to talk to the man, Gaby? He's not going to stop calling or coming by."

Gaby removed her glasses, and shoved away from the desk and stood.

"Gaby . . . are you there?" her assistant asked, concern in her voice.

"Yes, I'm here, Rosey. I just don't know what to tell you. I'm sorry you've gotten caught in the middle of this." Gaby replied. She picked up the mug of tea and walked toward the small balcony attached to the bedroom.

"That's not why I'm calling you. It's no big deal, I don't mind vetting the calls. But, it's only a matter of time before you have to see him again. You can't hide out forever," was her assistant's pragmatic reply.

"I'm not hiding. It's Thanksgiving break, and I'm using the time to have a break of my own. Aren't you the one always telling me I need time off?"

"And that's all this is, Gaby?" she asked, skepticism in her voice. "Just a break?"

"Look, Rosario, I appreciate the call. Really. And I appreciate you not telling him where I am. Don't worry about the rest. I'll take care of it."

Gaby pushed open the balcony doors and inhaled, taking in the early morning air.

"I'll see you next week, okay?"

"Okay, Gaby"

"And Rosario . . . thanks," she said, and quietly disconnected the call.

She knew she couldn't avoid Demetri indefinitely. It had been a week since she'd overheard his conversation and in that time she'd been stressed so badly, her stomach was constantly tied in knots and the occasional migraines that she suffered from had increased.

So much so that she'd decided to take the time off from school at Thanksgiving break off from the pharmacy, time for her to figure out what she had to do.

She wondered how long he'd been investigating her. Obviously he worked for some government agency, and she, along with Adam, was under scrutiny.

Nervous and beyond scared, she hadn't known where to go, who to turn to. Afraid, her first inclination had been to talk to Abigail.

However, when she'd tried, Hunter had reminded her that Abigail was out of town, taking care of one of her many philanthropic duties, working with underprivileged kids.

Despite the fear and worry gnawing a hole in her gut, Gaby hadn't felt comfortable confiding in Hunter when he asked, hearing the worry in her voice, if he could help. She'd been tempted to, but in the end she hadn't, not wanting to get him involved. When Abigail had called her later that night, after Hunter had given her the message, along with the voice mail she'd left on Abigail's cell, Gaby had been given time to think.

She didn't want to get Abigail involved in the mess she'd

been the one to create, either, so she hadn't disclosed what happened.

Abigail must have read something in her voice. When Gaby mentioned maybe taking a break, that she needed to get away to think, Abigail had volunteered to allow her to stay in her guesthouse.

She'd been driving home at the time, talking on her cell phone, and just before she turned the corner, she saw Demetri's familiar red pickup in her driveway.

She'd immediately done a U-turn and headed out on 1604 toward the Winters' home, gratefully accepting Abigail's offer.

So fearful that she'd come into contact with him, she hadn't bothered to return home, she'd made a hasty trip to Wal-Mart and picked up a few essentials, a few changes of outfits and driven back to the mansion.

Now, as she stood on the balcony, staring blindly, not taking in the elegance of the beautifully landscaped yard, with its magnificent oak trees, some whose leaves had begun to turn lightly golden, but mostly still green and lush, her mind turned over the events that had transpired,

"I can't hide forever," she whispered out loud. Turning, she walked back inside, just as the phone in the cottage rang.

Surprised, she wondered who would be calling. Few people knew the number; the phone was kept mostly for convenience's sake. She warily lifted the cordless from the base on the kitchen counter.

"You can't hide forever."

Gaby closed her eyes briefly, Demetri's deep voice eerily mimicked the words she'd just spoken aloud.

"What do you want?" She forced calm into her tone. No way in hell did she want him to know just how scared she was.

There was a short pause.

"Baby, look—"

"Please don't call me that!" she interrupted.

"Gaby . . . we need to talk," he said, his voice low. "I know what you thought you heard."

"Thought I heard?" her voice rose, shrilly, nearly hysterical laughter erupted. "What *I* thought I heard was you talking to someone about sending me to prison. That's what I thought I heard."

"I can explain—"

"Explain what? That you've been pretending to be interested in me, screwing me so you can help send me to prison? Is that what you want to explain . . . *Sweet*?"

"At this point, you don't have many options, Gaby. Either see me, or go to jail. It's your call."

Gaby closed her eyes briefly, fighting tears of frustration and betrayal.

"Fine. Where do you want to meet?" she asked, her words clipped.

"We can meet wherever you want."

She gave him the name of a café not far from the university.

"That's fine. I'll meet you there tomorrow, at noon."

"Fine," she said, and without waiting for a response, disconnected the phone.

Just as she had when Adam called weeks ago, the urge to rip the jack out of the wall and slam the phone against the wall was too hard to resist.

The resounding crash of plastic that rained in shattered pieces to the floor offered her little satisfaction.

Demetri was left with a steady bzzz tone in his ear when she abruptly hung up the phone.

He'd tried for a week to find her, even going as far as camping out on her doorstep.

He'd first gone to the university and was told she had taken the week off, prior to Thanksgiving.

He'd then gone by the pharmacy, and there was no trace of

her there. The CLOSED sign was hanging in the window, but he'd seen someone behind the counter. He'd banged on the door, not giving a shit who saw him, until finally the door opened.

Her assistant had warily allowed him in. He'd poured on all the charm he could, laying it on thick, trying to convince the older woman to help him find Gaby. His gut told him the woman knew where he could find her. Gaby wasn't answering her cell, despite the way he'd blown up her messages, and he was running out of time. Nick wasn't the type to threaten idly. Demetri needed to get to Gabrielle before it was too late.

He didn't know what he'd said, done, to convince the woman his intentions were good, but, when she'd written down a number where Gaby could be reached, he'd been so thankful he wanted to kiss the woman.

Now, his only hope was that she showed up. He wasn't taking any chances.

He drove to her house, but instead of going in the front, he drove up an alley. Lucky for him, Gaby lived in the older section of town, the section where things like alleys still existed. He parked the truck, kicked back the lever beneath the seat, and settled back.

If he had to stay there all night, he would. She wasn't going to try and sneak in and out before he could catch her.

21

Gaby returned home that evening, needing to give herself as many morale boosts that she could get. She wanted to be at her best for her confrontation with Demetri the next day, so she'd decided to leave as soon as she gathered her few belongings.

She had just stepped out of the shower and into her bedroom, one towel draped around her head, turban style, another wrapped around her body, when a sound alerted her she wasn't alone.

With a gasp, she grabbed the towel and clutched it to her body, before she saw Demetri lounging in her doorway, staring a hole in her.

"Adding breaking and entering to your list of crimes?" she asked, her heart slamming against her chest.

"To *my* list of crimes?" he asked, raising a brow. "That's more your style, baby, not mine."

"You bastard," she whispered and turned around swiftly, back toward the bathroom.

He covered the distance in three long strides and grabbed her shoulders. "I'm sorry . . . I didn't mean that," he said, turning her around to face him.

"Why is running the first thing you do?" he asked, his eyes going over her body. The heat in them irritated her even as her treacherous body responded to the desire burning brightly in his eyes.

"Maybe if everyone I came in contact with wasn't trying to use me, or have me locked up, I wouldn't have to," she bit out, angrily.

"I'm not using you, and neither am I trying to get you locked up. And right now, you'd do well to remember that I'm about the only one on a very long list who you can trust."

He grabbed her by the shoulders when she turned angrily away from him. When he tried to pull her around, she hauled a hand back and slapped his face so hard he felt his ears ring with the force of her strike.

"You fucking bastard," she ground out the words in a low voice, her nostrils flaring as she stared at him with contempt in her dark, pain-filled eyes. "You goddamn lowlife bastard! You're no better than the rest."

Her voice was low, controlled, as she enunciated each word, each one coming out crisp and clear. The words stung as sharply as the slap across the face.

"Come and sit down, calm down first. I—"

"Calm down? Calm down? How dare you?" This time she screamed the words, her face contorted in rage.

Before he could answer, she hit him again. And again, and again, her small hands balled into tight fists, she rained down blows on his hard chest, tears beginning to trickle down her face. "How dare you do this to me? I trusted you. I loved you, damn you!" The words were more painful than the blows to his chest, and Demetri felt his heart clench, break with each sobbing accusation.

"How dare you set me up, lie like you cared about me, get inside my head . . . my heart, and set me up?" she cried. "You ripped a hole in my heart." She stopped, drew in a deep breath. "I . . . I loved you," she whispered.

She continued to hit him with her fists, tears of anger and betrayal now running rivers down her face and Demetri took them all—the tears, the blows—until she finally stopped, her body slumping forward.

She would have fallen to the floor had he not caught her. Too tired to fight, she allowed him to take her down to the carpeted floor and pull her into his arms.

She renewed her struggles, weakly, yet he held on to her, refusing to let her go. Once the fight had drained from her, he felt her body go limp. He brought a finger beneath her chin, forcing her to look at him.

"Listen to me, baby, please . . ." her body stiffened and he sighed. "God, I missed you," he murmured and licked a trail up the soft skin on her neck before he reached her mouth. He straddled her over his hips and pressed her down on his body as he slanted his mouth over hers.

Demetri threaded his fingers though her hair, releasing it from the loose ponytail on top of her head, and continued to devour her lips, as his hands traveled a hot path over her soft curves.

He edged his fingers between their bodies and worked his finger deep inside her. She was moist. Her cream ran over his hands and he growled in satisfaction.

She wanted him as much as he wanted her, he thought, his eyes briefly closing, relief flooding him. No matter how angry she was, she still cared about him.

"No!" she said, tearing her mouth away.

Her hand went between their bodies and clamped down on his wrist.

She looked him in the eyes, hers red and swollen. "I don't want this and I don't want you."

But the need was strong now. Her scent had reached out and enveloped him. Her body, despite everything, was calling for his. She wanted him and he was going to give her what she wanted, what she had denied him—the two of them—over the last week.

He fingered her clit in soft circles, spreading her own moisture over the tightened bud.

She lifted her face to him, her chest heaving, her breath coming out in strangled gasps, her face set in determined lines.

"Von."

"Fuck!" The expletive was torn from him.

The unexpectedness of her using the safe word slammed into Demetri like a Mack truck. She'd never said the word, not once, in all the time they'd been together. No matter what he did to her, no matter what freaky pleasure he decided to deliver, she never stopped him.

For her to do so now stung. The rejection in her eyes was too painful for him to bear to look at. He stared down at her angrily and cupped her mound with her palm, ignoring her.

She became still, watching him, anger and defiance shining brightly in her dark eyes. Demetri leaned down to capture her full, kiss-swollen lips with his.

"You're no better than the rest of them," she bit out angrily before his lips could connect. "Adam, my mother. You're all the same." She turned her head away, but not before he caught the vulnerability, the incredible pain, in her expression.

Demetri stopped. Although he knew she wanted him—despite her anger, she wanted him—he also knew that she was beyond hurt and for him to force her to make love to him would only drive a deeper wedge between them, one that he might not be able to remove.

He drew in a breath. The smell of her sex washed over him, and he wanted to howl at the moon, but she had not only said the word but also was as hurt as though someone had stuck a knife directly in her heart.

He rolled away, his back on the floor, and closed his eyes.

He heard her scramble to her feet as he lay there trying to

get himself under control, trying to figure out how to get her to trust him once again.

"Who are you? I think I deserve to know the truth," she bit out, angrily.

There was a long pause before Demetri spoke.

"It started off as just another case, but it quickly turned into so much more than that."

Demetri slowly rose, but remained sitting, staring at her back as she stood with her arms crossed over herself, the gesture one of painful self-protection. As he began to speak, he saw her back stiffen.

"I used to be FBI, seven years ago. I left the bureau, didn't want anything more to do with it, and started a new life here, once my partner . . . left."

He told her of his involvement in the case, how his commander approached him, without telling her about Siobhan, simply wanting her to understand who he was and how he came into her life.

"I didn't know anything about you, Gabrielle, not when I took the case. I didn't know you were a woman with character, a woman who loved and gave of herself so freely." He took a few steps toward her.

"A woman I soon learned there was no way in hell could be involved in anything that would hurt or harm anyone, or one who would steal for greed. A woman I fell in love with," he finished.

She was quiet for so long that Demetri grew alarmed. He stood and walked toward her, hesitantly, lightly placing his hands on her shoulders, and turned her to face him.

"What do you want me to do? I'll do anything."

Her eyes widened. She bit the inside of her lip, a spark of surprise and excitement gleaming in her eyes. He could tell she was running the possibilities of what he was asking, the power he was offering to her, over in her mind.

"Take off your clothes," she stopped, drew in a deep breath. "I want you naked."

His cock thumped against his zipper at her words. The look in her dark eyes was filled with excitement, lust, and a certain amount of hesitation.

His eyes traveled lower and saw her body's response. Her plum-colored nipples were stiff and erect, had darkened and tightened with blood.

With his eyes on hers, he kicked off his shoes and slid his shirt over his head before unzipping his jeans and hooking his thumbs in the waistband to ease them off.

She grew bolder. The look of anticipation sparked in her eyes. She trailed a short fingernail down his naked torso, her hand shaking just the slightest bit.

Her fingers replaced his and, deftly, as though she'd done this a million times or more, unzipped his jeans all the way down and peeled the fabric away.

She lifted his shaft, cradling it in her small, warm palm. Demetri's eyes began to shut of their own volition against the sweetness of her touch.

"No, open your eyes," she said, and his eyes opened.

Her nimble fingers pulled his balls from within his briefs, fondling them, before her hands trailed back up to take his cock in hand.

Her fingers swept over the tiny eyelet, wiping away his sticky pre-cum.

"You'll do anything?" the question was a soft whisper from her lips.

After only a moment's noticeable hesitation, Demetri nodded his head.

She smiled and stepped away. "Take everything off." Before he could obey, she warned, "Slowly. And don't look away from me." She walked toward the bed and lay in the center.

When she spread her legs, one foot dangling off the side of

the bed, his cock thickened, his mouth going dry. A cough from her, and he raised a brow and did as she asked.

Once fully naked, he stood before her with his legs braced apart, arms at his side, dick painfully erect . . . and waited for her next move.

She stood and slowly circled him, as though inspecting him, as though he was a prize thoroughbred she wanted to purchase.

The thought sent a tingle directly to his shaft and his balls tightened at the thought of her riding him, of *her* taking the initiative, the lead.

She played the role of submissive perfectly, had learned what *she* needed, what her body craved in order to have earth-shattering climaxes . . . what would she be like as the one in charge? Demetri wondered. And could he allow her to be the one in charge?

Memories of his time at with the BDSM club, while undercover, ran through his mind.

During his "training," he'd had to undergo what it was like to be a sub, as well as a dom, but it hadn't prepared him for the actual experience, as intense as the training had been.

Being submissive to another, sexually, hadn't excited him in the least. However, the thought of Gaby being the one in charge was a different matter. He felt his erection swell even more.

He stiffened when her nails scored his back, before the tip landed at the dent right above the crease of his buttocks.

Her small hands began to stroke over the cheeks of his ass in light caresses before one of them slipped around his hips and grasped his balls, lightly massaging them.

He closed his eyes against the sweet sensation.

"Touch yourself." Her voice strummed with excitement, growing stronger, bolder as she stood behind him.

Demetri grasped his shaft in his hand and ran his palm over the thickened rod, stem to tip, his movements sure.

Her finger ran over his perineum, the soft skin directly behind his balls, with the tip of a finger as he manipulated his dick. He groaned when she again grasped his balls and moved to stand in front of him.

With her eyes on his, steady, she dropped to her knees, her eyes on level with his hand and cock as he continued to stroke himself.

"You've done this before, I see," she murmured, her thumb stroking across the sensitive eye in the center of his shaft, wiping away a bead of his cum.

He licked his lips, staring down at her. "I may have," he choked out the answer.

"No talking, *Demetri*," she chastened, and Demetri caught the anger that flared in her eyes when she emphasized his given name. "If you talk, well . . . the pleasure ends. You wouldn't want the pleasure to end, now would you?" she asked, her lips stretching into a closed-mouth smile.

She sat back on her heels and waited.

He'd taught her well, he thought, his eyes narrowing, and shook his head no.

She replaced her wandering hands with her lips and brought his balls into the warm wet cavern of her mouth.

"God," the word was wrenched from him before he clenched his teeth.

Gaby grasped the base of his shaft, near his balls, and circled his cock with her hand, dragging her fist down his length, ending at the round knob, and traveled back again, the same path.

When he groaned, she raised her eyes to meet his.

"God, you're killing me," he choked out the words.

The admission brought a pleased smile to her face.

She brushed the side of her face back and forth over the hair covering his groin, much in the same way he'd done to her on the many times he ate from her sweetness.

She gave as good as she got, quickly giving in to the sensual nature she had held so tightly in check.

"Take it," he rasped the words. "Take it into your mouth, damn it."

Peering at him from the corner of her eyes, she grasped his cock in both hands, opened her mouth wide, and engulfed him, deeply. He placed his hands on either side of her head and stared at the crown of her head when she began to ease his shaft in and out, in and out, of her mouth. Her tongue flicked out to lick his balls and tease along the seam of his cock in short little swipes, until she reached the head.

"Damn," he moaned, feeling his balls swell with cum, tightening to pain, when she swirled the very tip of her tongue along the rim and dipped into the eye, licking him clean. She withdrew from him, slowly, and stared up at him, lids half closed, her mouth wet with his pre-cum.

He shut his eyes against the sight, his heart racing as though he'd just completed a marathon, sweat dripping down his body.

"Do you like that?" The words whispered along his shaft while she gave nibbling kisses down the length as she played with his dick. "Because I do."

Her tongue shot back and forth over his cock with quick, nibbling caresses. If he didn't know better, he'd swear she was a pro, the way she was working his dick.

When Gaby lightly twisted his cock in opposite motions with her hands as she sucked on him, her cheeks hollowing, sucking him like he was her favorite lollipop, he placed his hands on the side of her face.

Demetri nearly detonated, right in her mouth. Although the need was strong, along with the heady image of his cum coating her mouth, he didn't want to come that way.

"Enough," he bit out, harshly. He lifted her in his arms, with a growl, and fell to the bed with her beneath him.

"Condom—" she said, breathlessly, her hand reaching blindly for the nightstand.

He tore his mouth from hers and opened the drawer, his hand searching for the elusive package. He found one and tore it open with his teeth, his eyes on her, hot and wanton, legs spread, and an erotic stamp of desperate need on her face.

Demetri guided the end of his shaft to her sweet, wet entry and fed her his cock, inch by slow inch. With every inch he gave her, it felt as though he was giving her a piece of his heart . . . his soul.

The moment was so intense, so surreal it transported them to a place they'd never been in their lovemaking.

"No dominant/submissive manipulations, Gaby. Just a man giving his woman pleasure, baby. A man loving his woman," he rasped.

Gaby nodded her head, her eyes bright, tears glistening, giving their chocolate depths a glimmering appearance.

When she nodded her head and shakily smiled, he felt the feeling completely unfurl within his chest, ready to burst free.

He pinned her with his gaze, his gray eyes dark, filled with lust and some other emotion, one that Gabrielle had to close her eyes against seeing, unable to take the intensity of the moment.

He fed her his dick, slowly, as he held on to her hips. Although she was moist, hot, ready for him, she moaned as he pushed past the lips of her vagina and invaded her. Once he was all the way in, when she felt the tip of his turgid shaft curve into the side of her walls, she looped her arms around his neck as he rode her.

He leaned down and brought his mouth to hers and she eagerly latched on, stroking her tongue against his in languid movements that matched his strokes within her body.

There was a difference in their lovemaking. Although her body was screaming for release, as was his, she knew, they took pleasure in their sweet lovemaking, by mutual, silent agreement drawing it out as long as they could, neither wanting their lovemaking to end.

When she felt her belly tighten, she squeezed her legs together, holding on to him desperately, her hands tightening, clutching the tops of his shoulders.

Crying into his mouth, giving in to her release, she heard his matching moan, and together they rode the crest of the climax in unison.

When Demetri came, he held on to her hips, his body trembling, his heart jackknifing against his chest, as he embedded himself as far into her willing body as he could.

He wanted to be so deep in her, she didn't know where she left off and he began.

For the first time ever, he resented the use of the condom, wanting the satisfaction of filling her with his seed . . . his life.

Finally replete, completely satiated, he slumped down on top of her. He reluctantly moved off her body, shifting to the side.

He turned to face her.

"Come back home with me?" the words were spoken low. Little inflection was in his tone, but in his eyes, Gaby saw a new awareness, as though he had come to some revelation about himself. She couldn't tell, in the dark, whether it was good or bad. Or some emotion in between.

"I want you in my home. In my bed," he said, carefully watching her.

"Yes," she answered. For her own reasons, she didn't want to stay in her own house. The fear that Adam would come by was an ever-present threat in her mind.

22

"You can trust me, you know. I would never hurt you."

When Demetri felt Gaby's back stiffen, he pulled her tight against him. "Baby, I would never hurt you, not ever again. Not purposely."

She turned to face him, pulling her lip inside her mouth. He touched her bottom lip with one finger and smiled lightly when she released it, looking at him, warily.

She'd followed him back to his loft and now, after another round of lovemaking, they were sated and he knew that he owed her a full explanation. Mainly, about why he'd left the FBI, among other things.

After they'd made love the last time, he'd brought her body close to his and they'd both fallen asleep, despite the turmoil, the tension, the anger she felt. She still lay with him, her arms around his, and his around hers.

He held on to the thought that she had to care for him, otherwise she wouldn't have given him a second chance, not after she'd already been betrayed by so many in her life.

He didn't want to ever be the cause of the pain he'd seen in her face the night she'd overheard his and Nick's conversation.

He knew she was beat up emotionally. He knew that he was one of the many who'd hurt her. One of many who'd used her.

Yet, she still loved him. He saw it in her eyes. Despite the pain, she loved him.

He would work around the rest. And he'd do his damndest to make sure that he and no one else ever hurt her ever again.

He'd watched her, closely, as she went about her routine.

You ripped a hole in my heart, Demetri. I loved you . . .

Her whispered words ran though his mind and shot to his heart, as direct and painful as a knife as he looked down at her.

Demetri rose and leaned against the headboard. He stroked the side of her face.

"Baby, when I took on this case, I did so for a reason."

He stopped and gathered his thoughts. The time for half-truths, and not sharing everything with her, was over. He knew that for her to ever trust him again, he had to open himself up. Completely.

Or as much as he could. Demetri knew his limitations. Trust, for him, had never been an easy thing to give or receive, due in part to his line of work, as well as his own background.

"I'm listening," she said, softly, encouraging him to continue.

"You already know who I am—who I *was* before I retired."

She nodded her head.

"What you don't know is why I agreed to this case. The woman I . . ." he halted, before continuing, "The woman I cared about was captured . . . hell, who am I kidding?" he asked running a frustrated hand through his hair. "She left with a killer. She left the agency . . . *me* . . . for a killer."

As he began to speak, telling her about his partner, and how the two of them had infiltrated a BDSM club after months of training, she sat up and leaned against the headboard, listening intently.

"Siobhan was a natural submissive. I was a natural domi-nant." His voice was nearly devoid of emotion, yet Gaby *felt* the pain he felt. "At least, that's what we were told."

"Isn't that normal? I mean, aren't men the dominant ones and women the submissive in those relationships?" Gabrielle knew next to nothing about the BDSM culture, only what she'd read in an occasional book, all of which was fiction.

"No. It's not a gender specification. Just a natural inclination, man or woman."

"How did you . . . train . . . in it? I didn't know the FBI had that type of training," she said and he laughed at the unexpected question.

The question, and the earnest look in her eyes, lightened the darkness he felt hovering whenever he thought of Siobhan and the case.

He leaned down and kissed her softly on the lips.

"No, the FBI doesn't have any specialty in BDSM training. Our training was . . . I guess you could say, 'outsourced.' " Again he laughed without humor. "A woman who was trained and heavily into the lifestyle began our initial training. She was the one who determined our inclinations. She was also the one who initiated us into the lifestyle."

"Oh."

"What?"

"How did she, uh . . ."

"How did she initiate us?" he asked, smiling, enjoying the jealousy he heard in her voice. Deciding that honesty wasn't always the best policy, he didn't go into specifics with her.

"Mostly psychological. The training wasn't only sexual. It was meant to break us. To *try* and break us, at least. To determine if we could infiltrate this select club. Not everyone could get in. The woman who trained us was not only training us but also indoctrinating us into the lifestyle. We had to be convincing. And we were." His voice was grim.

Gabrielle listened as Demetri dispassionately related to her how once the two of them had been properly trained, that their "instructor," who was also an informant, had gotten them into the club.

They'd entered as a couple, with Demetri as Siobhan's dominant. Although he didn't go into details on the true intimate nature of their relationship during the mission, Gabrielle felt a hard knot of jealousy swell in her chest, realizing, although he didn't say it, the two had been intimate. Beyond intimate.

As she listened, she began to understand more, at least peripherally, what it meant to be involved in this type of relationship. Despite the fact that they were undercover, the pair had to truly trust each other, to be convincing in their roles.

"The night we had the evidence we needed, the night the FBI was ready to swarm in on the club, Siobhan tipped the cult leader off. She left with him, as well. I tried to find her for months afterward until my supervisor pulled me off the case. When I refused, I was put on administrative leave." He ran a hand through his hair, anger tightening his features. "But I didn't give a damn. I was not going to give up looking for my partner."

"Did you find her?" Gaby was so caught up in the story, she held her breath wondering if he found her, and if so, what state he'd found her in.

"No. I haven't heard from her since."

She felt the raw emotion in his voice.

"I changed a lot during . . . particularly after, the mission was over. In ways I didn't even know I had," although he was looking at her, Gaby knew his mind was somewhere else. With someone else.

"The training and living the lifestyle messed with my head. It changed us both. I just didn't know how badly until the night she left me . . . she left the agency."

Gabrielle's gaze went over his face, watching the emotion flash across his rugged features in lightning-fast succession. She asked a question she already knew the answer to.

"Are you in love with her?"

She needed to know.

"I was. At least I thought I loved her, " he said, staring down at her, intently. "Until I met you."

The knot of jealousy loosened, and Gaby released a breath she hadn't realized she'd been holding. When he drew her close to kiss her, she willingly went into his arms.

"That's the reason I took the case," he said once he released her. "Nick promised to use his resources to look for Von. I couldn't say no," he said, and Gaby nodded her head, understanding his reasons.

"So . . . what do we do? Where do we go from here?" Gaby held her breath. She didn't know what the hell she was going to do, didn't really know what to do.

"Do you have to—" she stopped and breathed in deeply, before releasing the pent-up sigh. "I suppose you have to turn me in. Hell," she laughed, without humor, "you have enough on me alone to give your boss what he needs. What you need in order to find your . . . to find Siobhan," she finished and looked away, batting back the stupid burning of tears she felt in the back of her eyes.

"I'm not turning you in. Not for Siobhan, not for anyone."

Her eyes flew to his, surprise widening them.

"I care about you," he said, gruffly. The intense way he looked at her scared and excited her both at the same time. "I . . . I love you," he said and Gaby's heart swelled with happiness despite the tangled mess she was in.

"But, you have to trust me. I need to tell my commander—"

"No! You promised!"

He pulled her back, closer. "I promised you I would take care of you and that I would help you get out of this. But, you've got to trust me. You've got to trust that I know what I'm doing. We need Nick. He's the only one who can help you . . . *us,*" he emphasized, "right now. To do that, you've got to tell him everything you know."

He felt the indecision at war with her emotions.

"I don't know, Demetri. I'm so scared. What if—" she stopped.

"Nothing is going to happen to you. I promise you that." He said, drawing her into his arms, his face set. Although she went into his arms, Gaby wondered who he was trying to convince, her or himself.

23

Gaby glanced toward the clock mounted on the wall behind her.

"That's all for today, class. Why don't I let you all out early to get a start on your weekend?" She flipped the small switch on the side of the overhead projector, walked over to the door, and turned on the light in the large auditorium classroom.

She grimaced. Her throbbing headache seemed to intensify when the light hit her eyes.

Her comment was met with sounds of appreciation. She smiled slightly, despite the steady, throbbing pain beating at her.

"Go over the notes from chapters eight to sixteen, and pay close attention to the two clinical case-study handouts for next week's exam," she spoke as loud as she could over the sound of chairs scraping against the linoleum flooring in the auditorium and the hum of student conversations.

As the students began gathering their oversized bags and backpacks, Gaby turned back to her desk and gathered her things as well, closing down her laptop and placing it in her bag.

"I think I'll head over to the pharmacy. I want to get a jump start on the inventory before the weekend."

Gaby glanced over her shoulder when she heard Rosario speak from behind her.

"I don't think I'll be opening the pharmacy today."

Gaby rose from her crouched position and turned fully to face the other woman. "I'm not feeling well. I don't think I really feel up to going today."

"One of your headaches?" she asked, a frown wrinkling her otherwise smooth forehead.

Gaby offered a tired smile, "Yeah, haven't had one like this in a long time."

Rosario shook her head in sympathy. "You don't look well, Gabrielle." Her gaze went over Gaby, noting the dark circles under her eyes.

Gaby blew out a tired breath. "I feel worse than I probably look. At least I hope I don't look as bad as I feel."

"No, you're as pretty as always. You just look . . . tired," Rosario said, genuine concern in her voice.

Gaby hooked her bag over her shoulder. "I have a lot on my mind. A lot of work to do at the pharmacy as well as with finals coming up," she said and smiled tiredly at Rosario. "I've had to rely on my medicine more in the last week than ever."

"They're that bad?"

"Unfortunately, yes."

The two women walked out of the now-empty classroom together. "I'm going to head to my office to get a few things, and then I'm going home."

"That's a good idea. I'll still head on over to the pharmacy. Do some paperwork, put away some of the supplies we just got in."

"Why don't you take off as well? You work just as hard as I do at the pharmacy. We can start tomorrow morning, it's fine. Go have fun and do something," Gaby said as the two women walked along the nearly empty corridors.

"Nah, I don't have anything else to do. I have some studying to do for the board exam, that's the only fun I have on my agenda," she laughed, mentioning the test she was preparing for to receive her license.

"Are you sure?" Gaby stopped when they reached her office and faced the other woman.

"I'm sure. Now, you go home. Relax. Take a nice soothing bath, throw some good-smelling oils in there, put on some Al Green—" When Gaby chuckled, despite the headache pounding insidiously away at her, Rosario laughed. "Sorry, who is it you kids listen to now?"

"I don't know about the kids, but I like India Arie," she replied as she fished her key out of her bag.

"Okay, take a hot bath, put on some India Arie and relax. You just need to relax. Take a nap . . . read a book. Sometimes when I have something heavy on my mind, something I can't get through, a nice bath and soft music always help. That and the Good Book."

The older woman patted her backpack, where Gaby knew she kept a small leather-bound Bible. "Nothing is as bad as it seems, baby. Just have faith in yourself. And God. It'll all work out," she said.

When Rosario reached out and hugged her, Gaby, surprised, wrapped her own arms around the woman in return.

She felt tears sting the back of her eyes and blinked rapidly to ease them away before they could fall and eased away from the hug. Although she knew her own faith had come under fire lately, she drew strength from Rosario's beliefs.

"Thanks. I think I'll do that."

"Good. Call me if you need anything, okay?"

"I will. I promise."

Left alone, Gabrielle opened the door to her office and walked inside.

As soon as she did, she grabbed her head, as the pain intensified.

"God, I feel like hell," she moaned. Weakly she walked to her desk and sank down in the chair. She fumbled inside her bag for her medicine. When she located the bottle, she lifted it and wanted to cry when she shook the bottle and realized it was empty.

She opened drawers in her desk, searching for anything that would help the pounding go away. When she found an extra bottle of her prescription inside, she twisted the cap and emptied two of the small red pills into her palm and swallowed them dry, and lay her head down wearily on top of her desk.

Thoughts of Adam, her mother, and Demetri were the last things in her mind before she fell asleep.

When the shrill ring of her cell phone pierced the air, Gaby jumped and lifted her head from her desk.

Disoriented, she glanced around in her dark office and glanced out one of the small windows. It was dark, the sun had set a long time ago. Disoriented, she picked up her cell phone, depressing the small TALK button.

"Hello," she croaked out the greeting.

"Gabrielle?"

"Are you okay?" Hunter asked, concern in his voice.

"God, what time is it?" she mumbled, her voice slurred.

There was a short pause before Hunter said, "It's nearly six o'clock . . . Gaby are you okay?"

"I feel like hell, Hunter."

"You sound like hell, too." Hunter said bluntly, making Gaby laugh.

As soon as she did, she grabbed her head. The pain was there, not as bad as before, yet a dull ache remained, reminding her how she'd fallen asleep.

"I'm having one of my headaches, that's all."

"Don't you have your medicine?" Hunter asked. "I worry about you. You know you're supposed to take your pills as soon as you feel one of those things creeping up on you. Abigail told me they are debilitating for you." Gaby heard genuine warmth in Hunter's voice.

"I know, I know. Don't fuss at me," Gaby grumbled as she twisted her spine, easing the kinks out of her aching muscles from lying in the odd position. "I forgot them at home and had to wait until class was over to take them."

"Home is where you should be, now. Why are you still at the university? I called the clinic and that intern answered. She told me you were sick and went home. When I called your house, you didn't answer. I was worried about you."

"I'm fine, but thanks. Just a migraine," Gaby replied. "How's Abigail?" she asked, sitting upright in her chair.

"She's fine. Actually, she's the reason for my call," he said.

"Is everything okay?" Instantly, Gaby grew more alert. Abigail had been busy, busier than usual, and Gabrielle realized that she hadn't spoken with her friend in over a week. When she'd cancelled their weekly lunch date, her voice had sounded distracted, but Gaby hadn't thought anything of it. Over the last few weeks, they'd both been busy and she had actually missed Abigail and Hunter's anniversary party, simply because she forgot about it, something she had never done.

All her time had been taken up with Sweet. Although he was still working hard to find a way to help her, to locate the one who was calling the shots, the one had set up the scam, the time spent with him had been the happiest she'd felt in a long time.

Both he and his former commander, Nick, had warned her that although she trusted her mentor, until the case was solved, it was best she didn't share any information with her or anyone else, not even information about her relationship with Demetri. So many times Gaby had picked up the phone to call, bursting to tell her friend about her relationship with Demetri, and had flipped the phone down, disappointed and saddened that she hadn't been able to.

She'd promised Demetri and Nick that she wouldn't.

"Oh, she's fine. Just busy with her many causes," Hunter answered lightly, putting Gabrielle at ease.

"In fact, she's on her way home now. I thought it would be nice if you came over. Had dinner with us. It's been too long since we've seen you."

"Oh, thanks, Hunter. But I think I'll take a rain check. I think I'm just going to go home—"

"I won't take no for an answer. Come on. I ordered Spinoli's," he said and she groaned when he mentioned her favorite Italian takeout. "I ordered your favorite. Chicken pasta smothered in real Parmesan . . . and I think Abi made some of her famous ice tea you love so much, I think I saw a pitcher of it in the fridge. Come on, don't tell me that doesn't tempt you."

Just then her stomach growled and she laughed. She hadn't eaten since lunch and that was several hours ago.

Deciding a visit with Abigail was just what the doctor ordered, she agreed to come over and visit with the couple.

"Okay, okay. You had me at the chicken Parmesan! That and Abigail's tea? I'll be right over," she laughed along with him. "Give me twenty minutes and I'll be there," she promised.

"Great. I'll let her know," he replied. "And Gaby," he said, before she could press END on the call.

"Yes?"

"Make sure you come alone. We'll make this a family meal. Just like old times," he said, and Gaby smiled.

Hunter and Abigail had been more like family to her than her own, since the first moment the couple had come into her life.

"Okay," she promised softly.

She glanced down at her cell phone and noted the battery was low. She turned it off, wanting to conserve the last cell in case of emergency, a habit she'd gotten into since she had once gotten stranded with a flat tire and her cell phone had died.

"I'll recharge it in the car," she promised herself, tossed the small phone in her bag, and hurried out to her car.

"Well?"

"She's coming," Lee replied, a smile curving her lips as she hung up the phone. "He just called her. She'll be over in twenty minutes."

"I'll . . . I'll get everything ready," Adam said and turned to leave the room.

"Good," a voice purred behind him, as a manicured nail raked down alongside his face.

Adam turned, and pushed away from the arms that had snaked around his body.

"Is there something wrong, darling?"

Adam turned around to look at his lover, Abigail LeeAndra Winters. Or Lee, as she preferred he call her, when they were all alone.

In fact, he'd called her by her middle name for so long, she often had to reprimand him—severely in her own sadistic way—when he'd occasionally slipped and called her Lee in public.

She turned from him and lifted a tumbler filled with cognac to her lips. Adam knew without looking it was the finest, the most expensive. Lee would accept no less than the best.

"Is something troubling you, darling?" she asked, placing the glass down, arching one perfectly shaped brow, a look of faux concern etched on her perfectly madeup face.

And that's just what it was—fake. As much as he loved her, Adam knew that Lee's concerns were for herself and doubted she was overly worried about how he felt.

But he played the game with her. Without her, he was nothing. She constantly made sure he was well aware of that.

"Nothing," he murmured, glancing away from her, unable to keep eye contact when he finished his sentence.

"I just don't see why we have to kil—"

His words were cut off when she reached across and slapped him so hard, his head rang.

"It *has* to be done because you fucked up, Adam," she reminded him, and he nodded his head, touching his cheek.

Adam covertly watched her in a mixture of lust, anger, love, admiration . . . and an odd resentment. Had she not picked him off the streets, even when his own father refused to acknowledge him, there was no telling how his life would have turned out.

She was so clever, so damn clever . . . no one, not her rich friends, or even her clueless husband, had any idea just how twisted she was on the inside. All they saw was the educated, well-connected, sophisticated philanthropist. Although, after over thirty years of being married to her, he wondered how the man had remained so clueless about what his wife was really like.

No, all he saw, all any of them saw, was a woman to be admired. One others deferred to, a woman who had spent her life steadily climbing her way to top.

But Adam knew her secrets, her perversions.

She hadn't climbed her way to the top. She'd clawed her way from the gutter, and God help any fool who got in her way or hurt her.

His mother had learned that the hard way.

She turned to him, smiling. "Be a darling and go put the

food out. Hunter had it delivered already. It's on the kitchen counter. Our Gaby is on her way and I'm sure she'll be hungry. Make sure you put out the special tea for her. The one I made for your mother."

She grinned a purely evil smile and Adam's heartbeat increased, his stomach filled with knots. He reached inside his pocket and pulled out one of the small antacid pills he gulped down regularly, like vitamins.

When his mother had tried to contact his father, Lee had been the one to pay a visit. Although the doctors had given her a year to live with the inoperable cancer, Lee had hastened his mother along the way to death, something he hadn't known until years afterward.

He mentally shrugged. She'd been dying, anyway. The only unfortunate thing was that when Lee had returned for him, he'd already left, and it had taken years for her to find him. She'd taken care of him then, just like she promised his mother, and he'd been with her ever since.

"What are you waiting for?"

He bobbed his head up and down and turned on his heel and hurried away.

Once Abigail was sure Adam was gone, she went to the large mahogany desk and opened the drawer.

Pulling out the small, pearl-handled .45, she made sure the safety was securely on and placed the gun in the oversize pocket of her silk kimono.

Whistling cheerfully, she readied everything, set the dining room table, making sure everything was perfectly in place, laying out her best china and silverware.

Her forehead creased when she looked at the floral arrangement she'd had delivered. She rearranged several of the roses, the baby's breath, and greenery until it was to her liking and stepped back to look at her work. "I swear, if you want anything done right, you have to do it yourself," she groused out loud.

Once she finished setting the stage for Gaby's last meal, she stepped back and ran a critical eye over the setting.

"Perfect," she murmured, everything in motion. Once the setting was to her liking, she waited for Gabrielle to arrive.

24

"Hmmm, it smells delicious!" Gaby took a deep breath, inhaling the wonderful scent wafting out to greet her, as soon as she walked inside the Winters' home.

Abigail walked toward her to greet her, arms opened wide she engulfed Gaby in a short hug. The two women embraced and Abigail pulled back and ran assessing eyes over Gaby.

"You've lost weight."

"That's a good thing!"

"No, you're thin enough. Good thing I got Spinoni's. The pasta sauce alone is guaranteed to put at least five pounds on you," Abigail laughed and led a groaning Gaby into the dining room.

Gaby smiled as she glanced around at the opulent surroundings. She placed her bag down on the red silk chaise lounge in the corner. "Is this new?" she asked, running her hands over the silk-covered chair. Abigail looked up and nodded. "Yes, Hunter bought it for me for our anniversary. Which *you* missed the party for, young lady."

Gaby walked toward Abigail, watching her fuss over the table setting.

"Abigail, I'm so sorry I missed your party. Can you forgive me?"

Abigail wrinkled her nose. "I forgive you. It wasn't a big do, just an intimate party." She replied, a teasing glint in her eyes.

"Intimate?" Gabrielle asked, stopping herself from smiling. Gabrielle knew Abigail's idea of an intimate gathering was miles away from the average person's idea of intimate.

"Only about two hundred guests. Give or take," she said and winked. The tension eased and both women laughed.

"Here, why don't you have a seat? It's been too long since we chatted."

"The setting is beautiful," Gaby said taking in the beautiful ornate setting Abigail had arranged. "You didn't have to go through all this trouble!"

"When Hunter said he ordered for us, I was glad you decided to come." she said, "I know it's just the two of us, but I wanted to make it special," she said with a smile.

"Where is Hunter?" she asked, looking around for Abigail's husband.

"He won't be joining us for a while. I sent him out to get some wine. Silly man, knows I like the latest Vino Novello, whenever I eat Italian, even take-out Italian," she said, an affectionate tone in her voice. "You'd think that after more than thirty years together, he'd remember that," she chided her absent husband. "But, that doesn't mean we can't start our meal. I bet you're hungry! Have a seat. Let me get you something to drink," she said and strode over to the large hutch in the corner, lifted a large, crystal pitcher filled with tinkling ice and tea.

"I made your favorite," she said and poured the amber liquid into Gaby's tall frosted glass as she settled in the chair.

"Thank you, Abigail. Just what I need," Gaby said with a smiled and rubbed her temple.

"Sweetie, have you been taking your medicine for those god-awful headaches of yours? You don't look well," Abigail said. Her eyes glistened with concern as she examined Gaby's face.

Gaby sighed deeply, her hands cupping the cool glass. "Not really. I've had a lot on my mind," she admitted.

"Drink, it'll make you feel better, and we can talk while I dish up our plates!" she said, and Gaby nodded her head.

She tipped the glass to her mouth and took a grateful sip of the sweet, cool tea. She smiled once she placed it in front of her. "No one makes tea like yours, Abigil. One day you have to let me know your secret ingredient!"

Abigail turned to look at her, a teasing glint in her eyes, "Nope. It's a family secret."

"Well, if you ever decide to tell anyone, you know you can trust me, Abigail. I'll take it to my grave!" she laughed.

Abigail's eyes twinkled, "Well, since you put it like that, I suppose maybe I *could* be persuaded," Abigail responded, and winked. "Let me go and get the salad and we can start eating."

Gaby placed the glass down and hastily pushed back from her seat. "Let me help."

Abigail waved a manicured hand. "No, Gaby you sit down! I like taking care of you. You know that. Just drink your tea and I'll go and get the food," she admonished lightly. When Gaby hesitated, she said, "Gabrielle Marlowe . . . if you don't sit down, girl . . ." she said, placing one hand on her hip, a scowl on her face.

Gaby relented, threw up both of her hands, and grinned.

"Okay okay . . . I know not to mess with you when you get that look on your face."

"Good. Now be a good girl and finish your tea. You're making me think you don't love it as much as you claim!"

Gaby lifted the glass with a smile and took a healthy drink of the tea and sat back, idly looking around the beautiful, tastefully decorated dining room.

"So, don't you think it's about time you told me about your new love?" Abigail asked, her voice drifting from the kitchen.

"Not much to tell. Not really," Gaby tried to infuse as much nonchalance in her voice as she could as Abigail walked back into the room.

"Oh, come on, Gaby, spill! It's bad enough I had to hear about your new love from your ex. I think the least you owe me is your own rendition. Lord knows Adam's was . . . skewed at best."

"I can imagine." Gaby got up from her seat.

She was acutely uncomfortable talking about Sweet and their relationship.

"There's not much to tell," she insisted, taking a drink of tea.

"Well, not from where Adam stood. From what he says, he had quite a run-in with your new love."

Gaby lifted her glass and idly walked around the room, admiring its beauty.

"It was nothing. Adam came by the shelter to see me. Sweet . . . Demetri, was there. He didn't take kindly to the way Adam was acting," she said, and although she was uncomfortable with the conversation, she admitted to a bit of pleasure when remembering how Demetri had manhandled Adam.

"Sounds like he did more than 'escort' him out of the shelter, from what I hear."

Gaby grew even more uncomfortable. Talking about Adam was making her head hurt worse.

"Look, can we talk about something else right now?" she cut in and immediately apologized when there was a long pause. "I'm sorry, but I don't want to talk about Adam."

"Of course, Gaby . . . I understand."

Gaby blew out a sigh of relief.

She walked over to the whitewashed fireplace, lifting a portrait of Abigail and Hunter from their wedding day into her hands.

The framed photo was the only one on the ornate mantel-piece, and had been sitting in the same place for as long as Gaby had known the Winters.

Next to it was a photo in a smaller, less ornate frame of Gaby on the day she'd graduated from pharmaceutical school.

"Two of my most prized photographs."

Gaby placed the two frames back in the same spot and turned, smiling at Abigail.

She took a deep breath in, inhaling. "Mmmm, that smells wonderful."

Gabrielle's stomach rumbled in reaction when she smelled the aromatic scent of Spinoli's signature pasta.

"Feeling better?" Abigail asked, as she efficiently went about placing the food on the table.

"Actually, I do, quite a bit. Must be the tea," she said and walked toward the table.

"Good!" Abigail gave a huge smile.

Gabrielle shook her head, feeling an odd, light-headed feeling. As she walked toward the table, her legs even felt wobbly. She stumbled and shook her head.

"Come on, Gaby, sit down before you fall down," Abigail chastised, and gently escorted her the rest of the way to the table.

Sitting down, again Gaby shook her head to clear it, putting the light-headed feeling down to the fading headache and sheer exhaustion.

Between nights spent with Sweet and days filled with working and worry over the trap Adam had placed her in, her mind was a mess. Abigail sat down, placed the expensive linen napkin in her lap, and glanced over at Gaby.

"Eating will make you feel better, sweetie," she said. She lifted the sterling-silver spatula from the serving tray and ladled a healthy portion of the thick, rich chicken Parmesan onto Gaby's plate.

"Why don't we finish? Tell me more about this man you've been keeping hidden from me," she said with a smile, after placing a smaller amount on her own plate.

Gaby stared at Abigail.

The familiar gentle smile was on her face. The same concern was reflected in her light eyes. Yet . . .

Yet, for a moment a look was in Abigail's face that sent shivers down her spine. As she smiled, there seemed to be an eerie glint, almost maniacal, reflected in her eyes. She ran her eyes over her mentor's smile, noticing how wide it was . . . how practiced.

She shook her head again, casting the crazy thoughts from her mind.

She bit into the food and nodded her head at Abigail's questioning look, forcing a smile to her face, silently telling her she liked it.

She brought the glass to her mouth and took another drink of her tea, after Abigail refilled her glass.

"So, you and this man . . . Demetri?" Abigail asked, and Gaby nodded her head. "Demetri, it seems like you two have been having quite the flaming affair."

Gaby blushed. "I wouldn't exactly call it flaming, Abigail!" She laughed self-consciously. "And I would have told you about him," she said, reading the disappointment in Abigail's eyes.

She searched for a reason she hadn't told her mentor.

In fact, although Sweet had told her not to tell Abigail anything about the thieving, he had never told Gaby not to mention her relationship with him. That had been all on her part.

One part of her recognized that she herself hadn't quite come to terms with the relationship. The other part of her realized that their relationship was different, she'd never been with a man who made he feel the way Sweet did, in and out of bed.

The changes in herself had been a direct result of her relationship with Sweet, the growing confidence in herself as a woman was so new, so . . . special, she didn't want to share the cause with anyone. Not even Abigail.

For the time being she was happy to keep it all to herself.

She took a swallow of her food, and it hit her stomach with the force of a cement truck.

Nausea swelled, until Gaby felt like throwing up.

When moments ago she'd felt relaxed, so relaxed that she felt a bit lethargic, now she felt her heartbeat race so hard, it was as though she had just gotten through running a marathon.

She shoved the chair back. From what felt like a long distance she heard it scrape against the soft pine floor before it went crashing down onto the carpet. She grabbed the edge of the table and stared at Abigail, her eyes widening.

"God, I feel horrible . . ." she panted the words as her fingers tightly gripped the edge of the table.

The expression on Abigail's face remained calm and serene. She cocked her head to the side and was staring at Gaby as though she were a specimen under a microscope.

"Maybe you just need to drink some more tea, sweetie. I'm sure you'll feel better," she said and calmly poured more of the dark amber into Gaby's empty glass.

"No, no, Abi . . . I think I need to go. I feel, I feel . . ." At that moment the room spun around and the nausea rose bitterly in her throat, her mouth filling with its bitter taste.

She shut her eyes and stars flashed before her closed lids.

"Lee, hmmm. I think Gaby's had enough of your special tea."

Gaby turned her head. As she did, it seemed the action was completed in slow motion, the room spun around her, but she felt disconnected somehow, the whole scene in front of her held a surreal quality.

Her head felt leaden on her shoulders, she tried to move it, but the movement hurt. Her eyes darted back and forth between Adam's slow, approaching body and Abigail as she watched her, the smile, the one that seemed so full of concern, so loving, now seemed evil and mocking.

Adam reached the table, and instead of coming to her, as she thought, he stood behind Abigail as she sat in the chair. Gaby's eyes followed as Adam brought a hand to her shoulder.

"Lee?" she squeaked out the word. Out of everything, all the crazy stuff happening, him calling her "Lee" struck Gaby oddly. "Why?" she asked and stopped speaking when her chest began to burn, the effort to breathe making speaking difficult.

"Conserve your energy, sweetie. Lee is my middle name, remember?" she asked, as though it was nothing out of the ordinary, as though they were discussing the weather.

"Actually it's LeeAndra," she said, her nose wrinkling in distaste. "But I prefer to use Lee in certain areas of . . . business. Lee is my pimp name," she said and giggled. The sound of her laugh was unnatural and totally at odds with the normally cultured laugh, not to mention her referring to herself as a pimp.

What the hell was wrong with Abigail? Gabrielle wondered. What the hell is wrong with me? she thought, her vision blurring.

As her breathing grew harsh and painful, she couldn't keep her eyes off Adam's hand resting lightly on Abigail's shoulder, his fingers caressing the curve of her shoulder blade.

"Your what?" The absurdity of the situation hit her, and despite the pain and confusion, she stopped herself from uttering the hysterical laughter, realizing that whatever was causing the shortness of breath and dizzy feeling was only going to get worse.

She knew she needed to conserve what little strength she had. Clutching the edges of the table, she focused on the woman who she considered a friend . . . a mother.

"But why, Abi . . . why?" she asked, bitter tears slowly trailing down her face, both from the pain in her chest as well as the pain of realizing the woman she loved, the one person she never would have thought would hurt her, had proven to be the one who would ultimately hurt her the worst.

"Well, I guess there's no harm in explaining things now. Doubt you'll be around to tell the police, bitch." Adam laughed.

Her lids were so heavy, she desperately wanted to just close them, but she forced them to stay open. She turned her head enough so that she could see Adam's face.

"Shut up! You've fucked up enough. None of this would have been necessary had you done what you were supposed to!" Abigail said and slapped Adam so hard across the face, the imprint of her hand blazed sharply against his pale white skin. When he did nothing, Gabrielle stared back and forth between them, confused. No longer able to stand, she fell weakly into her chair.

"You just take her over to the sofa and lay her down, and I'll get everything in order," Abigail bit out.

Gaby was weak and unable to fight Adam off. He lifted her by the armpits and pulled her up with her legs dragging on the floor to the chaise in the corner and laid her down.

Abigail's chuckles mingled with Adam's low laugh rang in Gaby's ears as her body slumped, her head fell to the side, and darkness claimed her.

25

"What have you found out?" Demetri asked, without greeting his former commander.

"One of my informants finally came through with information on Adam Quick. He was adopted when he was eighteen."

"Damn old to be adopted isn't it?" Demetri questioned.

"Yes, but that's not the only odd thing about it. Says here he was adopted by a LeeAndra Winters," he paused.

"Kin to Hunter Winters?"

"I thought so at first. I ran all kinds of cross-checks, came up empty."

"Then who the hell is Lee Winters?"

"Well, after more digging, I found something else. LeeAndra is Abigail Winters's legal middle name."

"What the hell? Are you telling me that Abigail Winter's adopted the illegitimate child of her husband?"

"It appears that way. The records were closed, the way they are in some adoptions. Not really that big of a deal, except in normal adoptions the kid adopted isn't a grown man, and the one adopting him isn't the wife of the child's father."

"Is Hunter listed on the adoption papers as well?"

"No. Just Lee Winters. No other information was on the papers. It's plain fucking weird, no two ways about it."

"That's putting it mildly. Okay, if you find out anything else, let me know."

Demetri ended the call, and stared at the phone, a deep frown settling across his face.

None of it made any sense.

At that moment, his stomach clenched, nausea welling up in his throat swift and sudden. So overwhelming. Demetri stumbled as he stood.

Just as soon as it happened, the feeling passed, leaving him dizzy and weak for a moment.

A sick feeling, one different than the nausea, but just as deadly, settled in his gut.

He snatched up his cell and punched in Gabrielle's cell phone number. When it went to voice mail immediately, the deadly feeling in the pit of his gut increased.

He called the pharmacy and her intern answered. When he asked to speak to Gabrielle, the older woman told him she was ill and had decided to go home.

He raced out of the club, calling out to his manager to lock up for him, and broke speed records as he drove to Gabrielle's home.

When he pounded on the door, there was no answer. He cursed when he realized he hadn't brought the spare key. Taking out a pick, he picked the lock and ran inside, calling her name.

After a quick but thorough search of the house showed she wasn't there, he knew where she was.

His gut . . . his heart . . . knew.

He spun around and ran back to his truck, reversed out of the short driveway, and drove like a bat out of hell toward Abigail and Hunter Winters' home. On his way there he called Nick and gave him the Winters' address.

"Call the police, FBI, any goddamn agency you know and send them over right now!"

The nausea in his stomach returned and he gritted his teeth, grimacing, the sweat that dampened his forehead increasing and rolling down his face as he raced toward Gabrielle.

Gaby didn't know what drug Abigail had used to taint the tea, but, from the reaction her body was having, it was one that would kill her, she knew.

She could only pray that it was a slow-acting poison, and someone, God, anyone . . . would help her before it was too late.

She kept her eyes closed and took small, careful breaths of air, trying like hell to slow her racing heart and regulate her now-shallow breathing.

Stay calm, stay calm, stay calm . . .

She chanted the mantra over and over to herself in a desperate effort to save her life.

Which was a lot easier thought than done. But she had to try and keep her mind calm, focus on breathing in and out in slow breaths, and stay awake, similar to what those who practiced deep meditation did.

She'd read about the technique in school when studying the effects of anaphylactic shock, never believing she'd have use for it.

However, as much as she tried, Adam's and Abigail's voices, conversation, broke through her deep concentration. Rather than trying to tune it out, she listened.

"Okay, so what do we do now . . . how long will it take?" Adam began to wring his hands in nervousness.

"I've given it a lot of thought, Adam, and I think I've come up with the perfect solution."

"And that would be?"

"Seems here our poor Gaby was so overwrought with guilt

she came here to unburden herself and admit what she'd done to me."

As she spoke, Abigail moved away from Adam and Gaby, walking toward the other end of the room.

Adam glanced down at Gaby and she quickly shut her eyes. She felt his stare before he turned away and walked toward Abigail's voice.

Glad they were no longer paying her much attention, Gaby cautiously opened her eyes as far as she could and glanced around the room, desperately searching for a way to get away.

She tried to lift her hand, tried to reach for her purse near the sofa without their noticing as they argued.

"No, see, that's where you're wrong, dear stepson. It's not going to go down quite like that," she said. "You've fucked up one time too many. You've become a liability. One that I need to take care of."

"What the hell are you talking about?" he asked, stumbling as he took a hesitant step backward. "Let's stay to the plan. Kill her. Cops will think she committed suicide, just like you said!" he added, desperately, his voice coming out in a high terrified squeak.

Abigail cocked her head to the side, her brow furrowing as though considering his words. She then shook her head, and gave Adam a smile of pity. "Hmmm, no, that's much too complicated. I have a much better solution."

Abigail's hand went to her pocket.

Fighting to stay awake, through her blurry vision, Gaby saw the look of confusion and dawning fear and disbelief cross Adam's face.

She strained her neck to see what had caused the look. When she saw the familiar, diminutive gun in Abigail's hand, she bit back a strangled gasp.

"No, like I said, there's been a change of plan. New plan—I kill you with Gaby's gun and stage it to look as though Gaby, distraught, feeling guilty, lures you here, kills you, and then herself. Sounds perfect to me. Don't you think?" she asked, grinning widely.

Gaby closed her eyes, no longer able to keep them open, and sent a final prayer to heaven as she felt the darkness closing in on her.

Demetri killed the engine on his truck, less than a block away from the Winters' home, opened the door, and ran toward the gated mansion.

He glanced toward the circular driveway and saw Gaby's Honda parked there. A dark sense of foreboding closed in on him.

His instincts had proven correct; she was here.

He hoped like hell the sick feeling in his gut was wrong, and that she wasn't in any danger, but again . . . his instincts were telling him he was right.

He noted that although there were night-lights illuminating the path from the driveway and edging the grass, there were only a few lights on in the house.

He grabbed the wrought-iron bars and easily vaulted over the tall gate. Once he landed on the other side, he crouched down low and sprinted toward the side of the house.

As he flattened his body on the brick siding, he swiftly eased around the house, looking for a way in.

When he reached a large window, with lights on inside the room, he hunkered down even lower, squinting his eyes to try and peer through an opening in the wide wooden slats.

His eyes widened when he saw Abigail Winters standing within a few feet of Adam Quick, a small handgun held in her hand, pointed at him.

Demetri's eyes darted around the room and what he saw made his heartbeat race, a yell of denial lodged deep in his chest.

In the far corner, lying on a small sofa, one arm dangling off the edge, eyes closed, was Gabrielle with a deathly pallor, one he could see even through the window.

Adrenaline flooded his body.

He stood back, angled his upper body, and hurled himself at the window.

Demetri rolled to his feet, his feet crunching against the shattered glass as he stood and quickly assessed the situation.

He spared Gaby only a brief glance. She lay on the sofa, in the same position. He thought, for a moment, her eyes were open. But there was no time to think; he had to act.

He lunged toward Abigail and crashed to the floor with her. A short chop to her wrist and with a cry she dropped the gun, and it spun on the floor away from her. With his feet he kicked her. The force of his kick sent her several feet away from him and he went for the gun.

"No!" A guttural cry from Adam as he landed on Demetri and the two men struggled for possession of the gun. Demetri threw one well-aimed punch and it landed across the other man's jaw, a satisfying crack splitting the air as he shattered it.

Gritting his teeth, with blood streaming down his face, Demetri turned and faced Abigail and Adam, the gun trained at them both.

"What are you waiting for? Kill him! He poisoned Gaby!" Abigail screeched at Demetri, standing on wobbly feet, bracing her hands on the table, her breathing heavy.

What he'd seen could have been Abigail, in a fit of rage, seconds from killing Adam, or it had been that she had been the one to poison Gaby.

The decision was taken away from him when Adam launched himself at him.

Demetri aimed the gun and fired.

Adam turned to Abigail, his hand on his chest covering the hole there, the other held out toward Abigail.

"But, I . . . I loved you," he said simply, and fell to the floor.

Demetri didn't spare him a glance, and ran to Gaby's side, pulling her off the sofa and into his arms.

"Oh, my God, baby, baby wake up!" he cried, lifting her into his arms. He spun around, with Gaby in his arms and yelled, "Call 911, Abigail, we've got to get her to the hospital!" he yelled, hoarsely.

As he spun around to face her, he saw that the gun he'd dropped was now in the woman's hands.

Just as she had with Adam, she now trained the gun on him.

"I'm afraid I can't do that, Demetri," she said and pulled the trigger.

26

"I'm afraid I can't let you do that, Abigail."

Just as Demetri dropped and rolled, seconds before the bullet hit, he turned his head to see Hunter standing in the doorway.

In both of his shaking hands he held a .45 pointed directly at Abigail.

"Nooo!" Abigail yelled, seconds before he pulled the trigger and a whoosh split the air.

The bullet hit her dead between the eyes.

A look of surprise, and then disbelief, coupled with the smoking hole, spoiled her perfectly madeup face, before she crumpled in a heap to the floor.

"She was behind it all," the words seemed to be choked from him. "I couldn't let her kill Gaby."

Hunter calmly lowered his arm. The gun fell to the floor, the sound unnaturally loud in the room. Hunter walked over to his wife.

He glanced over at Adam, his eyes darkening as he saw the crimson pool of blood covering his son's chest, staining the pine floors, before he turned away.

Demetri warily watched the man as he lowered himself to the floor next to Abigail's lifeless body.

He ran his hands over her hair and swept it back into the elegant slipknot on top of her head as he rocked her back and forth in his arms.

Demetri placed two fingers under Gaby's chin, feeling for her pulse. Although faint, it was there.

He silently thanked God when he heard the screaming sirens just outside the house

Demetri swiftly stood and lifted a listless Gaby into his arms just as he heard the crashing sound of the front door shattering.

Seconds later the house began to fill with uniformed men and women.

"She's been poisoned," he yelled, shoving through the suddenly crowded dining room.

When two paramedics broke through the crowd, he reluctantly handed Gaby over to them.

As they strapped her onto the stretcher, he held on to her hand, tears flowing unchecked down his face, at the feeble way her hand held onto his.

"It's over, baby," he whispered the words, brushing the hair back from her forehead.

"You're going to be okay," he promised, reassuring her as well as himself, and stepped back, allowing the paramedics to whisk her away.

"They told me that after they pumped her stomach that the probable drug used in the tea was orphenadrine citrate," Demetri told Nick, running a hand through his hair as he paced up and down the waiting room in the hospital, adjacent to Gabrielle's room. "Norflex—it's a—"

"It's a white crystalline powder that dissolves completely in liquid," Nick broke in, and Demetri paused.

"How do you know about that? *Why* do you know that?"

"I'm sure there are plenty of things I know that you would

find odd," was Nick's reply. "It can be taken orally. It's a white crystalline powder that completely dissolves in liquid, but it has a bitter taste. But, as Abigail placed it in the tea, the sweetness would mask the bitterness. That would hold with Gaby's symptoms of convulsions, weakness, dizziness." He paused. "How is she now?"

"Better. The first day she was in and out of consciousness. They put her on Valium. It's the best treatment. Because of her symptoms, the potential for cardiac arrest was a threat, so they had to be careful. The wrong med and it would have slowed her respiratory system. Could have shut it down completely."

Demetri felt the remnants of paralyzing fear, realizing how close Gaby had come to dying, the fear filling him with a cold, dark rage toward the dead woman.

"Good," Nick murmured and continued. "We let Hunter Winters go. For now," he added.

Although Demetri knew he should be grateful for the man's intervention, one part of him hated Hunter as much as he did Abigail and Adam.

"He didn't know about his wife's plans to kill Gabrielle. But he damned sure knew she wasn't lily-white in her other operations. He'll have to come back in and testify."

"And Gaby?" Demetri held his breath, hoping she would be exonerated of any crimes.

When Nick sighed over the phone, he knew she wouldn't be let off easily.

"It's not that easy, unfortunately," Nick finally replied, mimicking Demetri's thoughts. "Although, I did manage to pull some strings."

"Meaning?"

"Meaning, although her reasons were understandable—wanting to help her mother—she's still guilty of fraud."

"She had no idea what Adam was doing, Nick. She was trying to help her mother. When she found out, she cut ties with

Adam, and was trying to help get the evidence needed to arrest him," Demetri broke in.

"Demetri, you know it doesn't work like that. No such thing as being a little guilty of fraud or not. Either you are or you're not. But," he said quickly, before Demetri could cut in. "But, as I said . . . I pulled some strings. With her promised testimony, her sentence will be commuted. She won't have to do any prison time, and I've arranged to have her testimony, as well as any subsequent legal action, in a closed file. As far as her license . . . I don't know if I can swing it. She will more than likely have it suspended. Possibly revoked."

Demetri breathed a sigh of relief. Although he knew how hard Gabrielle would take having her license taken, at least she wouldn't have a record or do any jail time.

He would be there for her, to help her deal with the rest.

He glanced up and noticed the doctor leaving Gabrielle's room.

"I've got to go . . . the doc's leaving her room," Demetri said and without waiting, ended the call.

As soon as Demetri saw Gaby's attending physician emerge from her room, he strode over to him, fear twisting his guts in knots, although he knew she was going to be okay.

"Is she awake?"

The doctor nodded his head. "She's awake. Tired, but awake. She's going to be fine. We have her on I.V. electrolyte fluids to replenish what she lost due to the vomiting," he told Demetri, gravely continuing. "It was a close call. Another hour or so and she would have gone into coma and heart failure. You got her here just in time."

Demetri shut his eyes briefly, and though he wasn't overly religious, he nonetheless knew that a higher being had intervened. He sent a grateful prayer of thanks heavenward.

"Can I go in and see her?" he asked. No matter what the doctor said, he had no intention of leaving without seeing Gabrielle.

"Sure, go ahead. I don't want to overtire her, so try not to stay too long. She needs to sleep, heal. But, she asked for you as soon as she woke about an hour ago, and I think seeing you is just what she needs," he replied. He patted Demetri on the back and left.

As soon as the doctor left, Demetri opened the door to the hospital room and quietly walked inside.

Tears, unbidden, sprang to his eyes as he approached her and he looked down at her lying on the sterile, narrow hospital bed. Her normally healthy, beautiful, dark honey-brown skin had an ashen quality to it and dark shadows underscored her closed lids.

She turned her head toward him and her eyes drifted open.

"Demetri," she whispered, the sound coming out croaked and dry. "You're here." She smiled a tired, drained smile and lifted her hand, placing it in his.

He grasped it, bringing it to his mouth, and placed a kiss in the center of her palm and returned her smile, his heart clenching in his chest.

Carefully, so that he didn't interfere with the I.V. attached to her arm, he sat on the edge of the small bed, desperate to be close to her, to assure himself that she was alive and well.

"No, don't move, you might hurt yourself. I have enough room," Demetri gently admonished her when she tried to move to accommodate his large body on the bed.

"How do you feel?" he asked, running anxious, worried eyes over her. Although the hospital bed was narrow, it seemed to dwarf her as she lay huddled in the middle, the white, coarse hospital-grade sheet up to her chest.

"I've felt better," she tried to laugh. When she did, she grimaced. "Definitely had better days."

"Don't . . . please baby, just relax. Don't do anything! God, I've never been so scared in my life."

He stroked her hair, content to be near her, running trembling hands lightly over her, as though assuring himself that she was okay. "I spoke with Nick," he told her.

He saw the question in her eyes and the fear on her face. He leaned down and kissed her, softly, reassuring her.

"So . . . what's going to happen?" she asked once he released her lips.

"I'm sorry, baby, but, you may have to surrender your license," he said and wished like hell he could take the pain away from her. "Even though you weren't involved in the scheme, had no knowledge of what Adam and Abigail were doing, the fact that you knowingly used the methadone for your mother, without a prescription . . ." he let the rest of the sentence dangle.

"Yes. I know. I was wrong," she whispered, tears in her eyes.

"Your intentions were good, baby. You only wanted to help your mother," he said, trying to console her.

She took a deep breath and raised her chin, "I wasn't really helping her, in the end. I know that, now," she said, and he was proud of the way she took responsibility for her action.

"However, with the promise of your testimony, your sentence will be commuted. I'll make damn sure of that," he promised and she kissed him in gratitude.

"Nick assures me you won't have to do any prison time, or go to trial, in exchange for your testimony." She nodded her head in gratitude. "And, he'll speak on your behalf to the university, so you don't lose your job," he finished.

Although she'd only been awake for a short time, she felt her lids droop, exhaustion claiming her, draining her.

Everything hadn't processed, she knew it would take time and healing, both physical and mental, before she would be strong enough to face the consequences of what she'd done.

But, with Demetri by her side, she felt she could face those consequences when the time came. Gabrielle sighed and closed her eyes, leaning into Demetri's side as he sat on the edge of the bed, drawing strength from him.

* * *

"You have a visitor, Ms. Marlowe," Gaby's eyes lifted and turned toward the door of her hospital room, a smile on her face, expecting to see Demetri in the doorway, ready to take her home.

When the nurse moved to the side, instead of Demetri, Hunter stood there, an uncertain look on his face.

She nodded for the nurse to allow him to enter.

Once alone he turned toward her. "How do you feel, Gaby?" he asked, not coming any farther into the room. "They told me you were being released today."

She licked dry lips, her heart racing as she glanced at the man she'd known as long as she had Abigail, a man she had once considered a substitute father of sorts, married to a woman she loved like a mother.

The pain returned, not physical, but one that hurt ten times worse than any physical wound ever could.

"I've been better," she murmured and saw him flinch. "Come in," she invited him into the room.

He nodded. Instead of coming to stand by her, he walked toward the window. She knew it was difficult for him to look at her, just as hard as it was for her to look at him, the two of them caught in a situation neither knew how to talk about.

"All this time, I knew it was her. I knew she was behind what Adam was doing," he said, gazing out of the window.

The shock had worn off, yet still, she found it difficult to believe that Hunter was Adam's father. Demetri had filled her in on what he'd learned from Nick, as well as the information Hunter had willingly given Demetri's former commander, about Hunter's connection to Adam.

She sat down on the edge of the bed and drew in a breath, staring at his stiff back.

"He contacted me less than a year ago. I didn't even know he existed until then. When he showed me a picture of his mother, I knew he was mine. She and I were . . . involved . . .

years ago. Around the time that Abigail had her first miscarriage," he said and turned to look at her.

Gaby nodded her head, remembering what Abigail had once told her, that Hunter had had an affair.

He stared at Gaby. "I, I met Adam's mother the same way I met Abigail," his gaze was thoughtful, as though he were trying to measure his next words carefully. Yet, what he said next surprised her and she knew her shock showed. "I met Abi when she was working the streets," he went on, laughing a humorless laugh at Gaby's painful look of surprise.

"It was something she wasn't proud of. She preferred that people thought that, although she'd grown up in poverty, she'd chosen more noble ways to pull herself out," he said and shook his head. There was a fierce set of pride in his eyes when he looked at Gaby again. "And she did. She turned tricks, yes, but, she was never a fool. She fought hard to be her own woman, never allowed anyone to use her."

He turned back to face the window. Gaby felt it was easier for him that way, saw the difficulty he had keeping eye contact with her.

He straightened his sloping shoulders. "Anyway, when Adam showed up in town, he asked for a job. I had to help him, he was my son. He'd told me he had gotten into some trouble. That he needed to get away."

Hunter admitted that he knew Abigail was involved in some type of scam, but that he didn't know she had intended to harm Gabrielle, that he would have never believed it if he hadn't overheard her talking to Adam weeks before.

He turned back to face her and slowly walked toward her. "It took me a while before I realized what was going on. And as much as I loved her, would do anything for her, I couldn't let her hurt you. You were always like a surrogate daughter to me, Gaby," he said. When he reached a hand out as though to touch her, she flinched.

His hand dropped away.

"When she called me, told me she wanted me to order food for dinner, at first I didn't think much of it. Was glad, in fact, that she was reaching out to you. The two of you hadn't seen each other in a while," he said and stood. The look he gave her was one of sorrow and pain.

"But, I knew. I knew in my heart . . . she was going to hurt you. I couldn't let her do that. As much as I loved her, I couldn't let her do it," he said, his simple statement said so much.

Abigail felt tears burn the back of her eyes, swamp her vision.

She was still trying desperately to understand what happened, who Abigail really was, and why she would hurt her. Trying to come to grips with the painful realization that she hadn't ever really known her, that Abigail hadn't ever truly cared about her, that so many people in her life had never really cared about her, with the exception of Demetri.

With Hunter's words, a part of that pain was released. She would probably never understand who Abigail really was, but in the end, despite his love for her, Hunter had proven that he did care about her. More than she ever imagined.

When he reached for her, she allowed him to pull her into his arms as the two hugged each other tightly, both allowing the tears to fall for a woman they both loved, yet never truly understood.

Epilogue

Gabrielle held Demetri's hands above his head, fingers laced together with her thighs straddling his hips as she slowly rode him.

A sigh of pleasure escaped from his mouth, as she gently rolled her body against his, sliding up and down his naked shaft in easy, lazy glides.

She smiled down at him, a purely feminine smile of pleasure and power.

She lowered her head, closed her mouth around his, and nipped his lower lip with her teeth.

He groaned and felt her smile around his mouth, before suckling the rim, pulling it into her mouth.

"Brat," he admonished, huskily, a lazy, half-smile lifting the corner of his sensual mouth, when she withdrew from his mouth.

She knew she was driving him out of his mind with every bounce of her butt against his groin as she rode him. And she was getting just as much enjoyment out of the giving as she he was from the receiving.

She leaned back down as her hips continued to bounce and grind his dick and teased him, allowing the tips of her breasts to brush back and forth over his mouth.

He bucked forward, trying to grasp one of the swinging globes, but she laughed and pulled away. Although he could have, he didn't break free of her hands, allowing her to continue to "restrain" him.

"What, you're not going to come and get it, big boy? What's the problem, mama got you on lockdown?" she taunted. She leaned down and ran her tongue over one of his tight, male nipples, suckling the kernel into her mouth until it stabbed against the roof of her mouth with her steady nursing.

"No . . . this is your show," he groaned the words, referring to their interlaced hands. "But, I don't know how much longer I can go on like this," he stopped, drawing in a harsh breath when she reached a hand between them and began to fondle his balls as she fucked him. He slowly released the breath.

"Damn . . . you're killing me, Gaby," he said between clenched teeth. The muscles in his throat stood out in stark relief, the veins pulsing as she stroked downward and ground against him in short little tight circles.

"But, what a way to go," she whispered and he groaned again, in lusty agreement.

"I'm sorry, baby, but I need to come."

She only had time to gasp when he unlinked their joined hands, grasped her by her hips, and lifted her off his cock.

He flipped her over until she landed in a soft thud on her backside beneath him.

"No fair, you said it was my show!" She frowned in faux indignation.

Her fake anger was swallowed when he slanted his mouth over hers, grasped her beneath the knees, and pushed her legs up until they were spread wide, and surged into her.

"Ummm," she moaned into his mouth as he stroked into her

in hard, pounding thrusts, so far up in her that she felt his balls, tight, swollen with cum, tap against her ass.

He grimaced, sweat easing down his face, his chest, and landing on her body as their bodies writhed together, grinding and giving each other what they both needed, loving each other until the hazy film of lust blurred his eyes.

His arms shook, his body trembled, as he stroked inside her, not from the weight of holding her up, but from the sheer emotion that rolled over him in hot waves.

"I need to come, baby," he grunted, staring down at her.

Gaby bobbed her head up and down, with her neck thrown back, her eyes tightly shut. "Yes," she spoke in a broken whisper, in agreement.

His strong hands held her securely as he repositioned her on his cock, his fingers biting into her buttocks as he brought her into hot alignment with his shaft, stroking in swift, steady strokes until her orgasm slammed into her.

As she cried out, she heard his answering cry loudly match hers as he shouted his release with her, slamming his cock deep into her until she nearly blacked out from the pleasure.

When she came back to herself, he was withdrawing. His seed had filled her in hot, sweet waves deep within her womb.

He buried his face in her neck, holding their position, locked deep inside her long after the orgasm claimed them, until finally he slipped out, and drew her in front of his body, holding her protectively in his embrace, his soft penis nestled against her buttocks.

When her heart had calmed, she turned to face him, idly running her fingers through the dark hair on his chest.

"You know, I think a few of your male students have a crush on you." As he spoke, she felt the low hum in his chest, as she laughed.

"What are you talking about?" She raised her face and looked into his eyes.

"You know exactly what I'm talking about. Some of those young boys are crushing on you. Isn't that how they put it?" he asked, raising a brow.

"Whatever," she mumbled and felt her cheeks warm.

"I think I liked it better when you were Professor Marlowe, not Doc Marlowe as the kids have taken to calling you. Too damn familiar," he said in mock anger. "And speaking of that, when are you going to change your name at the university? The minute those young boys know you're mine, the sooner they'll realize you're off limits," he grumbled, but Gaby saw the hint of a smile playing around the corners of his mouth.

She held up her left hand for his inspection.

"Between this, and your auditing the graduate class . . . I'm pretty sure they know," she laughed.

This in question, was a two-carat, emerald-cut, diamond platinum wedding band. In the early morning light, the flawless diamonds in the ring sparkled, and seemed to wink at her.

"Hey, I've always wanted to further my education. Why not sit in on one of my wife's classes? Total waste of a benefit, if you ask me," he replied, grinning unrepentantly.

Within a week of her release from the hospital, Demetri had proposed. Within a month they were married. Six months later and Gabrielle still couldn't believe the changes in her life. Mostly for the better, she thought, smiling at the man beside her.

She'd gotten her mother into a rehab clinic and with a finality she felt deep in her spirit, knew that it was up to her mother if she chose to accept help, Gaby no longer felt any lingering misplaced responsibility. She'd done all she could for her. The rest was up to her mother.

Nick's promise to find Demetri's former partner, she could tell, had lifted a dark burden from him as well, and he no longer wore the familiar necklace with her ring, as a constant reminder of how he'd failed to help her.

Everything hadn't turned out perfectly. She had been forced to surrender her license. However, Nick had helped her maintain her position at the university. She was happy to turn the pharmacy over to Rosario, and found her an assistant to help run the community pharmacy.

"I love you, baby. God, how I love you."

Gaby smiled and lay her head on Demetri's chest.

In addition, Demetri and Gaby had learned more about the woman Gaby called friend, as well as mentor, in the time since the ordeal.

The mother, before she died, had contacted Hunter, in a letter. In the letter she'd told him all about his son, and where to find him, in the group home he had been placed in, when she'd known she was dying, but Abigail had hidden the letter and gone to see the woman herself.

When she'd returned, Adam had run away from the group home he'd been placed in.

When she found him, she'd taken him off the streets, and pretended that she cared for him, telling him that Hunter wanted nothing to do with him. Just as she had with Gabrielle, she'd befriended him, although in a way she never had with Gaby.

She'd also begun to have sex with him and eventually involved him in her criminal activities.

Gaby felt sympathy for Adam, despite what he'd done and tried to do with her. She herself had fallen victim to Abigail's charms, and had believed the woman truly loved her. That she cared about her.

Gaby inhaled a shaky breath, fiercely holding back the sadness she felt at how wrong she'd been.

When Demetri kissed her, gently, gathering her into his arms, she allowed the tears to fall.

"It's okay, baby, let it out. It's okay," he encouraged, running his hands over her naked back. The soothing movements and gentle way he held her allowed her to finally release the emotion she'd had building for years.

Like a dam that had finally broken, the flood of tears that gave way was violent in its intensity. She allowed the tears she'd held back for so long, too long, to freely run.

She cried for the young girl she'd been, the one who'd never known true motherly love, one who'd desperately needed a female figure, a mother figure to love and take care of her.

She then cried for the woman she'd become, one who still sought her mother's approval. So much so, that she stole for her.

And finally she cried for the woman she now was. These tears weren't sad ones, filled with remorse and pity. They were tears of relief, mixed with joy.

She had been so closed off to everything, yet desperate for love, for acceptance. Now, she felt whole.

She reached up and softly kissed Demetri, smiling past the tears that blurred her vision.

"I love you," he whispered, the look of love in his eyes nearly as blindingly bright as the diamonds on her finger.

"I know," she whispered back.

A smile of happiness and contentment was on her face, as she lay her head back on his chest. She was a new woman. Changed in ways she never imagined, yet free. Free to embrace life, to test her boundaries, push herself.

Most of all, she was now free to accept and embrace the strong woman this incredible man had shown her she was, all along.

Turn the page for a preview
of Kate Douglas's novella,
"Chanku Challenge,"
from SEXY BEAST VII!

On sale now!

1

His thick paws made barely a sound as Nick Barden trotted along beside his mate. He and Beth followed three of their packmates along the service road running near the large wild wolf compounds at the sanctuary run by Chanku shapeshifters Ulrich Mason and Millie West.

At some level, Nick realized he should be loving every second of this chance to run free in the beautiful northern Colorado mountains—here he could take this form without fear of discovery or attack, without the stink of the city burning his sensitive nostrils.

Instead, he hardly noticed the myriad scents and sounds teasing his wolven senses—not the fresh mountain air or even the altogether unique freedom of running as a wolf through dark, pristine forest. No, he was much too aware of the female beside him to appreciate any of it.

Too aware of her displeasure and her silent disapproval to notice the scent of fresh game or even his own unique abilities in this powerful body.

Nothing he did seemed to please her. Not anymore.

His ass still hurt from Ulrich's screwing the other night, but when he looked back at the way he'd been acting for the past week, he figured he'd deserved what he got and then some. The power play Beth had talked him into had backfired—more literally than he'd expected.

Couldn't she see that Ulrich Mason wasn't the problem? He'd never done anything to Beth that wasn't perfectly kind and accepting. Beth's misplaced animosity was totally unfair, all part of her own convoluted baggage. Baggage she needed to deal with now if she and Nick wanted to remain part of this close-knit pack.

If he didn't love her so much, Nick never would have gone along with her stupid wishes.

There was no denying the fact he'd eventually enjoyed Ulrich's powerful response to his stupid challenge. Sex with a dominant male was worth the pain, worth the pure sense of humiliation Nick had suffered.

It had raised his level of arousal even higher.

He wished Beth would lay off. She'd focused her anger on him now, instead of on Ulrich, and it was so thick he could practically see it vibrating in the air between them. In fact, her anger was just about the only thing they had between them anymore. She'd shut him out ever since he'd blocked her constant bitching that night, even though Nick was the one who had ended up paying for the failure of Beth's stupid plan. When he chose to follow Ulrich's lead rather than hers, it meant getting his ass reamed out in a reactive display of dominance by the old guy.

Okay. So he got the message, along with some really great sex. Now why couldn't Beth figure it out? There was no point in challenging Ulrich. Nick didn't want to fight him. For one thing, he really liked and admired the man.

For another, he'd lose.

Ulrich was smart, he was cunning, and he was strong. He had age and experience on his side, and he was a born leader whether he was in his wolf form, snarling with teeth bared and hackles raised, or staring a man down from his impressive height on two legs. No matter, it was something Nick knew he'd never be able to pull off in any form.

Why couldn't Beth accept him for what he was? In this society, this world of Chanku, he was just a pup. Barely twenty-four years old, he'd been nothing but a loser on the streets of San Francisco. Why did Beth seem to think his ability to shift would make him anything different?

Was it the fact he'd killed that guy to protect Tala? Was that why Beth expected him to be more aggressive? If that was the case, she was dead wrong. He'd killed without thinking, shifting before he even knew he had the ability.

And he'd bonded with a woman he loved before either of them really thought about the permanence of their act.

He watched Daci, Deacon, and Matt trotting together up ahead. The three of them had slipped into an amazing union, and they weren't even mated. He and Beth were mates, yet they hardly spoke to each other. He missed the easygoing relationship he'd had with Matt and Deacon, missed the freedom and the fun they'd all had together, but he missed Beth most of all. Missed the beautiful, shy young woman he'd fallen in love with.

He glanced at Beth and realized she watched him. Was she reading his thoughts? He'd been blocking . . . or at least he thought he was.

She veered off the road and trotted down a narrow trail that led deeper into the woods. Nick hesitated then decided to follow her. She stopped after a short distance and turned to face him, standing in a brilliant ray of late afternoon sunlight, dead center in the middle of a small meadow.

He halted a few feet away, ears flat, tail down. It was easier this way, acting the submissive role with Beth. It seemed to make her happy, though at this point he hardly cared.

She shifted. He faced her for a moment, still the wolf. She

stared at him, her dark brows crinkled in that way she had, her arms folded over her bare chest like a disapproving teacher. He held her gaze for a moment longer. She didn't move. Didn't say a word.

Oh, hell. If he wanted to see what she wanted . . . Nick shifted and stood on two feet, wary and uncertain.

Beth raised her chin and stared at him. Sunlight poured across her beautiful olive skin and raised red highlights in her long, dark hair. Her amber-eyed gaze, so much like his own, bored into him. He held her stare.

"It's not working," she said, clasping her hands over her smooth belly. In control, as always. Naked, beautiful, standing there with a sense of entitlement, of power, like an Egyptian goddess here in the midst of the Colorado forest.

"We never should have bonded. I want out."

Her words, a statement, not a request, came as a relief. At least he wasn't the only one who felt that way.

Unfortunately, it wasn't an option.

He actually smiled when he answered her. "Great. So do I, but it's a little late for that, Beth. You heard what Tala said. A pair bond is forever. You wanted me, you've got me."

She jerked back as if he'd slapped her. "You don't want me?"

Not at all surprised by her contrary question, Nick shook his head. "You're supposed to be the one who can tell when a guy's lying or telling the truth. You tell me."

She shook her head as if some of the fight had gone out of her. "I can't tell anymore, Nick. Not with you. It doesn't work with you."

"Does it matter? You just said you want out. You've shut me out for days. We don't have sex with each other, even after a run. It's pretty obvious you don't love me anymore." He was standing up straighter, feeling taller than he had since they'd first linked, even though every word he spoke chipped away more of their bond. "So, I guess my answer's no, Beth. I don't want you. Not anymore. Not the way you are now." He shook his head, no longer smiling.

"I loved a girl who was sweet and kind, who cared about me, about the future we planned together. All you care about now is power. You're twenty-one years old, Beth. You're a baby in this pack, just like me. You have no power. Not over me, not over yourself, and definitely not over any of the others. Get used to it."

He stared at her for a long moment, holding her gaze until she finally looked away. Obviously, this conversation was over.

He shifted. *I'm going back to the others. You can come if you want to. Or not.* Nick glanced over his shoulder and watched her face. She looked brittle, like she might shatter as easily as glass. He felt bad about that, about hurting her, but he didn't trust her. Not anymore.

He still loved her, though. Goddess help him, he loved her.

With one last look, Nick whirled around and raced back along the trail. Dry grass crackled beneath his feet. A gentle wind blew and leaves dropped all around, but he focused on the trail ahead. He didn't want to think of the young woman he'd left behind.

He left her standing in the meadow, looking stunned and alone. At least she wasn't angry at him now, but he didn't feel like he'd won a victory. No, he just felt empty.

Empty and very much alone.

It was the ear-splitting *rat-a-tat-tat* of a woodpecker working away on a thick branch overhead that finally jerked Beth out of the fog Nick had left her in. She sat down hard on the rough ground and dropped her forehead to her knees.

Well, what the hell did you expect? That he'd beg for forgiveness? That he'd say everything was just hunky-dory?

No, in all honesty, she had to admit he'd behaved much more admirably than she had. First sign of trouble, and all she'd wanted was out.

Of course, the trouble was all of her own making.

It wasn't easy to run away from yourself. Beth lay back in the dried grass and scratchy pine needles and stared at the tiny bits of blue sky visible between the canopy of leaves. The woodpecker stopped its pecking and flew away. She heard the sharp buzz of a bee searching for one last flower before winter and felt the cool brush of air across her naked thighs and belly.

Her nipples tightened from the chill, and she thought of that first time with Nick, when he'd drawn her nipple between his lips, pressed it with his tongue, and held it against the roof of his mouth.

She'd never felt anything so sweet, never known love like that in her life. When he'd filled her, when he'd stretched her with his length and width and pressed deep inside, she'd expected pain, a repeat of the violation that was all she'd ever known.

She'd felt only pleasure.

He'd chased away the memories. The nightmares, actually. Nightmares she'd lived with ever since she'd been a sixteen-year-old virgin and her stepfather had raped her. That one brutal, agonizing act on the eve of her mother's funeral had taken more from her than any girl should have to give.

No one man should have the power to defile a person's entire life, but her stepfather had managed. He'd taken what should have been hers to give, and he'd ruined it forever.

Then she'd met Nick. Gentle and kind, he'd offered her friendship, and then he'd offered love. They'd chosen together to cement their relationship with the mating bond. Beth hadn't had any doubts then. She'd thought Nick was the one who would keep her safe, the one to take the darkness that covered her soul and strip it away—and for a special but much too brief time, he had.

If only she hadn't joined Tala that night when they had sex with Ulrich. It wasn't Ulrich's fault he was older, that his age and even his general appearance reminded her of her stepfather. He hadn't hurt her. Anything but . . . in fact, Ulrich had given her pleasure.

Maybe that was the problem—the fact she'd had a wonderful sexual experience with a man similar enough in looks to her stepfather had to totally reawaken the memories.

Without realizing it, Ulrich had brought back all her ghosts. His had become the face in her nightmares.

It wasn't fair to Ulrich, but it wasn't fair to her, either. She'd thought those nightmares were a thing of the past.

Now they were back, worse than ever. Nick could have been the answer. He could have fought her demons if he'd been man enough, but he wasn't willing to challenge someone he saw as a mentor. He'd chased away the nightmares once. For some convoluted reason, she was certain that if he challenged Ulrich and won, they'd be gone forever.

Or would they?

Now she'd never know. Nick had looked totally disgusted with her, and she really couldn't blame him. It wasn't fair to ask something of a guy that just wasn't part of his nature. Why couldn't Nick, the Nick she'd fallen in love with, have been enough? Why did she need to make him into something he wasn't?

It wasn't fair to him. Not to her, either. Like an absolute idiot, she'd managed to chase away the best thing that had ever happened to her.

The sun disappeared behind the hills while Beth lay there on the hard ground. Pebbles dug into her butt and pine needles poked her thighs and back, but she couldn't find the energy to move.

Where would she go? Nick wouldn't want her back. Not after what she'd said to him today. He'd barely tolerated her since that fiasco the other night when he'd ended up getting royally fucked in the ass.

She wasn't sure if he'd actually liked it or not. In some per-verse way, Beth had. She must be totally sick to have gotten so turned on watching Ulrich slam into her mate the way he had. The sex had started out so brutal, so typically male, but Nick hadn't fought. He'd merely bowed his head and accepted Ulrich's pounding violation—accepted it and eventually climaxed from it.

In fact, all of them—Ulrich, Matt, Nick, Millie, and even Beth—had achieved something amazing with their simultane-ous orgasm, but it hadn't really mattered. Nick had blocked her long before his climax, just as she'd blocked him. That night, aroused, angry, frustrated with each other, they'd essentially severed the special link that bound them together.

Neither of them had attempted to reconnect since. It was like cutting off part of her body, going through the motions each day without Nick's thoughts in her head.

He'd slept in Matt's old room that first night, and the next couple nights since, sharing the cabin but not her bed. She missed sleeping beside him. Hated running beside him and not connecting. She felt the pain in every part of her body, but the place it hurt most remained the hardest to touch.

Her heart actually ached. What had she expected? That he would promise to challenge Ulrich? Even if he won, what would that solve?

Beth opened her eyes. A narrow sliver of moon was rising. It was almost entirely dark, and still she lay shivering on the hard ground. She thought of shifting, of just staying the night in the woods as a wolf, but somehow that didn't seem right. Not with the convoluted thoughts swirling darkly in her mind.

Instead, she folded her hands over her waist and closed her eyes against the moonlight. Naked, vulnerable, her body cold and aching with the night's chill.

Alone, with nowhere to go.